S0-BDM-747

VOW

A LORDS OF ACTION NOVEL, VOLUME 1

K.J. JACKSON

Copyright © K.J. Jackson, 2016
This book is a work of fiction. Names, characters, places, and incidents are products of the author's imagination or used fictitiously. Any resemblance to actual events, locales, or persons, living or dead, is coincidental. All rights reserved. No part of this publication can be reproduced or transmitted in any forms, or by any means, electronic or mechanical, without permission in writing from the author.

First Edition: May 2016
ISBN: 978-1-940149-16-5
http://www.kjjackson.com

K.J. Jackson Books

Historical Romance:

Stone Devil Duke, *A Hold Your Breath Novel*
Unmasking the Marquess, *A Hold Your Breath Novel*
My Captain, My Earl, *A Hold Your Breath Novel*
Worth of a Duke, *A Lords of Fate Novel*
Earl of Destiny, *A Lords of Fate Novel*
Marquess of Fortune, *A Lords of Fate Novel*
Vow, *A Lords of Action Novel*

Paranormal Romance:

Flame Moon
Triple Infinity, *Flame Moon #2*
Flux Flame, *Flame Moon #3*

Be sure to sign up for news of my next releases at
www.KJJackson.com

DEDICATION

– AS ALWAYS, FOR MY FAVORITE KS

– BONUS DEDICATION: TO MY DEAR FRIEND, S.

Sometimes the extraordinary happens.

When the extraordinary happens to someone you love dearly, words cannot even express the happiness felt. I am so lucky. One of my dearest friends that has been in my life since I was four years old (three, depending on who tells the story), has found a soulmate, and I am awed, as always by her spirit.

This is fitting, because this particular book is not only about love, it is about letting people into your life—choosing who becomes your family—bound by love, laughter, tears, babies, and memories far too many to count. And I, personally, have been fortunate enough to choose one of the great ones.

So to say I am happy for you, S., is an understatement.

To S & J & G & B, I raise my glass high, beyond ecstatic that you have found each other, forged a family, and you will get live this crazy adventure of life together (and you know, too well, how crazy it can get!). I couldn't be more proud in your ability to love. May it always shine brightly in each of your lives.

{ CHAPTER 1 }

Putrescence infested his nostrils, invading upward, dulling his wits.

Unable to hold back any longer, Caine Farlington, younger brother to the fifth Earl of Newdale, pulled free from his pocket a small, round silver vinaigrette, flicking it open under his nose and leaning back. The half-rounded rungs of the rickety chair creaked, threatening to snap under his frame.

Casual. He had to portray casual even if he couldn't breathe. It was crucial.

A long whiff of the spice and vinegar, and Caine dropped the vinaigrette from his nose, slipping it back into his jacket.

The sharp stench of sewer and rot instantly flooded his nose again. No reprieve.

He had been in a sufficient number of brothels in the East End in his day. But this. Nothing like this. Filth. Decay. Timbers half rotted above him, threatening to collapse at any moment. Liquid dripping down along the wall next to his head, even though it wasn't raining. Half of the floor wooden planks, half of it indiscernible muck.

Squalor. A word that did not come close to doing justice to this devil's den.

Caine let his elbow slip off the arm of the chair in slobbery drunk fashion as a barmaid clad only in an apron and thick skirts clattered two mugs onto the askew table. He made sure to move his hand slowly, missing the handle of the mug three times before making contact and lifting the tankard to his lips.

He swallowed a gag. Even the blasted ale was rancid in this place.

Fletch's grey eyes shifted to Caine from across the table, the other tankard hiding his friend's cringe as he swallowed. Good man. Caine hadn't been able to let the vile liquid breach his lips. But Fletch did.

If anyone could play the role of gutter-drunk rakehell, it was Fletcher Williams, Marquess of Lockston.

Fletch's left eyebrow cocked ever so slightly at Caine.

Caine knew his friend would be laughing at him if the business in this whorehouse weren't so gravely serious.

That they had even gotten past the burly guards had been a feat. Drunk, a fool, he would have played any part to gain entrance to the auction. Caine had been terrified he'd missed it until they made entrance and found an open table in a dark corner, and he had recognized the place still buzzed in anticipation of the upcoming sale.

Caine's eyes haphazardly swept the room. Bustling crowd—surely more crowded than this place saw nightly. Half-dressed women draped over disheveled drunks, a few of the girls slipping sticky fingers under jacket lapels to snatch coins.

But there were a handful of patrons sitting serious, sober, and impervious to the debauchery around them.

Those were the men Caine knew he needed to worry about. The sober ones. Here for a purpose—not just for the entertainment, the sport of it.

A ruckus started at the far end of the room by the bar that stretched almost across the depth of the building.

The bar ended just to the left of a door that flipped open. Caine could see it was an interior door leading to stairs. A tall man dressed in shiny peacock colors emerged, raising a silver-encased cane high in his hand. He tapped the cane on the top seam of his ridiculously tall, purple satin hat as he walked along the edge of the room, jumping onto the stage that centered the room.

"Gentlemen, and to the rest of you scrubs, welcome. You have waited long enough. It is time we offer this night's entertainment." His arms swinging wide in flamboyance, the barker's voice boomed over the laughter of the women and the grunts of the men in the room. His face cracked into a wide sneer—almost vicious—emphasizing the wide gap from four missing front teeth.

The man waited several beats for the crowd to quiet, then spewed with enthusiastic aplomb, "Virgins, virgins, virgins. I know you've been waiting. And let me assure you, these were worth the wait. Integrity, gentlemen. All verified to be clean and unspoiled by our own Ma Betty. Highest price, gentleman. You know the rules." He paused, bowing slightly for effect before splaying his arms wide, his cane flourishing out to the side. "Welcome to the Jolly Vassal, lads—it be virgin time."

The point of his cane landed to the right of the bar, and the door he had come through swung open again.

Caine's breath stopped.

A hulking thug stepped through the doorway, pulling a rope with him. The room erupted, and a splattering of men in front of Caine stood, vying for a glimpse of what was attached to the rope.

Long seconds passed before the thug stepped up onto the stage, truly just a wobbly platform along the edge of the room. He tugged the rope as he stepped behind the barker.

Caine leaned far to the side, his breath still frozen. At least from this angle he could see most of the stage.

The rope snapped, dragging three girls single file up onto the stage. All three girls had the long rope tied about their waists, each of them clad only in a sheer, threadbare chemise that hid no skin from the eyes of the crowd. Heavy veils—almost hoods—covered the girls' heads, hiding their faces from the room.

"Shit." Caine hissed out his held breath. He had known the veils were a possibility—the mystery of the faces spurred higher bids, while hiding the tears and terror—but Caine hadn't wanted to take the slightest chance. He couldn't afford to. Not tonight.

The first girl stepped farther onto the stage where Caine could see her clearly. Too short. Too rotund.

The second girl. Tall. Very tall, gangly. Elbows like razors popping from her skinny arms as she tried to cover her body. Not her.

The thug behind the barker moved to the rope slacking between the second and the last girl and jerked it, yanking the third girl fully onto the platform. She stumbled over the lip of the stage and fell with the force, her long blond hair tumbling out from under the veil to curl around her body.

"To yer feet, wench." The thug snapped the rope.

Half on her knees, the blond girl staggered across the stage away from the man, her bare feet gaining traction. But before she could reach the far end, the thug pulled the rope, jerking her to a stop. He strode across the stage and grabbed a fistful of her hair, shoving her against the wall next to the tall girl.

His stomach churning, Caine's eyes ran over the last girl's body.

The hair. The hair was the right color, had the right waves to it. Right height. She wasn't scrawny, nor did her frame carry any extra weight. She stood proudly. Not trying to cover herself with nervous palms stretched wide like the other two.

She just stood. Still. Solid. Not even a twitch under her translucent bright pink chemise.

Caine swallowed, forcing breath into his lungs.

It had to be her. It had to be.

Only his Isabella would have poise like that in this god-forsaken place. On that god-forsaken stage.

The jeering from the crowd reached a pitch, and the barker raised his cane, smiling, waiting for the mouths to quiet.

"These be the three beauts, lads. We done ye well, as I said we would." The gleam in the barker's eyes shone as brightly as his purple hat. The bastard was clearly relishing the current affair. "Nothin' but the best from the Jolly Vassal. Tell yer friends."

Fletch set his tankard down hard onto the table, ale flying and drawing Caine's attention from the stage.

Both of Fletch's eyebrows were raised. Caine nodded, tapping three fingers on the table.

Fletch's eyes travelled from Caine's fingers to meet his eyes. He nodded, understanding exactly what Caine was telling him. Fletch turned back to the stage.

Caine stared at the three figures lining the back of the stage, his jaw clenching. The visceral need to smash every single face in this hellhole into the ground ripped through his body. He leaned forward, his chin dropping to his chest as he tamped down on his rage.

Rage would not serve him at this point in time.

Only money would. And that, he had plenty of.

It was time to get his love back.

~ ~ ~

Shoved into the carriage by the rope-holding brute from the stage, she landed in a thud at Caine's feet. His love's wrists were still bound together, and the veil sat like a hood over her head. The translucent chemise draped around Isabella's body offered only a thin layer between her and the chill of the night.

Caine fought the instinct to grab her arm, help her up, cover her in his warmth.

He looked to the thug, his mouth drawing tight. "That will be all."

"Ye be able to control 'er?"

"Yes."

The thug stood there, staring at Caine, his hand not leaving the carriage door.

Caine dipped into an inner pocket and pulled out a shilling, flipping it to the man as he knocked on the carriage roof.

The horses started moving before the carriage door closed. Caine leaned forward, quickly pulling the dark curtains on the windows. One lamp by his head lit the interior.

The jolt of the carriage sent Isabella scampering, her hands flailing about, trying to find her way to the bench across from him. Whimpers came between gasping breaths as her bare feet kicked at the squabs of the bench, and she tried to make herself as small as possible in the corner.

Caine shifted to her bench, grabbing her thrashing arms. "Bella, Bella. It is me."

She fought him, growling, kicking at his legs.

"Bella."

She tried to wrench herself from his grasp, screaming.

A kick, and her heel dug hard into his side.

Grunting, Caine shifted without freeing her arms, wedging his leg over her thighs, and effectively stilling her kicks.

Her head flew back and forth, the whimpers increasing. She couldn't see.

He realized she wasn't listening because she couldn't see.

"Bella. It's me." Keeping one hand clamped onto her wrists, Caine grabbed the veil covering her head and tore it from her face.

He froze.

She froze.

Eyes impossibly large, she stared at him, only her heaving breaths cutting through the silence.

"Shit."

She cringed, her captured body trying to curl away from him.

He dropped the veil to the floor, shoving off from her as he punched the back of the opposite cushions. "Bloody fucking hell."

He turned back to the crouching girl and his fists slammed into the cushions on either side of her head. Growling, he leaned over her.

"Where the hell is she? I just spent a fucking fortune on you. And you're not her. She was supposed to be there. That was the damn place. The only damn place and you were bloody well supposed to be her. They said Bella. Bella. They said you were Bella. Who the hell are you and what did you do to her?"

He saw it then. Her entire body shaking in the shadows. Vibrating. Terrified. Terrified of him.

It halted his rant.

Her eyes were wide open. Watching him. Waiting for whatever he was about to unleash on her. But she didn't hide from it. As terrified as she was, she was one to meet her fate as it came to her.

He pushed himself from the cushions, sinking to the bench opposite the girl.

He stared at her for a long moment in silence. "You are not Isabella. They said you were Bella. Where the hell is Isabella?" He knew he wasn't keeping the desperate rage from his voice—the accusation—but blast it, she wasn't Isabella.

She shook her head.

"What, girl? What? Bloody well speak."

Her bare arms tried to cover her body, but her wrists still bound by rope prevented the movement.

"Bloody hell." Caine grumbled, grabbing the dagger he had along his boot and leaning forward, slicing through the rope in one ripping motion.

Her hands flapped, shaking from the rope like it was locust on her skin. She wrapped her arms around her body, covering her chest and belly as she drew her legs up underneath her, shrinking into the corner.

But her eyes didn't leave him with the movement. No. The wide eyes stayed fixed to his face. Her mouth opened, her words a shrinking whisper. "You look for Isabella? They confused us."

Caine sat upright, leaning forward, but stayed on his bench. He didn't need to scare her more than she already was. "You met Isabella? You know where she is?"

"We were together in the carriage." Her soft voice shook. "Isabella has blond hair, like me—my height?"

Caine nodded.

"One of them, those men—those vile men—he asked our names, but he did not hear me—not correctly." Her words were creeping slowly, barely audible over the clomping of horses' hooves and the racket of the carriage wheels. "He called us both Bella. Bella one. Bella two. Then they all did the same with our names."

Caine held back the need to shake her. Shake her until answers flew fast. "So where the hell is Isabella? They only sold you tonight. You and two others that looked nothing like her."

Her head dropped as her arms tightened around her body. It was the first time her look had left him.

Caine's eyes narrowed. "Where is Isabella?"

The girl didn't lift her head, only shaking it, silent.

"You know where she is. Is she back at the whorehouse? Was she in there?" Caine couldn't hold himself back and he jumped over to the girl, grabbing her shoulders and shaking her. He was bloody well losing time traveling away from the brothel. "You have to tell me. Tell me if she was inside that place. Tell me where."

The girl gasped in a whimper, her head bobbing from his shaking.

"Speak—dammit, girl—speak. Where the hell is Bella?"

"Dead." The word blurted out, loud and rash.

No. God no.

His hand flew up to slap her.

She instantly cringed away, and Caine caught himself in mid-swing—right before his palm hit flesh.

His hand hovered next to her cheek. "You're a liar."

Tears streaming, her head swung back and forth. "I am not."

"You are mistaken." The words slipped past his gritted teeth.

Her wide eyes, now wet, rose to him. "She looks like me? My hair color? My height? Our bodies?"

"Yes. But you are lying. Confused. Isabella is not dead. I would know. I would feel it."

The girl yanked an arm free from the tangle of her body, thrusting the back of her hand in front of his face.

"Her hand. Did she have a mole on her left hand? Right below her knuckle? Right here?" She pointed to the skin below the knuckle of her ring finger.

Her words hit him, blasted through his gut.

His body staggered backward, collapsing on the opposite bench. "What…how do you know that?"

"I stared at her hands in the carriage. After they took me. I stared at them for hours and hours and hours. I could not lift my eyes. So I stared at her hands. Soft hands. She had truly soft hands, so soft."

It was Isabella.

There was no doubting it. The girl knew her. Knew the hand, the knuckles he had traced a thousand times over in a different land, in a different life.

His head fell back on the cushions, numb.

He had been so close. So close.

The words the girl spoke made sense in his mind, but could not travel down to his body. He couldn't feel it. Not yet. Not his love gone from this earth.

"You are…you are sure?" He could not move his head to look at her, could not smooth the roughness of his voice.

"She died. I saw her."

Each word sliced into Caine's chest, robbing him of his breath, of his heartbeat.

She moved, sitting upright on the bench, threatening to stand. "What—"

"Sit. Shut your mouth." His growl sent the girl back into the corner, wrapping herself into a ball.

Caine's head fell back, his eyes closed against the horror.

His love. Dead.

He had stayed alive for Isabella during the war. For her. And now she was dead.

Thick silence swelled in the carriage, seeping into every corner to suffocate the air.

Ten minutes. An hour. Caine had no idea how much time passed before he heard the girl's voice slip into the silence, a whisper against the pain ravaging his chest. Against the failure pounding in his brain.

"What…what are you going to do to me?" The trembling words broke through the air.

His head dropped, his eyes finding her in the corner. She had not moved a muscle. "Do to you?"

"Yes."

"Nothing."

"Nothing? But…"

Caine leaned forward, his voice hard. "Do you want me to do something to you?"

She snapped back, hiding her face from him.

Dammit. How many times was he going to send the pitiful creature cowering?

He shook his head, damning himself. If Isabella were sitting across from some strange man, at his mercy, how would Caine want her to be treated?

He sighed. "I am not going to hurt you, girl. What do you want? Where do you want to be delivered to?"

Her head flew up, her eyes wide as her mouth opened and closed several times before sound made it past her lips. "Truly? You are letting me go?"

He nodded.

"Home. I want…I want to go home."

"Where is home? Somewhere here in London?"

"I am in London?" Her hand flew over her mouth, fingers dragging across her lips. "I…I did not know that…I am from Wiltshire—the village of Marport. My father is the local vicar."

Blast it. That was at least a twelve-hour carriage ride away. His night and the next day would be gone. But that would also place him by Isabella's home in Somerset. He could go to see her mother and father, tell them the news, even if he wanted to put it off as long as possible. He still did not fully believe it himself.

He settled his hands on his lap, tempering his voice from the pain beginning to cut through his shock. "Then I will return you to Marport. What is your name, girl?"

"Ara Detton—Arabella Detton."

Caine shook his head.

Of course, dammit to hell.

Another Bella.

{ CHAPTER 2 }

Ara pulled the edges of the dark jacket tighter around her ribcage. Light had started to filter into the carriage, but the warmth of the sun had done little to heat the air in the past hour.

The rustle of the jacket sent the scent of the man across from her floating up from the fine fabric to her nostrils. The complexity hit her, cinnamon, alcohol, pine, apple, spice and something she couldn't identify, something of male, something that brought the range of smells into a whole. Somewhat akin to her father, but much deeper. A man that lived life. Not a boy. A man.

Whatever it was, it was oddly comforting.

Her eyes lifted, opening to the morning rays sneaking past the edge of the dark curtain after trying unsuccessfully to sleep for the last four hours. For the first of those hours, she had sat huddled, shivering in the thin, bright pink rag they had thrown over her in the brothel, unwilling to believe the man who had bought her was truly taking her home.

It wasn't until he had moved to drape his jacket over her that she had relaxed. Slightly. She had still kept her head down, her eyes closed, her body still. She didn't want to remind him she was in the carriage. Didn't want to give him a reason to change his mind. Didn't want to give him a reason to take what he had bought.

She had no idea she was worth so much as a virgin.

But it wasn't her the man had bought. He thought he was buying Isabella.

Isabella.

Ara's eyes squeezed shut, fighting back the memories of the girl she had just spent days with. Of the terror. The helplessness. Rage at the injustice that could turn nowhere but inward. Shame. Desperation. Everything she had felt during their journey, she had seen reflected in Isabella's eyes.

Everything except for the stillness of death. That alone had belonged to Isabella's vacant stare.

Ara had survived. And the nightmare was now solely hers.

"How did they take her?"

Ara's eyes jerked open to the man across from her at the soft words, his voice almost unrecognizable from hours ago when it had been harsh and furious.

Her mouth dry, Ara cracked her lips. "Isabella?"

He offered one nod, staring at her.

She opened her mouth to answer, but the one word had sapped every bit of liquid from her mouth. And when was the last time she had eaten? She couldn't even recall. The mealy lump of bread had been at least a day ago—had that been all?

Ara slipped a hand up from under his jacket, pointing to her mouth with two fingers. "W-water?"

The man looked around the carriage and then leaned across the bench he sat in to flip open a flap of wood on the side of the carriage. He pulled out a silver flask, removing the stopper and holding it out to her. "It is brandy. I have no water, only this. But it will wet your mouth."

She nodded as she fumbled her arm out above the jacket. Now that she was covered—haphazard as it was—she wasn't about to let any more of her body show than necessary. Only her bare feet peeked out onto the bench from under the jacket, and she meant to keep it that way.

She grabbed the flask, the edge of it hesitating on her bottom lip. She had never had brandy before. Father had always said it was a sin. But if it was all this man had, it would have to do. How bad could it be?

She took a long sip, the instant relief of moisture on her tongue disappearing as the brandy turned her mouth to fire.

He snatched the flask out of her hand just before she gagged, coughing and spewing droplets of the brown liquid onto the back of his jacket. Cough after cough, and she swallowed hard, trying to clear the flame from her tongue.

"I apologize. I should have known." Concern etched his brow.

Ara shook her head, still trying to gain control of her throat. "There was no way you could have. I did not know."

He held the flask up. "Try again?"

"No. No." She leaned back into the corner of the cushions, hiding her arm and drawing his jacket up to her neck.

Relaxing back onto his bench, he set the stopper onto the flask, but then thought the better of it and drew a healthy swallow before securing the stopper in place.

Ara watched his face. Not a flinch as the liquid descended. The man clearly did not think brandy was a sin.

His look lifted to her, his eyebrow cocked. "Isabella?"

Ara's breath stopped in her chest. "I am sorry, I do not know how they took her. She was already in the coach when I was shoved in. She never told me."

He nodded, silent, and his head dropped. Ara watched, waiting as he stared at the bottom left corner of the carriage for minutes.

"You. How were you taken?" His eyes stayed solidly on the dark corner.

"I was walking home."

"From where?"

"The market in our village." Her voice halting, she looked out the small crack beside the curtains to the passing fields. "I dropped the bread. The eggs. They all cracked. That was what I worried about for hours—the bread and the eggs. Birds picking at them. Mice. That we would not have them for dinner. I did not understand what was happening. Not until they…"

Her eyes closed, her head softly shaking. "I still do not understand…why…why do this…"

"There are bad men in this world, Miss Detton."

She opened her eyes to look at him and found him staring at her. His eyes were blue. A light blue that did not match his dark hair. Her fingers tightened the jacket to her chin. "You. You are not one of them?"

He shrugged. "Does being an utter failure equal bad?"

"No."

"I think that decision depends upon the one who was failed." His fingers went to the bridge of his nose, squeezing as his eyes closed. "And since she is dead, the judgment is quite clear."

Ara licked her lips, moisture finally returning now that the sting of the brandy had subsided. "Why do you think you failed her? You did not take her, did not put her into that…that…place."

"No. I merely abandoned her. She did not want me to leave for the war—go to the continent—and I took far too long to come home. I thought I was protecting her, staying away after the war ended until my head was right."

"You are a soldier?"

"Was. She begged me not to go, said I was abandoning her. I promised we would marry when I returned, even though I could have chosen not to go. But I did not want to fail my men. Instead, I failed her."

"When were you last with her?"

"I have not seen her in more than two years. I returned only weeks ago, and when I arrived at her home, I found out she had been taken. Mere days. I missed her by only days. If I had made my way to her without stopping in London, she would be with me now—protected. I was too late. Too damn late and I failed her."

His head dropped again, and his hand slid flat across his face, hiding his eyes.

Ara had no reply, no words for the man. Nothing to comfort him. Nothing but the guilt in her chest that she was the one sitting here, in this carriage, in the place meant for his love. The wrong woman. Without Isabella's death, Ara could very well be chained up by an old lecher right now. Or ripped apart. Or dead.

The guilt swelled, settling heavy into her chest.

She had escaped, but at what cost?

Silence filled the carriage the remainder of the day, but Ara did not mind. She had begun to realize she was still numb, her mind still impervious to all that had happened to her. Once she was home, safe, in her bed, then she could think. Then she could dwell, move on. Once she was safe with her father.

Pangs of hunger twisting her belly, Ara stared out the carriage window as she had for most of the day. The curtains had been pulled aside, and she had watched clouds set in, rain brewing, and then she saw it.

The stone wall trailing up a hill, jutting in and then crumbling. A wall that kept nothing in, nothing out. She had passed that stone wall countless times on the way to Widow Bellington's farm. Widow Bellington always kept the plumpest chickens, and she had been to her home hundreds of times over the years.

Air she had held hostage in the pit of her lungs exhaled. She was almost home. Almost.

"You recognize something?"

Ara's head swiveled to the man. She hadn't realized he had been watching her.

"I do. I have walked this lane countless times. May the driver stop at the next crossroad? We are very close to my home, and I would prefer not to appear with…" Her voice trailed off, not wanting to offend.

"Accompanied by a strange man?"

She nodded. "I mean no offense, but father—"

The man's palm whipped up, stopping her. "I understand."

Moving to flip open the door in the roof of the carriage, he repeated the request to stop to the driver.

The man sat down, his voice soft but stilted, as though the words were mere motions he had to bear his way through. "Do know, Miss Detton, I take solace in the fact that, at least for you, the horror you have gone through will have a happy outcome. You are welcome to take my jacket, cover yourself until you get home."

"Oh." She blinked, looking down. "I had not even considered my dress." Ara looked up to him. "I will take it, if it is not too much trouble. I have come to appreciate the slight modesty it affords me."

"It is yours."

A sad smile curved the edges of her lips. "Who are you?"

"Caine Farlington."

"I do not know how I can possibly begin to thank you for your generosity, Mr. Farlington. All I have been able to dwell upon today is where I might be in this very moment had circumstances been different in that brothel. Had you not been the one to purchase me."

He nodded, a sudden shine blanketing his blue eyes. He had stifled it all day, but the pain she saw in his eyes in that moment gripped her heart, crushing it until she felt it would explode.

Ara cleared her throat. "I know I am not the one to decide it, but you are not a bad man, Mr. Farlington. You are, truly, the furthest thing from it."

Another nod, and he looked to the window. He didn't believe her, that she could see. But she had said the words that needed to be said, at least from her mouth.

"How did she die?" His face still to the window, his whisper barely made it across the short distance to her.

"What?"

He looked to her. "I did not ask you before. I meant to. How did she die?"

Ara's gaze flickered to the passing trees, giving her precious seconds to steady herself from her stomach that flipped, threatening to heave at the question.

A deep breath, and her eyes found his. "They gave her something in a bottle—laudanum—I am not sure. She fell asleep, and she just stayed asleep. She died."

"No."

"No?"

"You are lying."

Ara's eyes fell closed as she took another bracing breath. "I am not." She opened her eyes, meeting his hard gaze. "I held her hand, Mr. Farlington. It went cold under my fingers. Her breath stopped. It stopped, and her head dropped to the side. I saw peace take over her body…it was quiet…soft."

The carriage slowed to a stop.

"She was not alone?"

"She was not."

His face ashen, he held her gaze. Held it for seconds that stretched into eons. But Ara refused to look away. She would give him this. If nothing else, she could give him this kindness.

Finally, he nodded. "Thank you for telling me, Miss Detton."

He opened the carriage door and descended, turning back to help her down the step the driver had pulled. He dropped her hand, and Ara resettled his jacket about her shoulders, wrapping the front flaps closed as best she could.

He inclined his head. "I wish you well, Miss Detton."

Ara could only nod, her throat clamped against all sound. She turned from him, stepping on her bare feet to the grass alongside the lane to avoid the rocks on the road. Home was only minutes away.

She walked, hearing Mr. Farlington's low voice mix with the driver's. His driver mentioned encroaching darkness and a coaching inn. Their voices trailed, and when Ara looked over her shoulder, the black carriage had already started to move once more.

Stopping, she watched it until it disappeared behind a line of trees.

She turned forward, her feet moving quickly and bringing her stone cottage into view.

Home. She was finally home. Safe.

{ CHAPTER 3 }

The carriage slowed, jerking as the horses jumped against tightened reins.

Dammit. What now?

All Caine wanted was to get to Somerset. They had left the coaching inn at the first light of day to move onward to Isabella's parents. To tell them the news. Her parents had been frantic a fortnight ago when he saw them—and he was sure they would now be beyond desperate for news of their beloved daughter.

Caine had sworn to them he would find her. And as much as he would abhor telling them what had happened, he wanted nothing more than to get this business done as quickly as possible.

"M'lord."

Caine flipped the trap door in the roof as the carriage came to a stop. "What is it, Tom?"

"The side of the road, m'lord. I don't want to interfere, but…"

Caine could see his driver pointing to the right. He went to the side of the carriage, pulling aside the deep blue curtains to search the side of the road.

A stacked stone wall lined the road, the land rolling down into a gentle hill just beyond it. Bleating sheep dotted the hill.

"Tom, what?" Caine growled. He didn't have time for looking at sheep.

"Just behind the wall, m'lord. I can see it from up here. Mayhap you can't down there."

Caine's eyes flitted back and forth along the top stones of the wall.

He saw it. The gaudy pink. Bright, shocking against the deep green of the pasture. Just a slice of the fabric—lifted by the wind—but there it was.

He flew out of the carriage before Tom could descend and open the door. To the wall in a second, his hands landed on top of the stones, knocking several loose. His gaze dropped with dread.

The piece of fabric was attached to the whole chemise.

The whole chemise was attached to Miss Detton.

Her face was buried in the dirt, but even from his poor angle, he could see the streaks of blood on her neck. Her legs splayed crooked, prone, her bare arms huddled under her body for warmth.

"Miss Detton? Ara—Arabella?"

Ever so slowly, her head moved, sliding sideways. She cocked her face to the side, looking up at him through the slit in her left eye, swollen with blackness.

The slit closed, her face turning back down to the earth.

Caine jumped the wall, his hands going gently to her shoulders, turning her over.

She whimpered in pain at the movement, her body trying to cringe from him, but not able to move.

Her bottom lip was split. Both eyes blackened. Her cheek swollen. Blood smeared everywhere about her face. And that was just what he could see. The way her body moved—or didn't want to—he could tell she had cracked ribs, and her shoulder was possibly out of place.

"Good God, Ara. What the hell happened to you?"

"Die. Leave…leave me." Her voice was only the faintest cracking whisper.

"Who did this to you? How did you get here?"

"Crawled." Her mouth closed, lips trembling against pain. "Leave me…die…I want to die."

"No."

"Please." Her hand shaking, she raised it and gripped his arm with far more strength than her broken body should have allowed. "Please…please, let me die. Leave me here… please."

"You are not going to die, Ara. I will not allow it."

She tried to shake her head, the slightest tear slipping down her temple.

"No, Ara. No." Caine couldn't stifle the rage exploding in his gut, and his fist slammed into the ground. "Who did this to you?"

"Father. Sins. My sins. I am a sinner. Die…let me die. Please."

His knuckles smashed into the ground again.

A breath to control himself, and Caine looked up to his driver. Tom stood on the other side of the wall watching, waiting. "Help me get her to the carriage, man."

Tom nodded, jumping over the wall and helping to lift Ara as gently as possible into Caine's arms. Swinging his legs over the wall, Caine carried her to the carriage as Tom ran ahead to open the door.

"Where to, m'lord?"

"A coaching inn at least two towns away, Tom. At least that far—farther if we can get to one with haste."

~~~

Ara opened her eyes, instantly confused at how little light came into her sight. She tried to open her eyes farther.

They didn't pull wide. They couldn't pull wide.

Pain. Needles around her eyes. Throbbing. Her cheek revolting against the slightest twitch.

"You are awake."

Ara tried to turn her head. Was that a pillow under her neck? And water dripping along her jaw, pooling behind her ear?

"No. Do not move. It will be easier for you if you are still."

Ara found the source of the voice through the thin slits the skin around her eyes afforded.

"Wh…where?" The one word stuck in her throat, travelling upward with a slow exhale.

"My driver found you on the side of the road. You are in a coaching inn in Shillington. I am Caine Farlington. Do you remember me?"

She nodded.

"No. Again, do not move. I can see it pains you." He dragged a wet sponge along her cheek, the water stinging. "I am almost done cleaning you. You said your father did this to you?"

She didn't want to acknowledge his question. Acknowledge what had happened.

After everything. After being taken. After the wretched thugs. The nauseating smells. The invasion of her body. All she had wanted was to be home.

Home and safe and warm. It was all she wanted.

But then her father.

Her mouth cracked open, and she could feel the tender skin on her lips tear, fresh blood seeping onto her tongue before she could get words out. "I am a whore…not his daughter…he has no daughter…no daughter…"

So soft, she could barely hear her own words in her head.

But Mr. Farlington heard her. He grimaced, the deep-set frown on his face tightening. His hand jerked on the sponge.

"I…I told him. It was so hard to speak the words, but I told him. They never…I am still a virgin. But he…he…"

"He what?"

"This." Her eyes closed, she drew breath against the pain the words caused her. "Disowned. This is what he did. I am no longer his daughter."

Mr. Farlington's head shook as he lifted the sponge from her face and turned, dunking it into a bowl of water. He turned back to her.

"I am your guardian now, Ara. You are a distant cousin from Devonshire. My brother is dying, so I have taken over running the estate. No one will question it when I settle you in a townhouse in London as a relative. You will have a small staff, a chaperone. All of it above reproach. Do you understand what I am telling you?"

She heard his words, but couldn't trust them. Couldn't trust anything. Not anymore. Not after her father. "Why?"

He turned, looking away. Looking at something Ara couldn't see through her swollen eyes.

He did not look at her as his voice eased past the pounding in her ears. "Because it is the way of right."

"Why? Why could you not let me die? I want it."

"I do not know why, but I need you to live, Ara." His eyes whipped to her, a hard glint in them. "You will heal. And you will hold your head up, Ara. You will not let this become you, do you understand?"

She stared at him, not able to believe his words.

"I will not give up on you, Ara, as long as you do not give up on you. Tell me you understand."

She nodded.

But she didn't understand—not a single thing that had happened to her. Not one of the horrendous moments. She would never understand how men could be so heinous.

But she could lie. She could survive.

And if Mr. Farlington was right, maybe one day she could hold her head high again.

~ ~ ~

"My lord, thank the heavens you are home."

Caine set aside the numbers he had been poring over, the vellum crinkling as he set it on the fat ledger on the left of his desk. Disappearing into the numbers of the estate had been his only solace during the past month since Isabella had died, and his annoyance at being interrupted set his shoulders tight.

He looked up to see Mrs. Merrywent step into his study, pulling the heavy door closed behind her.

Caine's butler had announced her only a second before she had rushed past the man and into the room. It was far too late into the night, and it was his study, but Mrs. Merrywent was not one to bow to propriety. She had always skirted on the far reaches of acceptable behavior, which was why his younger sisters had so adored her as their governess.

Propriety aside, Mrs. Merrywent was also unfailingly loyal and prided herself on her discreetness. Caine could think of no other more fit to be Ara's chaperone.

Mrs. Merrywent looked about his study, her eyes reaching into every corner. "You are alone?"

"I am. Is something amiss with Ara?" He had checked in on Ara and Mrs. Merrywent several times during the past month to make sure everything was running smoothly in the new household. He had set up Ara in a respectable house on Gilbert Lane, but he had not visited them in the last week and a half.

"Yes. You need to stand, my lord. Action. You need to move, to come with me."

Caine's chair flew back, hitting the wainscoting as he jumped to his feet. "Where is Ara?"

"I cannot get her to leave the spot, my lord. I have tried. She had the driver bring us there."

A chill ran up Caine's spine. "Where is Ara, Mrs. Merrywent?"

"She is in the East End, outside a brothel, my lord. Or that is what it looks to be."

"What? Dammit to hell, Mrs. Merrywent, it is the middle of the night." Caine shot from behind the desk, grabbing his dark jacket from where he had draped it along the back of a side chair.

"I know, my lord. I could not stop her. She has been there for hours. Since nightfall. I never would have let her get in the hack if I had known where she told the driver to go. She refuses to leave."

"You need to return to the Gilbert Lane townhouse, Mrs. Merrywent." Caine shoved his arms into his jacket.

"I will come with, my lord. You trusted me with her— she is my responsibility."

"No." The word was sharp, but he didn't care. He didn't want to have to worry about getting two women out of the East End in the middle of the night unscathed. "And not a word of this to anyone. Concoct whatever story you need to, to hide Ara's absence from the staff."

"Of course, my lord. Not a word."

Caine stepped past her, yanking the door open.

Mrs. Merrywent grabbed his arm. "She is in front of a place called the Jolly Vassal, my lord, it is on—"

"I know the place, Mrs. Merrywent. Thank you." Caine paused to incline his head, his voice a deadly warning. "Not a word. To anyone. Ever."

Her hand dropped from his arm, her face solemn with her nod.

A half hour later—far too long for Caine's liking—his black, crestless carriage came to a stop down the block from the Jolly Vassal.

Caine jumped from his carriage and ran up to several stationary hacks. Disregarding privacy, he started yanking open the doors of the coaches to check the interiors from the street side, hidden from where a group of hackney drivers huddled with a bottle of brandy.

Two empty hacks. One with a whore on a man's lap.

He ripped open the door of the fourth hack. His heart dropped.

Ara.

Wide eyes whipped to him. She twisted around from her kneeling position in front of the opposite window.

Before she could say a word, Caine jumped into the carriage, slamming the door closed. "What in the bloody hell do you think you're doing, Ara?" Fury laced each word as they sliced into the staleness of the carriage.

"I—"

"No. No excuses. There is no excuse for this. For here. For being here." He grabbed her shoulders, fingers digging into her flesh as he lifted and shoved her onto a bare wooden bench.

She instantly struggled, smacking his chest as she wedged her feet up to kick him away.

Recognizing the panic he was causing her, Caine released her, dropping back onto the bench across from her, his hands high and unmoving to calm her.

His breath seething, he stared at her, trying to control the savage storm in the pit of his stomach. She wore a pretty yellow muslin walking dress, demure, the top lace reaching high across her chest, but the whole of the outfit sat in complete contrast to the dark night. Blond strands from her upsweep scattered askew, her green eyes wary and her face flushed from the scuffle. The last traces of the beating from her father had disappeared from her cheeks, but Caine could tell by the way she held herself to the side that she had just aggravated her wrecked ribs. Or more appropriately, *he* had just aggravated her injuries.

"I am getting you out of here, Ara."

"No."

"No?"

Her hands came up, her fingers rubbing her forehead, hiding her face.

Caine waited.

With a growl, her arms dropped, her eyes finding Caine in the dim light escaping from the windows of the closest building. "No. I saw them. I saw them—those men that took me. I saw them. I was at the market this afternoon and I saw them." Her words flew frantic, furious. "They were in a coach and they had a girl with them. She was young. And crying. And looking out from the carriage window. And I saw."

"Saw what?" Caine's voice softened, but he said the words carefully, giving her no rein to think that her current actions were in any way acceptable.

"The look. The exact look I know. I saw it on her, and I know it too well. The look of disbelief. Of desperately wanting someone to see her. Help her. Save her. The fear. The confusion."

"So you came here?"

"I followed them. I stopped a hack and told him to follow the carriage to wherever it went. It came here." Her eyes drifted from him to the building across the street. "I tried to get Mrs. Merrywent to stay at the market but she jumped in with me." Her eyes jolted back to Caine. "Mrs. Merrywent—where is she? She left—I would not go with her."

"She is safe. She came to me. But you put her in danger, Ara. This area is no place for either one of you."

"Oh. I did not mean to put her in danger."

Damn, she was too innocent. Even after what she went through. Yet it didn't temper his ire. "You are sitting across from a brothel, Ara—what type of area do you think this is?"

Her head snapped back as though he had struck her. "I did not think—"

"Exactly. You did not think. Now we are going to get out of here."

"No."

"You keep saying that word, Ara, and I am getting tired of it." He pushed from the bench, reaching for her arm to drag her out of the hack.

She was quick, her fingers wrapping around his wrist just as he grabbed her upper arm. "They are selling that girl tonight, Mr. Farlington."

Caine froze, his face right above hers. "How do you know that?"

"I have been waiting here, watching and listening for hours. Men pass by and they are drunk and they talk. There is to be an auction tonight. They put a damn description of her in an invitation."

Her head shook and then her voice went to a whisper as her wide eyes lifted to meet his gaze. "Did they do that with me? A description in an invitation?"

Caine could not lie to her. Whatever she was doing here, whatever she was searching for, she needed the truth. "Yes."

Her lips drew in, and she half nodded, half shook her head as her eyes closed. Caine could see her inhale, trying to calm the tremble in her body.

"What did you think you were going to do here tonight, Ara?"

Her eyes opened to him, the intensity in the green orbs startling. "Get her out."

Caine dropped his head with a long exhale. He loosened his hold on her arm, but did not move from his position above her as he met her glare. "How?"

"I do not know." Her hand fell from his wrist. "But I am going to do it. Sneak up the back. Grab her when they drag her out. I do not know. But I am going to get her out."

"You cannot do this, Ara."

"I can."

"You cannot. They will kill you. Or take you to sell you again."

"I do not care what you say, Mr. Farlington. I have to get her out. I will figure out a way. I cannot let this happen to her. She is just a girl. A girl." She looked up at him. Fire in her eyes. Her voice vehement. "It is the way of right."

Caine stared at her. She was not only an innocent, but now she thought she could snatch a girl from a brothel. Caine sighed. And she was going to do it with or without him.

Better that she do it with him.

"I will go in and buy her, Ara."

She blinked, shock shaking her features. "You will?"

"Yes."

It took a long moment, and then she nodded. "Thank you. And I am sorry I kicked you."

Caine offered a slight nod to her apology, then ran his fingers through his hair, glancing over his shoulder to the brothel. He wished he had Fletch with him. That was not a place to be in alone, dressed as he was.

He looked back to Ara. "What does she look like—the girl?"

"What? Why do you need to know?"

His eyebrow cocked. She couldn't be that innocent, could she? She had been in the brothel—she knew exactly what happened in there. "They sell more than one at a time, if they have them. Just like when you were—" He cut himself off as her face tightened at his words. "They like a big production."

Her face relaxed slightly. "Well then, you must buy all of them."

"I cannot. It is not done, Ara."

"But you must." Her eyes went wide, begging as she scooted to the edge of the bench.

"They will not allow it." His head shook. "And if they realize I am not buying one for my own…pleasure, they will make me pay for ruining their sale."

"What do you mean, make you pay? Why can you not just purchase all of them?"

Caine rubbed his eyes. Blasted innocence. "They will beat me, toss me into the gutter if I am lucky. Much worse if I am not. These men—there is no room for honor or respect in this world, Ara, and the spoils of virgins must be sold for the purpose, or they have no business. If they have even a second of doubt as to why I want to buy one, I am at their mercy."

"Oh." She sank back against the wood where squabs of cushion once existed, her hands twisting together above her belly. "Well, I do not want that."

"Thank you."

She closed her eyes, her face tilting back as she clunked the crown of her head on the board behind her. She knocked it three more times.

He reached over and grabbed her knee through her skirts. "Stop. You will not injure yourself, Ara."

One more clunk, and her head rested on the wall of the carriage.

Caine removed his hand. "So what did the girl look like?"

Ara's right eye cracked open. "Only one?"

"One."

She opened both eyes and brought herself to a ramrod straight posture, her voice low, haunted. "She was small with dark hair that hung very long. She had such frightened eyes—huge—except you will not be able to see her face, will you, with the veils?"

Caine shook his head. "Was she taller than you?"

"No. Maybe a head shorter as far as I could tell from the distance. It was only a glance when the carriage door opened and she was sitting."

Ara leaned forward, one knee going to the floor of the hack, and grabbed his arm. "You are positive you cannot find a way to buy more? It is just that they—"

"We can only save them one at a time, Ara. No more. It is too dangerous."

"You are firm upon that?"

"Do you want them to toss me out here—to find you in the process and drag you back into the place? For it is a very real possibility, Ara."

She recoiled back onto her bench, fear at his scenario—or his harsh tone—flashing across her face. "No."

He forced his words softer, but could not loosen the hard set to his jaw. "Then we save one at a time, Ara. No more."

"Thank you." She nodded, attempting to produce a small smile, but it only twisted into a frown on her lips. Caine realized in that moment how distraught—horrified—she was for any of the other girls about to be sold.

He couldn't blame her. But he also wasn't aching to be beaten to near death and robbed this night. So he would do what little he could. He could get one out.

Opening the door of the hack, he jumped into the street. He helped Ara from the hack and quickly ushered her along the street to Tom and his waiting carriage.

Depositing her inside, he paused before turning to the brothel and stuck his head into the interior of his carriage, his hand gripping the door. "Just concentrate on the one, Ara. And remember, you were the one. It will make a difference."

She nodded again, the frown still set in place.

Caine closed the door to the carriage, wondering if saving the one would truly sate her.

He guessed not.

{ CHAPTER 4 }

The day had brought forth too much—far too many memories.

Caine drained the last brown drops of brandy and clunked the tumbler to the table. He reached out, wrapping sloppy fingers around the bottle of brandy.

Damn the memories.

The exact moment Ara's voice had told him that Isabella was dead. Telling her parents. Their faces contorting in grief. His failure to bring her home. The guilt that would not loosen its hold on him.

He had not expected the memories to rush upon him as they had. But the second his carriage had pulled away from the simple cottage of the girl they had saved last night, Misty, the memories had overwhelmed him.

It had taken the rest of the previous night and most of the day on the muddied roads to reach Misty's home. And far from Ara's father's reaction to her return, Misty's parents had pulled her into their arms, overjoyed that she had been returned home. Even after the girl told them what had happened, Caine had not seen the slightest waver in their gratefulness for their daughter's safe return.

Caine had watched Ara closely during those moments in the cottage. She had refused to let Misty go into the house by herself, wanting to protect her if need be. Watching the joyful reunion, Caine had waited for jealousy to spark to life in Ara's eyes, but there was none. Quite the opposite, tears streamed down Ara's face with genuine happiness that the girl had been wrapped in the comfort of her father's arms.

It was only as they left the cottage that Caine caught a glimpse of the heart-wrenching sadness taking over Ara's eyes.

Ara had hidden it in the carriage. Pretended to sleep while the daylight turned to darkness. But Caine could see she was awake the whole time. Awake and twitching against whatever was in her mind.

Apparently, the resurgence of memories was not for him alone.

His own memories had stewed for a month, skillfully avoided by him at every turn. Yet they had not left his head. Instead, they had festered, not dissolving away to nothingness as he had planned for them.

Glass clinked on glass, the last of the amber liquid dripping from the bottle as Caine stared at the wall in front of him. Just on the other side, Ara was ensconced in the room next to his at the coaching inn they had stopped at halfway back to London.

Ara had wanted to push on through the darkness, but as none of them, including his driver, had slept during the day or the previous night, Caine had insisted they stop.

That had been a mistake.

The moment he had entered his room, the silence had crushed him. He had stopped moving, stopped the busyness, and he paid for it. Far from all of his usual distractions in London, Caine could not defend against the onslaught of pain that came with the memories of Isabella's death. The last hours of silence in his room had only strengthened the failure that constantly gnawed on his chest, refusing to yield.

His head tilted back, a swallow of brandy sliding down his throat.

A scream pierced the air, snapping Caine upright.

"No, Crow—Crow—not her—not the Crow—not there—"

The words, the scream, were coming straight through the wall from Ara's room.

Caine fumbled to his feet, snatching his white linen shirt from the chair. He jabbed at it, trying to get his arms though the holes—failure. Damn shirt. Damn brandy.

More screams.

Flinging the shirt to the floor, he grabbed the candle from the table. His feet sloshed, weighted down by invisible mud. Too slow. Ara was in trouble and he was too slow.

Three tries to turn Ara's doorknob, and he finally managed to crack open the door. It had taken only seconds but felt like an eternity, every motion heavy on his limbs.

Ara screeched, again and again, and Caine found her in the darkness, her body thrashing on the bed.

"God no—no, no, no—not the wolves. Not the wolves. Crow. Please. Not the wolves. No. Please crow." Another stinging scream.

Caine's muddled mind took in the dark room, searching for an attacker. Someone that would make Ara scream, crazed.

"Ara." His voice was no match for the wail that filled the room.

He lifted the candlestick in his hand, scanning the shadows again.

Only Ara in the room.

Caine's sluggish eyes landed on Ara, and he finally realized she was asleep, terrorized in her dreams. Her next scream stunned him, a cold, brutal chill invading his spine. He had seen men in the war, their legs being sawed off, bullets tearing them apart from the inside—but their screams were nothing like this. Whatever horror was in her mind was tearing her apart, chunk of flesh, by chunk of flesh.

He knew he was too damn drunk to help her properly, but he didn't have a choice. Muttering a line of blasphemies under his breath, Caine closed the door behind him and set the candle on the small table next to the fireplace.

Shrieks, three in a row, rang in his ears, smothering the room, and Caine rushed to her as fast as his sloth-feet would carry him. The sheet twisted along her legs as she kicked, her bare feet jamming into the wall by the bed. The top half of her body was covered only by the simple white chemise—damp with fear—that she had stripped down to. Her hands flailed above her head, slapping onto the headboard, battling unseen demons.

Caine stumbled, landing on the edge of the bed, and grabbed Ara's writhing shoulders. Her hands flew up at the touch, fighting him, her screams reaching a new pitch.

"Ara, wake up. Ara."

"No. God no. Not the wolves. No, no, no. Crow. Please no. Don't do it. Please. No, no, no."

"Ara, it's only me. It's Caine. Wake up. Ara."

A scream, and she attempted to crumple into a ball, trying to disappear away from him, but the tangled sheet along her legs held her captive. It aggravated her savage terror, and her whole body convulsed, trying to both fight him and escape him at the same time.

He shook her. "Ara."

The shrieks intensified.

Blast it. She sounded as if she were being tortured. There'd be a knock on the door soon if he didn't quiet her, and rightfully so.

He grabbed her face in his hands, his nose touching hers. "Ara. Wake the hell up." His voice overtook her screeches.

His hands on her head tightened. "Wake up, Ara."

She stilled, silent.

Blood pounding in his ears, Caine watched as her eyes cracked open, the long lashes fluttering.

It took seconds before her eyes focused.

Caine pulled his face away from hers, giving her room, but did not drop his hands from the grip on her head.

Confusion filled her eyes, crinkling lines along her forehead. "Mr. Farlington?"

"Caine. I think we are well past Mr. Farlington, Ara."

She blinked hard, confusion still thick in her green eyes. "Caine?"

"Yes?"

Her trembling fingers came up, wrapping along the back of his hands still clamped to her cheeks. "These are your hands?"

He nodded with an exhale of relief. Reality was settling into her mind. "Yes."

"Why? What are you doing on my bed?"

"We are in a coaching inn. Do you remember where we were?"

Her fingernails dug into the back of his hands for an instant, then dropped to the bed as her eyes fell. "Misty. We were delivering Misty."

"Yes. And we are in a coaching inn on the road back to London. Do you remember?"

"Yes." Her eyes came up to him. "I was dreaming?"

"You screamed of crows and wolves."

She drew a gasping breath that covered a sob.

Caine knew she was awake, knew he could drop his hold on her, but the tremors still vibrating through her body made him keep his hands in place. "You are safe. Do you understand? Safe."

She nodded, her cheekbones rubbing against his thumbs. "I am sorry. I tried to stay awake. I tried. But I was too tired."

"You have been awake for days, Ara. You need to sleep."

"My mind in sleep is traitorous." A quake rocked her entire body, and her head fell as she gulped back a sob. Her chin stayed down, but her wide eyes lifted to him. "Mr. Farlington, I do not want to ask. But…"

"What is it?"

Her hands came up, gripping his wrists. "Your heartbeat…may I listen to it?"

His head tilted. Even with the brandy fogging his brain, it was an odd request. "Why the heartbeat?"

"At the townhouse. When they attack in my dreams and fill my brain, and my body hurts I fight so hard…I listen to Patch's heart after, it thumps, and it takes away the shake in my body. It is outside my body and constant—something to hold onto to even me. It will not take long, I swear it."

His chest tightening at her words, he silently dropped his hands to grab her body, wrapping her onto his lap as he shifted on the bed, setting his back against the wall. Drawing her legs up to her belly, Ara curled onto his chest, making herself small as she shoved her blond hair aside to lay her ear on the bare skin above his heart.

In this position, one arm wrapping along her back, the other holding her head tight to his chest, Caine could feel the constant trembles in her body—and also feel as they eased. But she did not fall asleep. The constant tickle of her eyelashes against his skin verified she was refusing to close her eyes again.

"Who is Patch?" The question had been forefront in his mind in the long minutes since she had mentioned the name.

He could feel her cheek rise in a smile against his chest. "I found a dog. He followed me from the park across the street to the townhouse the first week I was there."

"And you let him sleep with you?"

"Yes, when I need him to. Though the bugger has decided that should be all the time."

Caine chuckled, aware that the laugh was delayed by his still brandy-soaked mind.

"Caine, will you teach me? I do not want to be innocent anymore."

His muscles froze.

Even in his sodden state, he knew he had best tread carefully with that question. "What do you mean, Ara?"

"Your world. London. This world I do not understand."

Caine exhaled, his body relaxing. Of course it was an innocent request. It always was with Ara. She was old enough to be relatively savvy of the world, yet she had been exposed to so little by her father.

"It is the sounds. The smells. The sights. The people. It is so big and I walk around, trying to understand it all. But it is so much. There is gold gilding on some of the doors, and then I walk ten blocks, and I am standing in front of buildings like the one they took me to. All of it is so far beyond what I knew in Marport."

"You were to never speak the name of that town again, Ara."

"I cannot even with you?"

"Never. You need to forget everything of your life before a month ago. You swore you could do it."

She shook her head. "Even that I do not understand. The demand must have a reason."

"I cannot have anyone question that you are a distant relative, Ara. I do not want you ever tainted by your past. This is the easiest way. The only way. You come from a tiny village in Devonshire. You are a fourth cousin, descended from the youngest of my great, great grandfather's four brothers, Richard. That is all anyone ever needs to know of you."

She nodded, falling silent.

Minutes passed, and the tremors had nearly ceased, only the slightest shiver running periodically along her arm.

More minutes ticked by, and Caine could not stop himself from questioning his own demand of Ara to forget everything she had ever known. And then his blasted mind went rogue and wandered unwittingly to a month ago—to the very moment he knew Isabella was lost to him.

Damn, he missed Bella.

The brandy in his mind sucked, pulling him into the hell of memories.

The ultimate cruelty of her death was that she had been waiting for him. Protecting her virtue, her innocence—and that was the very thing she had been stolen for.

Before Caine left for the war, Isabella had never allowed more than a kiss. He had never held her like this—like Ara was on his body.

Never had her body draped over his.

Her heartbeat thudding on his chest.

Her lips near to his skin, her warm breath heating his bare nipple.

Ara.

At that moment, her head tilted and she looked up at him. Innocence in her eyes. Innocence like Bella's.

Without thought, he dropped his head, taking her mouth under his. He sensed for a moment she resisted him, resisted the kiss. But by the time the deterrence registered through his soused senses, she was leaning into him, gently offering her mouth to his.

His tongue swept across the softness of her lips. Hell. So sweet. Bella was sweet like that. His tongue breached her lips, and she opened her mouth to him, taking him in, pulling him into her essence.

Her nipple, taut against her chemise, was suddenly under his fingers, his palm moving to cup her breast. How had his hand even landed there? He rolled her nipple, pinching it. A murmur at the touch rumbled from her throat into his mouth, sending his cock rock hard.

His senses took over his brain. His mind nothing but nerve endings being stoked. Her fingers moved against his bare chest, wrapping around his neck, curling into his hair. A thousand wildcats could tear at him, and he wouldn't abandon this kiss.

The hand he had wrapped around her waist moved downward, his palm landing on her thigh, his fingers pulling up her chemise. His thumb swept the inner stretch of her thigh, the skin prickling under his touch.

No resistance. She only purred under him, her tongue twisting with his, her body arching into his. His thumb moved upward, breaching the hair at the juncture of her thighs. Soft. Wet. Throbbing.

He swallowed the gasp that escaped her at the touch. He stroked through her folds, finding the hard nubbin waiting for him, plying it, making her hips ride his hand in rhythm, her body begging. He continued his onslaught, her moans begging him insistently for more until she shuddered violently, screaming into his mouth and then gasping for air under him.

His hand on her nipple dropped, and he freed himself from his breeches.

Hell. What he was doing was so wrong. Wrong. But Bella was so sweet, so pliable in his arms. Her skin rippling under his fingers. Her thighs clamped around his hand, contractions still rolling from her core.

He needed to take his love right now. Right here. They had waited too long. Years too long.

He grabbed her hand, setting her shaking fingers along his shaft, guiding her to stroke the length of him.

Exquisite. Her fingers both strong and gentle against him.

His mouth moved against her lips. "Yes, Bella. There. Yes. Bella."

Both of her hands flew up, hard against his chest. Hands he needed down below. Touching him. Stroking him.

Nails bit into his skin. Her face twisted from him, her lips gasping for air.

She was fighting him. Fighting to get away from him.

The fact sank through the tar in his mind—through the thick haze of lust and brandy blurring his thoughts.

"No."

The one word pulled him into reality. Into the present. Bella wasn't in his arms.

Ara was.

And she was trying to twist away from his clamp. Escape him.

His hands instantly dropped from her.

She scampered to the far side of the bed, tugging her chemise over her knees and ripping the sheet up over her body in one frenzied motion.

How long had she said no? How long had she tried to free herself from him?

Dammit to hell.

She stared at him, the sheet up to her chin, heaving. Her lips, plump and bruised, opened and closed, her tongue licking her lips as she fought for breath.

But she wasn't afraid. He could see that. No fear in her eyes. What he saw was accusation—hurt?

Had he hurt her? Blasted ass that he was, he couldn't even think straight enough to know if he had hurt her.

His hand went out to her. "Ara—"

"You called me Bella."

"I what?"

"You called me Bella. You thought you were with Bella."

His own words from seconds ago barreled into his mind. He had.

Of all the bastard things to do, he had called her Bella. He had touched her, then called her Bella.

His hand dropped from midair.

"I…I cannot be Bella for you, Caine. I cannot." Her voice crept across the bed, shaking, distraught, but with a trace of pride that would not be denied.

Caine stood from the bed, shoving his erection under the flap of his breeches. He went to the door quickly, yanking it open.

He paused, his head bowed as he stared at the floor of the hallway, not able to turn back to her.

"I apologize, Ara. There is no excuse for how I just violated you. I apologize. Please know that I will never touch you again."

He stepped from the room, quietly closing the door behind him.

Two steps into his own room, he collapsed backward onto his closed door.

He was a bloody bastard.

{ CHAPTER 5 }

Caine peeked over his shoulder into the interior of the carriage.

Damn. Ara was still slumped in the corner, dead to the world. Even after he had been extra obnoxious with noise as he descended from the coach. He turned to his driver. "Tom, could you please carry Miss Detton into the townhouse and up to her room?"

"Oh." Surprise shot across Tom's face before he stifled it. "Of course, m'lord."

Caine knew Tom was entirely curious as to why Caine wasn't about to carry her in—or more sensibly, wake her. But Caine wasn't about to do either of those things.

Ara hadn't slept the rest of the night at the coaching inn. He had heard her pacing, and then the sounds of her bed creaking to no end. And he knew full well she was past exhaustion, as was evident from the deep, dark circles under her eyes when she entered the carriage in the morning.

So no, he wasn't about to wake her now that she was finally asleep.

As for carrying her into the townhouse…he had sworn to never touch her again. He wasn't about to break that vow mere hours after making it.

Caine moved to give Tom space to lift Ara out from the carriage and then looked up the stairs leading into the Gilbert Lane townhouse from the mews.

Mrs. Merrywent stood holding wide the rear door of the townhouse, her hands agitated, as a medium-

sized, short-haired dog—black, with haphazard patches
of brown and red and white—ran in front of her tapping
feet, yelping. Patch. The yelping grew frantic when Tom,
grunting from the awkward motion, stepped down from the
carriage with Ara sound asleep in his arms.

"Quiet that mutt, Mrs. Merrywent," Caine snapped in
a loud whisper.

She bent her plump frame and picked up the dog,
tossing him backward into the house. He was back to the
doorway in an instant, yelps flying until Mrs. Merrywent set
her fingers on his nose.

She shifted aside as Caine and Tom moved up the three
stairs and into the hall outside the study in the back of the
townhouse.

"Miss Ara, is she not well?" Mrs. Merrywent scurried
after Tom until he stopped, and her hand went to Ara's
forehead.

"She is asleep, Mrs. Merrywent. Nothing more. Just
exhaustion."

Her head shaking, Mrs. Merrywent turned to Caine.
"Good heavens, I have been worried to hades and back on
her. Where have you been with her? It has been days, my
lord—days of worry. Where have you been?"

Caine rubbed his eyes. He knew full well the woman
was building herself into a tirade directed at him. "I will
explain all, Mrs. Merrywent."

Mrs. Merrywent rounded him, hands on her hips. "You
have charged me to be her chaperone, my lord, and stunts
such as this undermine the very job you pay me to do. If
you thought to hire me, only for me to look the other way
when it comes to you taking that sweet child to only the

devil knows where, you had better rethink my employment. And you had better rethink your responsibilities as a gentleman. You had assured me—"

"I do not require a scolding, Mrs. Merrywent. I will wait in the drawing room and explain all once you have her settled."

Tom cleared his throat. The man was still standing behind Caine, holding Ara, her head propped against his black coat. The noise hadn't stirred her in the slightest. Ara was slight, but Caine knew Tom was uncomfortable carrying her. Not to mention the mutt was jumping on Tom's leg, trying to get to its mistress.

Caine waved his hand, ushering Tom past him. Mrs. Merrywent harrumphed pointedly in Caine's direction and then bustled in front of Tom, leading him through the hallway to the stairs in the foyer. Caine followed, stepping into the front drawing room to wait as promised.

His back to the large front window of the townhouse, Caine's eyes swept about the room. It had been well appointed—whether by Ara's or Mrs. Merrywent's taste, he couldn't be sure. Soft colors, a few nicely chosen pieces of simple-lined furniture. No trinkets.

The whole of it presented much better than the obtuse gold and shine that had been stuffed into each corner and splattered onto every surface in the room when he had purchased the house a month ago. Judging by the restraint of the current furniture, Caine doubted Ara and Mrs. Merrywent had spent even a third of what he had allotted them for new furnishings.

He spun, his nose almost touching the glass of the window as he stared out past the quiet street. He had chosen this house specifically for its calmness. Little traffic on the road, and a peaceful park across the street. Quiet and gentle. Ara deserved that after her ordeal, and it was exactly what he would have hoped for Bella to have, had she survived.

Caine's eyes were fixed on a couple strolling through the wide park across the street when Mrs. Merrywent entered the room, pulling the door closed behind her.

His eyes did not leave the man and woman stopping by a row of shrubbery. "She is settled?"

"Yes. That mutt of hers is already splayed on her chest, his ears perked to the slightest threat. He did not take kindly to your man carrying her in, my lord."

"I gathered that." Caine turned from the window, looking to Mrs. Merrywent. "The dog—it helps her?"

Her eyes went to pinpricks, her head tilting. "What are you asking me, my lord?" Mrs. Merrywent always was an astute one. She'd had to be to keep his sisters in line.

"She is exhausted for a reason, Mrs. Merrywent, and it has absolutely nothing to do with what you are dreading happened."

"What did happen, my lord?" Her hands landed on her hips.

The brandy had dried from his veins, but Caine's head still pounded, and he could do without Mrs. Merrywent's accusing tone. He sighed. "Ara was determined to help the girl she saw in the market. Helping the girl was the only way she was going to move from that place and not do something foolish."

"That building—that was the place you found her a month ago?"

He nodded. When he had hired Mrs. Merrywent, he had told her every detail of Ara's ordeal, so Ara herself would never have to retell the tale.

"I guessed as much. And what happened to the girl she wanted to help?"

Caine shrugged. "I bought the girl and we returned her to her home near Oxford. Ara insisted on accompanying the girl to her family. The mother and father were grateful to have their daughter returned. That is all that happened."

"Then why is Ara so exhausted?"

"We were in separate rooms in a coaching inn last night, and she had a nightmare."

Mrs. Merrywent's hands clasped in front of her, her demeanor suddenly agitated. "She had a nightmare?"

"It was not just a nightmare, Mrs. Merrywent, it was terror." Caine shook his head, the sounds of Ara's shrieks still echoing in his ears. "Terror that did not let her go. I have never seen anything like it. I could not calm her. I had to shake her awake. And still then, it took far too long for the tremors in her body to cease." His fingers went to his eyes, rubbing the memory from them.

"The crow and the wolves, my lord?"

His eyes snapped to Mrs. Merrywent. "Yes. So you have heard it as well?"

"Yes. Did you not know, my lord?"

"Know what?"

"How to calm the terrors?"

"Calm the terrors? There is a way?"

"Yes." Her palm swung up, waving in the general direction of the rooms above. "Come, I will show you."

She walked out of the drawing room without waiting for his agreement. The woman was far too impertinent. Unfortunate that she was invaluable. Even if her pay came from him, her loyalty was clearly with Ara, which Caine could not fault her for.

He followed Mrs. Merrywent up the stairs, hesitating in the open doorway to Ara's darkened room.

Much like the drawing room, Ara's bedroom had been decorated with restraint—simple, yet elegant. Several upholstered chairs dotted the large room, their fabric a soft, solid blue. Unadorned straight lines of a writing desk and a wardrobe completed the chamber.

His eyes rested on Ara. Deep asleep, she lay curled on her side, her arm hugging Patch to her chest. The dog's head lifted, looking back and forth between Mrs. Merrywent and Caine, but he was not alarmed enough to give up the cozy spot.

Mrs. Merrywent waved Caine into the room, waiting to speak until he stood next to her, looking down at Ara.

"Here. It is this spot," Mrs. Merrywent whispered as she brushed Ara's blond hair away from the back of her neck. The tips of Mrs. Merrywent's weathered fingers settled onto the skin just behind Ara's ear where her hairline started. Mrs. Merrywent looked up at Caine. "When she screams, all one has to do is press and hold this spot, right behind her ear. It calms the terrors, if you can get to it before she starts a-thrashing. Once that starts, it is nearly impossible to get a finger on there to calm her. I have had to sit on her in order to do so. But it will calm her. It always does."

Mrs. Merrywent lifted her fingers from Ara, gave Patch a stroke along the white spot on the top of his head, and then ushered Caine out the door.

Caine waited for Mrs. Merrywent to close the door. "How do you know of this—how did you discover that spot?"

She shrugged. "I learned it by accident in those first weeks after you hired me. My hand just landed there once, and it worked. So it is what I do. She returns to sleep, peaceful. The oddest thing."

"And the terrors stop—just like that?"

"Yes. Peculiar, but true." Her head cocked to the side. "I had thought you knew about the terrors, my lord, about how to help her."

"No, I did not."

Of course he didn't. He truly did not know anything of the girl on the other side of the door. He had been too consumed during the past month with his own grief for that.

He knew nothing, other than that he had just been a bastard to her.

Maybe it was time to change that.

~~~

Ara took a deep breath, steadying her thudding heart. A simple conversation. That was all that was necessary, and she could be on her way. Simple.

She stood alongside the doorway to the study where Caine's butler, Mr. Riggers, had left her after announcing her to Caine. Mrs. Merrywent had disappeared to the back of the townhouse, hoping to chat with Cook during their short stop, as the two were old friends from when Mrs. Merrywent was governess to Caine's sisters.

Ara couldn't quite get her feet to turn the corner into the study. Odd that the butler had left her here, but there appeared to be much activity bustling about Caine's household that Mr. Riggers was more concerned about.

She inhaled. Two steps in, talk to Caine quickly, and she could be on her way, her conscience at ease.

Two weeks ago, Caine had apologized profusely during the carriage ride back to London from that coaching inn. Heat spread up her neck at the memory.

Not that Ara blamed him for the events of that night. She had been a very willing partner in what they had almost done—until he had called her Bella. Once his dead love's name was uttered, it had been easy to recognize how very misguided both of their minds had been in that bed.

She had fallen asleep in the carriage, the awkwardness thick between them. And since then, Ara had not seen Caine once. Avoiding her was fine. While she was entirely grateful for his assistance—for a home to live in and food to eat—she could live her life quite comfortably without the mortification of having to see the man again.

It was unfortunate that the matter of the finances concerning the household he had set her up in would not let the avoidance continue. The finances needed his attention, as the current state of her allowance did not sit well with Ara.

Just a quick conversation.

One last breath, and she picked up her feet, spinning around the corner. Her jaw slightly dropped when she saw the depth of the study. She had not realized his townhouse was this enormous. This room alone sat two stories high—much more of a library than a study. Thick, leather-bound volumes lined two of the walls, the tomes stretching neatly up to the mahogany coffered ceiling.

"You should not be here, Ara." Caine's low voice brought her attention downward, and she found him sitting in a wide leather chair, a tumbler of amber liquid in his fingers balancing on the armrest. His usual dark jacket and waistcoat absent, he wore only black trousers and a white linen shirt, gaping at the neck.

He didn't look up at her, his eyes stayed on the low embers in the fireplace next to him. "It does not do that an unmarried woman visits the home of a bachelor."

Ara took two uneasy steps in, hovering by the doorway. "But you are my guardian, and Mrs. Merrywent accompanied me. I thought that would be within the bounds of propriety."

He shrugged.

She shuffled three steps farther into the room, still closer to the door than to Caine. "I came to ask you a question about the affairs of the household you have given me charge of."

"What of them?"

"It is more than I need—the allowance. I am not sure what to do with the remaining funds. Should I forward them back to your man of affairs, tell him to adjust the amount needed to run the household? Or I could—"

Ara cut herself off as his head lifted and he finally looked to her.

Agony etched deeply into his brow, his eyes hollow with dark circles above the line of his cheekbones. She had seen that look before. It mirrored the one in the carriage when he learned of Isabella's death.

Without hesitation, she sped across the room, her soft peach skirts flying forward to brush onto his knees as she stopped in front of him. Her right hand went to his upper arm, her thumb pressing through his linen shirt into his muscle. He jumped at the touch, looking down to her hand.

She tightened her grip on him. "Caine, what has happened?"

He looked up, his blue eyes a fierce growl, but then his focus settled on her face, softening with weariness.

"Tell me."

His eyes shut. "My brother. He has passed."

Ara stifled a sad gasp. She knew from Mrs. Merrywent that Caine's older brother had been dying of consumption for some time. Caine had never mentioned his brother, so Ara had assumed there was little affection between the two. Clearly she had been wrong.

Her heart constricting at seeing his pain, Ara stared at him. The way he reacted to her hand on his arm was warning she should do no more. But she could not curb her innate impulse—her need to comfort this man.

Without a word, she reached out her other hand, slipping it behind his neck. She gently tugged him forward. The cords of muscles along his neck reacted, resisting her.

She slipped her gloved fingers up into his hair, pulling with smooth force. After a willful second, he relented, letting his body move forward. Ara didn't stop the pull until his head was clasped to her chest. Even though he sat and she stood, his height made the top of his head reach the curve under her chin.

His body remained tensed, ready to escape, so Ara wrapped her right arm around his shoulders, holding him fast to her.

Her heart crushed for not only his loss, but also for the very fact that his body instinctively refused simple compassion.

But once there, he stayed in her arms, his breath hot on the bare skin above the lace trim of her bosom. No tears. No words. But slowly, his arms came up, wrapping around her waist, holding onto her as if she were the very last buoy in a vast ocean aching to pull him under.

She stood silent, clutching him for what seemed like forever, when it truly could have only been a few minutes.

His arms loosened around her waist, but before he could pull himself away, Ara cleared the lump from her throat.

"I am so sorry for your loss, Caine. Can I do anything to help you?"

His arms dropped from her body as he shook his head, leaning back in his chair. His fingers went to his eyes, rubbing. "I am sorry, Ara. That was unseemly of me."

Her brow furrowed. Why in the heavens was he apologizing to her at the moment? "Unseemly?"

His eyes cast downward as his head dropped, his voice rough. "My show of weakness. I did not know what you were doing. I should not have allowed that."

Weakness? What did that mean? The hug? Did he think a hug was weak? Ara couldn't fathom the thought.

Caine's head remained down, so she knelt before him, balancing on the heels of her boots as she looked up to him, finding his blue eyes that were attempting to stay averted from hers. "Are you telling me you have never been hugged before?"

He looked to the side, staring at the highly polished, gleaming planks of the floor. "Of course I have been hugged, Ara. Do not be obtuse."

"No, I mean in comfort, Caine. Compassion. You were never injured and hugged as child? Never lost a pet or a toy and held onto your mother's skirts?"

He shook his head, looking at her like an extra eyeball had appeared on her forehead.

"Not even by a nanny?"

"Affection was not something that was appropriate in our household, Ara." He rubbed the back of his neck, his blue eyes—usually so sure of everything—darting about awkwardly. "We have always been sufficed with bows and curtseys and handshakes."

Her hand went on his knee, squeezing as she stood, trying to move past the moment for his sake. She hadn't meant to make this any harder for him, and her questions obviously made him uneasy. One more thing she did not understand of his world. "I am sorry if I made you uncomfortable. But again, please, is there anything I can do for you to help?"

He shook his head, but then his eyes caught sight of his desk. He sighed. "The correspondence. It is too much, too many notes of condolences that need to be replied to. Too many notes of congratulations on the title." His eyes came up to her. "Congratulations, Ara. My brother is not even in the ground yet, and they are congratulating me."

"Let me. I can go through them, respond with politeness no matter how insulting to your brother's memory they are. It is a simple thing I can do for you."

His eyes narrowed on her, suspect, but after a moment, he nodded silently, his head heavy.

Hours later, her eyes bleary and her forefinger stained with ink, Ara looked at the piles in front of her on Caine's desk. The "answered" pile was now much taller than the "still-to-be-answered" pile. Good progress. Caine had been in and out of the study all day, seeing visitors in the formal drawing room at the front of his townhouse.

Mrs. Merrywent had kept herself busy helping the staff where she could, and Ara currently had her on a quest to fill several plates of food for Caine before he made his way back to the study after the latest visitors. Ara hadn't seen him eat anything all day, only refill his glass of brandy between visitors, and she suspected he hadn't eaten breakfast as well.

Ara set the quill next to the inkwell and thumbed through the small pile she had left to answer. The corner of a bright red card slipped out of the stack, stark against the whites and creams of the other paper. Near the bottom of the pile, the color was odd enough that she pulled it free, fingering it in her hand. It was addressed to "Mr. Farlington," not to "The Right Honourable the Earl of Newdale," as were most of the other letters.

She slid the sharp point of the pen knife under the black wax, breaking the seal and unfolding it. A quick scan of the contents, and Ara's hands began to shake.

Her breathing stopped, her heart wild. She couldn't drop the note, couldn't move a muscle against the tremble rolling through her body.

"Ara? What is amiss?" Caine ran the steps from the doorway of the study to her side at the desk, his hand landing on the back of her shoulder.

Ara couldn't speak, couldn't look up at him. Her eyes refused to move from the crooked writing on the note.

"Ara?" Caine ripped the card from her hands, reading the words. "Bloody hell. The bastard that owned that place is dead. How do they know who I am?"

His hand dropped from her shoulder, leaving a cold spot that sent a chill down her spine. Her stomach started to flip as Ara gasped, again and again, trying to get air into her lungs. What was Caine talking about? Who was dead?

Caine dropped the note, grabbing both of her shoulders and turning her to him. He bent, putting his face directly in front of hers. "Breathe, Ara. Breathe."

Her head shook, eyes shut tight and air still not reaching her lungs.

"Ara, open your eyes."

Her eyes cracked to him and she found his blue eyes, locking onto them.

"Breathe."

It took long seconds, but Ara managed to gain control of her breathing, the need to vomit passing. She nodded at him, still not able to speak. His hands dropped from her body and she sank back against the wooden slats of the chair she sat in.

Caine tilted his head to the note. "This was in the correspondence?"

"Yes." The word squeaked out.

He stared at the red paper, his voice low, murderous. "An invitation to a virgin auction."

"Yes. Tonight. What did you say—who is dead?"

"The old owner of the Jolly Vassal. Apparently, reprehensible new management had taken over."

His jaw flexing, Caine's eyes turned to fire as though he tried to burn the paper just by looking at it. Ara's mind spun into a tornado of grey—so many thoughts and reactions and emotions flying together in a whirlwind, that she was unable to grasp at anything. Unable to form even the simplest thought.

Caine's gaze lifted from the paper to her. "What are you doing this evening, Ara? I find I am suddenly in need of escaping the onslaught of preparing for my brother's funeral."

Guilt and horror that had done nothing but build upon her in the past six weeks settled in heavy, finding a place on Ara's shoulders. She knew exactly what Caine was suggesting, and she grasped onto the idea, gripping tightly to it. She nodded. "I am available."

"Good."

Something raw and uncontrolled flickered across Caine's blue eyes. But it disappeared, replaced with determination before Ara could guess at it.

He stood and curled his fingers around the red paper, crushing it. "Make sure Mrs. Merrywent is apprised of the situation. She must accompany us this time."

Ara nodded again, clasping her hands in her lap, trying to stop the quaking.

She straightened her spine, attempting to yank herself together into an able, composed woman. She had to do this. For the girls that were about to be sold. For her own guilt at what she had not done in that brothel six weeks ago.

There was nothing more important.

{ CHAPTER 6 }

Ara fingered the dark velvet drape, her middle knuckles pressing against the cool glass of the carriage window. She cracked the fabric just far enough inward to have an angled view of the street.

The usual shadowy mayhem scattered the streets—drunks staggering toward the painted women with their skirts hiked high, young kiddeys waiting for the perfect opportunity to slip a hand into an unguarded pocket, and an argument spilling into the muck-covered street with heated vows of deliverance to vile ends by characters lacking the sobriety to even lift fists.

She saw it all clearly now.

The prostitutes that would try to hide their profession with long skirts and innocent eyelashes. The privileged attempting to cover their wealth by awkwardly fitting into their footmen's free day clothes. The gangs of boys blending into the shadows of the buildings, ready to pounce—vultures on the slightest weakness. When in the light of day, all of them strove for an innocent veneer. Veneers Ara once believed.

But nearly six years of watching the carnival of depravity had taught her much of the world. This world.

The world that had ripped her from her innocent life in the countryside. And she could now recognize the squalor and the riches and the perversity that drove the underbelly of this world, so short a distance from her own home on Gilbert Lane.

Ara's gaze lifted from the street, taking in the lanterns burning brightly in the third floor of the decrepit building she kept in view. They always stopped the unmarked carriage in this spot specifically so she could have clear sight to the brothel. A block to the east and one to the north, the coach was pulled to the left side of the street so Ara could observe the building from an inconspicuous spot.

She hated this part. The waiting.

Even with the guards around the carriage, her heel tapped uncontrollably on the carriage floor. The sound did nothing to break Mrs. Merrywent's slumber as she had propped herself up as usual in the corner. The woman had an uncanny skill to sleep in any position, any time of day.

Ara and Caine had learned through the years that several of their guards had to be in ragged clothes, positioned along nearby buildings as soused sailors, and several more had to be discreetly spaced around the carriage, their size, eagle eyes, and dark clothes an instant deterrent to anyone bold—or stupid—enough to approach the carriage.

But even with all that—all the precautions—something could go wrong. It had before.

The time a young boy had snuck under the carriage, slipped into the coach, and had a small knife on Ara's neck before she had even realized the side door had opened. Mrs.

Merrywent had boxed the boy's ears before he could do damage.

The time Caine was smacked on the back of the head with a club in the middle of the street. It had sent Caine to the mud, and sent the girl he had just bought screaming, running for ten blocks.

And then there was the debacle with the girl that wanted to be a whore, and had been happy to end up in the brothel. She had taken none too kindly to being bought and freed. So they had delivered her to a more reputable brothel closer to Charing Cross.

But all of those events had happened early on. Ara and Caine had gotten smarter with the passing years and now had this endeavor controlled—as much as possible when dealing with blackguards and perverts.

Buying virgins would always be dangerous, but at least they mitigated the risks where they could.

Yet Ara's foot still tapped endlessly. It always did until Caine was safely inside the carriage.

This was taking an inordinate amount of time tonight.

A tiny bell clinked three times, the high chimes interrupting Ara's thoughts. Her eyes dropped to the front door of the brothel and then swung to the alleyway on the left of the building.

She stared, breath held, until Caine appeared from the shadows. His arm was wrapped around the shoulders of a short girl draped in a flimsy chemise. Good. He got her.

Ara exhaled a long breath.

Caine quickly ushered the barefoot girl across the street and along the block to the carriage.

Within seconds, he lifted the girl into the carriage and followed, plopping himself down on the bench opposite Ara as the carriage wheels started to roll. Mrs. Merrywent sat up, alert, and Caine lit the interior lantern. Ara gave him a quick glance to make sure he was whole and then turned to the girl.

The girl was whimpering softly and tried jerking away as Ara lifted the red veil covering the girl's face.

Scared eyes. Terrified. The girl's head swiveled, darting about for escape.

Ara swallowed hard. This one couldn't be more than fourteen. They had been getting younger and younger during the past year.

She tamped down on the rage swamping her chest. These first seconds were critical for how the night would unfold.

"Child, you are safe. Safe." Ara grabbed the girl's shoulders, dodging her face about to get in front of the girl's eyes. "You are safe. I swear it. The man that bought you will not touch you. No one here will hurt you. Do you understand?"

The girl wouldn't focus on Ara, fear swallowing her. Ara gave her a shake, setting her nose almost onto the girl's face. "No one will harm you. I swear it. I have been where you are, and you have no reason to be frightened. Not anymore. We are taking you away from here, somewhere safe. Do you understand?"

The girl finally looked into Ara's eyes. One timid nod.

"Good. Good girl. What is your name?"

"Va…Va…Valerie," the girl stuttered, fighting for her voice.

Ara dropped her hands from the girl's shoulders, but did not break eye contact with her. The girl had snapped out of her shock, so Ara softened her voice, coddling as much as she could manage as the carriage bumped down the streets. "Valerie, may I cut your ropes? I can untie them, but it will take longer."

Valerie nodded again.

"I am going to pick up a knife, but I am not going to hurt you with it."

Ara grabbed the dagger that sat hidden between her thigh and the wall of the carriage. The blade sharp, she worked through the scratchy rope quickly. She tucked the dagger and rope back by her side.

Silent, Caine handed Ara the cloak that had sat next to him on his bench.

Ara wrapped it around the girl, tucking the front of it down to her shins. "Are you hurt, Valerie? Anywhere?"

The girl shook her head.

Ara only half believed her. "Any hurt at all? Now is the time to tell me, Valerie, if you have been. We can call a physician to tend to you if so."

"No. I be bruised, nothin' more." Valerie's eyes swung from Ara to Caine and back again. "Who—who ye be?"

This was good. The girl wanted to know who they were. It often took hours for that question to arise. "My name is Ara. And we have a few options for you."

"Options?"

"On what you would like to do next. It is your decision." Ara smoothed back the thick brown hair that had fallen in front of the girl's right eye. "We can bring you to your home, wherever you are from, if you think

they will accept you back after this. If you do not think
that is possible, you can start a new life here in London. I
will be your guardian until you are of age to marry or find
employment if that is what you would wish."

Valerie nodded slowly. Ara could see her debating, see
how her eyes had tightened when she mentioned the girl's
home. "Have you been away from your home for long? Do
you think they will accept you at home after this?"

Slowly, tears rising in Valerie's doe eyes, she shook her
head. Her face dropped, the tears falling to the heavy wool
cloak on her lap.

Ara's arm went around the girl's shoulders instantly,
tucking Valerie against her side. Her free hand stroked the
thick hair along the side of the girl's head. "Then do not
think on that, sweet child. You will come home with me
and we can discuss everything after you have eaten and slept
and taken a hot bath. Then you will think on it when you
are ready. Will that do?"

An awkward nod came from Valerie's huddled form.

Ara squeezed Valerie harder into her hold, letting the
girl sob onto her shoulder. Lifting her head, Ara looked
across the carriage to Caine.

He had waited in silence, blending into the cushions
as he always did. The mere presence of a male in these
situations was more than many of the girls could take, so
terrorized had they been. So he waited and watched, ready
to assist, but never inserted himself into the situation. He
had done his part, and now it was Ara's turn to do hers.

Her eyebrows rose at him, silently asking the question
she no longer had to vocalize.

He nodded with shrug. The auction had gone fine—as fine as purchasing a virgin in a brothel could go.

His eyes left hers to stare out past the curtain he had pushed aside.

She stared at Caine's profile, the strong angular lines of his jaw, the dark hair curling along the back of his loose cravat. He still had the build of an athletic man, his shoulders only broadening during the six years since he had come into her life. His odd blue eyes set off by his strong nose, the tip of it slightly lifting. His was the face she now knew better than her own.

A familiar pit sank into her gut, rubbing it raw.

Ara tried to ignore it. Now, with the girl sobbing on her shoulder, was not the time.

But she could not push the worry from her mind. Something was wrong with Caine. He had barely looked at her tonight on the way to the brothel, and now he was avoiding her stare. A stare that could usually make him flinch—or at least make him groan with a smirk, if nothing else.

A deep sob shook the girl. Ara glanced down at her.

Not the time to wonder on Caine. This was serious business at the moment—it always was. Ara never breathed properly until they were five blocks past Charing Cross.

Whatever had set Caine's eyes into evading hers could wait.

She would have to pin him down about his avoidance in the morning.

~ ~ ~

Ara leaned back in the cushioned chair, letting her shoulder blades sink into the comfort. Her back still knotted in tension from the previous night, she said a silent thanks for the cushion.

She had never once complained about the hard wooden chairs in Caine's study, but one day two years ago, this chair had appeared to the left of his desk where she always sat when they were discussing business. He had never mentioned its sudden appearance, but she had seen the smile touch the corners of his mouth when she sank into the softness of the light turquoise fabric the first time. Ara was positive it was more comfortable than any chair in her own home and had thought more than once about asking him if she could steal it to the Gilbert Lane townhouse.

Her fingertips tapped along the side of her jaw as she scanned through the neat column of numbers again on the paper, mentally calculating. She leaned forward and set the paper on a pile along the edge of Caine's behemoth walnut inlaid desk, picking up the next set of expenses from the stack in her lap.

She loved this most in the world—sitting between Caine and the fire, Patch holding down her toes, and the numbers in front of her. There was not a safer place in the world. And her mind could be occupied by the simple black and white of the numbers. No nuances to discover, no agendas hidden, no human cruelty she could not grasp.

Numbers did not lie. Numbers she understood.

She had always been good with mathematics. Her father had given her the task of keeping his ledgers when she was young and he had discovered how good she was with numbers. So while peculiar, the progression of Ara's involvement in Caine's affairs had happened naturally over the years. She had continued to help Caine with his correspondence after his brother died. Then his mother had stolen Mr. Riggers to be butler at her townhouse, and Caine had asked Ara to help run his household during the transition. From there, Ara's involvement grew.

She knew Caine's household accounts, knew his schedule, and little by little, he asked for her to put extra eyes on the affairs of the estate. Caine's man-of-affairs had been his father and brother's, and the man's eyesight was failing, which also meant that the numbers had started to fail to make sense. Caine's loyalty to the man meant he needed a covert way to check the numbers, rather than risk his man's pride by having one of Caine's stewards involved.

So Caine had enlisted Ara's help. And years later, Ara was ingrained in all of Caine's affairs and spent hours with him every day.

Ara blinked the dryness from her eyes and set the last of the papers from her lap onto the desk, looking to Caine. "I only had those few corrections. We are done with these?"

"Yes." He kept his head down, quill scratching along a piece of vellum.

"Excellent." She set her elbows wide on the chair's arms and clasped her hands. "Then I have a new topic to discuss."

His gaze lifted to her, the first time he had actually looked in her direction since she walked into his study this morning. His eyes instantly widened. "You look…"

Her eyes darted about, wishing there was a mirror in the room to wipe off whatever he saw on her face. "What?"

His head shook, and she could see his eyes try to unsuccessfully flicker away. He blinked hard, his face hardening as he gathered himself from whatever thoughts he was having. "Exceptional. You look exceptional today."

A flush ran up her neck. Blast it. She hoped she wasn't glowing outwardly at the compliment.

At least she thought it was a compliment. Maybe she was inferring that merely because she was in love with Caine, and had been for the last six years.

A humble smile touched her lips. "I have a meeting with the Duchess of Dunway after I leave here." Her fingers ran across the bare skin above the bosom of the deep mauve silk dress she wore. A slight ribbon of white lace set off the slope of her breasts, much lower than she was accustomed to. "I plan to wear the latest emerald filigree pieces first, as I think they will suit the duchess's eyes quite well."

Caine nodded, his eyes dropping to her chest. "So Mrs. Merrywent's idea has been working well?"

"Very much so. It is so much easier to sell the designs by modeling them." Ara fingered the silk of her skirt. Since she had begun modeling in-person the jewellery that Greta created, the finery in her wardrobe had expanded.

Ara marveled once more at the good fortune bestowed upon them when they had saved Greta from an auction at the Jolly Vassal. Greta had been seventeen, one of the first girls that they had rescued—and also a Dutch orphan whose father had been the preeminent jeweller to William V of Orange.

Trained by her master goldsmith father, Greta had inherited not only her father's delicate skill with metals, but also his aesthetic for creating beauty. He had died when she was fifteen, and she had been sent to live with a distant aunt in Essex. An aunt that had sold Greta to the thugs from the Jolly Vassal only months after she had arrived.

So Greta had moved in with Ara, and after a few years, Greta had determined the best thing she could do to contribute to the household was to create jewellery and train the other girls in goldsmithing. Thus, the Vakkar Line of jewellery was established.

Smoothing the crinkle she had made in her skirt, Ara looked to Caine. "And this dress sets off the colors of emeralds. I was just happy Greta finished the bracelet of the parure in time for the meeting with the duchess. She worked through the night."

Caine's eyes suddenly dropped from Ara's chest to the desk and he fingered the piece of vellum in front of him. "But I assume your meeting with the duchess is not what you wanted to discuss? Was there something more about Valerie? You said nothing was amiss with the girl when you arrived, but are there concerns?"

"No, she is settled. She was clear-eyed this morning after a bath, and Mrs. Merrywent has already taken to coddling the girl. I believe she will stay at my house for a few days, and then we will move her to the Baker Street house with the other girls—it usually helps the transition, being able to spend time with others who have overcome her same situation." Ara's voice caught. "She is just…so young."

"Too young."

The growl in Caine's voice startled her. She had not thought he was truly listening to her.

"Yes. I just did not expect one so young."

He looked up at her, his blue eyes searching her face. "It hurts your soul?"

Ara nodded. Why did he always know what she was thinking? Was she truly that conspicuous?

He cleared his throat as his look dropped down once more to the desk. "Yet that is not the topic either?"

Ara swallowed, trying to ignore, for the moment, the injustice on innocence she had seen last night. She stared at Caine's ear, where strands determined to escape the neatness of his dark hair curled along the top. "Why have you been avoiding me, Caine?"

His fingers on the vellum froze, but he did not look up at her. "We have just spent the last two hours together, Ara. Your grasp of the meaning of avoidance is somewhat suspect."

A chuckle stuck in her throat. "Do not be impudent, Caine. Your eyes have barely met mine once since I arrived."

"It is not like you to unbridle your imagination."

"No. Except that you were the same way with me last night. You said not but five words to me on the way to the brothel."

"You counted?" His head remained down as the corner of the vellum dropped from his hand, his thumb beginning to drum on the wood of the desk.

"Yes. So why the avoidance?"

Ara waited, the silence of the large study echoing in her ears. Only an occasional pop from the fire on the far wall broke through the deafening sound. She knew he hated it when she let silence sit between them, and she was not above using it to her own advantage. Caine had been avoiding her, and she intended to find out why.

The quiet stretched thin until Caine sighed, his hand curling into a fist. "I must wed, Ara."

"What?" Her spine cracked straight and she blinked hard, not sure she had just heard correctly. Patch jumped to his feet at her shins, his ears cocked.

Caine's eyes snapped to her. "I have to wed. It was decided. The Newdale estate will not survive past another five years without an infusion of funds. Funds that will only come through a sizable dowry or a wealthy heiress."

Her jaw slackened as Ara shook her head. "But…but how—why? Your estate has always been healthy. I have seen the numbers a hundred times over."

"You've never seen these numbers, Ara." Caine's fingers ran through his hair, fully mussing the neat strands. "The mines are failing. Unless we can explore—dig and find new deposits, there is not enough coal in the current mines to support the estate in five years. The seams we have extracted from are too narrow, and becoming more so. Exploration will be expensive, but I can put it off no longer."

Her face felt light, as though all blood had drained away and her head was about to float off her body. "So… you have been putting off marriage?"

His look whipped away from her, landing on the portrait of his dead brother, the last Earl of Newdale. "I have known for the past three years the mines were failing." His words were low, measured.

Panic wrapped around her shoulders, tightening the muscles running up her neck. Panic she ignored, forcing her voice even. "Does your mother know?"

"She does not know about the mines, only about my intention to wed. She has been given instructions to

identify the women of interest, with the caveat that they
have substantial dowries or income behind them." His eyes
went upward with the shake of his head. "You can imagine
her reaction."

Utter delight. Caine's mother had been haranguing
him to get married for as long as Ara had known him. And
for as long as she'd known him, he had resisted his mother
at every turn. Ara knew very well that he still loved Isabella
and no other woman would ever be in his heart.

But Ara had also known this would happen someday.
Of course Caine would have to marry.

She just hadn't imagined today would be the day.

He had to marry. He had to produce an heir. Even so,
she had never let her mind rest on that fact for long. She
ignored that inevitability every time it popped forth, never
truly believing Caine would marry.

And why? What had she hoped for? Nothing.

She had never dared hope for anything, so she would
never have to suffer the soul-crushing disappointment that
she was experiencing at this very moment.

She swallowed hard, stilling every part of her body.

Hide everything.

Just like she always had. Just like she was good at. Do
not let Caine know her heart had contracted, shriveling in
her chest.

She managed her voice to neutral. "And the mines?
Who knows about them?"

"No one except for Mr. Peterton, the mine foreman,
and now you."

Ara's mind raced. "But what about the Vakkar Line?
Greta's designs are just starting to flood the ton, and now

that she has trained many of the girls in goldsmithing, they have been working so quickly, and the profit—the growth of orders has been much more than we ever dreamed. Surely those profits can help with exploratory excavations?"

"It is not enough, Ara."

"But now is the time for you to wed? Why now? When did you decide this? You have said nothing about—"

"You do not know every damn thing I do, Ara." His fist slammed onto the desk, his glare landing on her.

Her mouth clamped shut, stung.

She gave a weak nod and stood, going across the study to the fine mahogany box she had set on the sideboard when she came in. Her head down, she pulled on her gloves and tucked the box stacked with three velvet layers cradling three sets of jewellery into her arms.

She snapped her fingers, and Patch sidled her skirts. Without another glance to Caine, she walked out the door of the study.

Her front teeth clamped onto the inside of her lip as she tipped her head to Mr. Wilbert, Caine's most recent butler.

"Ara, stop."

Mr. Wilbert's left eyebrow rose at her with Caine's barked order from the study.

Silently, she tilted her head pointedly to the door. It wasn't the first time she had left Caine's townhouse with him mad at her. Nor would it be the last.

Mr. Wilbert opened the door wide and Ara escaped down the stairs to the first of two waiting carriages. Caine must have had other business he was going to attend to today. *Such as landing a wife.*

"Felix, will you please gather up Mable?" Ara looked up at her tall coachman as he helped her up the stairs of the carriage. "I think she went to speak with Cook when we arrived."

"Of course, Miss Detton." He closed the carriage door and disappeared.

Ara settled the fine, but nondescript box onto her lap. These last three parures Greta had designed were special—masterpieces. Ara wondered as she did almost daily at the fate that brought Greta into her life. It had only taken a few short years to build the Vakkar jewellery enterprise, solidly built upon Greta's mastery. And not only had it created a business that could financially support the girls as they came in from the auctions, each of the girls that chose to be trained by Greta had gained a trade that offered them the chance to choose their own path in life without dependence on a man.

Ara balanced the box with the reverence the creations of beauty inside deserved. Greta was a genius, and now it was Ara's turn to sell her genius to the world.

She looked out the carriage window, annoyed she had to wait for Mable. But Caine always insisted she have a companion wherever she went, especially when she came to his home. He still did not want her reputation tainted—no matter that Ara was at his home every day of the week.

She shook her head. Caine was worried about money, yet he employed someone solely for the purpose of trailing after her. She never would understand all of the nuances of his world.

Her foot tapping wildly on the floor, she realized she had to calm down before she set herself in front of the

Duchess of Dunway. Two times she had met the woman, and while the duchess was nothing but kind, Ara couldn't afford to be a wreck in front of the lady. If she liked them, the duchess would be the highest peer to wear Greta's designs, and it would create an onslaught of interest in the Vakkar Line.

Ara forced her rabbit foot to stop its thumping. Her head dropped back onto the cushions, and she stared at the black velvet stretched tight across the ceiling of the carriage.

He couldn't have meant it.

Caine couldn't truly be intending to marry.

He couldn't.

Where at first she was stunned, her heart had now started to pound forcibly in her chest. Had she made a mistake six years ago?

Ara had not wanted to be a replacement for Isabella in Caine's mind. She didn't want love that was not rightly hers—love that belonged to another woman, especially when that woman was dead.

But if she had let Caine do more than kiss her—touch her—that night long ago in the carriage inn. If she had let him take her. She would be his right now. He was too honorable not to make that so.

Why had it mattered so much to her back then that he still loved Isabella? If she had just ignored her pride, ignored how his uttering the word "Bella" had sliced through her chest.

If only she could have ignored the wrong in that moment, Caine would be hers right now. Not set to marry another. She had been so proud those many years ago. But now...

Instead, what had she become to him? A burden? A responsibility his guilt had never allowed to set free? His secretary? She took care of so much of his business—his correspondence, his reconciliations, his household staff matters—that secretary could very well be how he regarded her.

His secretary. And an occasional partner in saving virgins from the auction stage. That was what she was.

Which would be acceptable, except that all she had done during the past six years was fall deeper and deeper in love with him. And subsequently, she had gotten very good at disguising that fact every minute they were together. Disguising it because Ara knew Caine was still in love with a dead woman.

A woman who never deserved his love in the first place.

And if Caine knew the truth of what had happened in that brothel six years ago with Isabella, he would never forgive Ara. Never forgive her cowardice. Never. And she couldn't risk him not being in her life at all.

The carriage door opened, jarring her from her thoughts.

"We be off to the duchess, then, miss?" Mable jumped into the carriage, her sweet youth filling the carriage with an energy that would eventually serve her well past being a maid. She would make an excellent wife someday—enthusiastic, yet sweet and loyal.

Damn. She had to stop thinking about marriages. About love.

She had to concentrate on calmness. On sereneness. On elegance. She would bring nothing but those things before the duchess.

Too much was at stake.

{ CHAPTER 7 }

Caine leaned back into the thick leather of the wingback chair that Ara had set into her study years ago. The only masculine thing in the room, Ara had been half-giddy the first time he had walked in and seen it.

Ara had not said a word about it, but had watched him walk through the study to the chair with a grin she tried to—but could not—suppress. He had toyed with her, pandering about the room, shifting from spot to spot in the study just to aggravate her anticipation. But once he had finally sat in it, he realized the care she must have taken in having it built. It fit his frame, his body perfectly.

And the deep brown leather had only worn into soft comfort throughout the years. Yet it still was the only masculine item in the room—the only allowance Ara had made in the sea of soft yellows and greys—a room that reeked of soft femininity.

Not that he could blame her. She dealt with women, with gentleness, with turning girls into proper young ladies. Her study reflected that.

Caine needed that right now. Needed to be reminded what gentle femininity looked like.

Three weeks of balls, dinners, and parties—and all of the brash young chits that came with the soirees—had him on edge. He was quickly verifying why he had avoided the marriage market all these years.

Ara would resettle him. She always did. But in the last three weeks, she had avoided him at every turn. The

few times he had seen her, she had been curt, quick to her
business, and then gone. He was accustomed to seeing her
almost every day, and now, nothing.

He knew he hadn't been as delicate with the news of his
need to wed as he would have liked to be, and she still had
not forgiven him for it. That much was clear.

Ara walked into the study carrying one of the simple
mahogany jewellery boxes she had ordered made specifically
for Greta's designs.

"Caine. Mr. Turlington said you had arrived. I had not
expected you. You have been scarce these past few weeks."

Caine stood, his eyes sweeping over Ara from toe to
face, and his head tilted at what he saw. Late afternoon
usually found her in a serviceable muslin dress, grey or dark
blue, and dealing with the girls, running the households she
managed, planning with Greta the Vakkar Line, or working
to balance all the finances. Not walking into her study
dressed in a slim, hunter green gown that set the color of
her eyes off to a perfect glow.

Uncontrollably, his look glided down and up her body
again. No. She certainly did not appear in a gown that
hugged her curves far too closely and cut far too deeply
across the swell of her breasts.

Her words finally reached his mind. He had been
scarce? Caine bit back his instant reaction and sat back
down in his chair. "You know what has been occupying my
time as of late, Ara."

What looked like a sad smile flickered across her face,
but it was gone before Caine could read it properly.

"I do." She set the box onto the rosewood desk in front
of him, moving to stand next to his chair. "Please, look, it

is Greta's newest design. I am so proud of her, but she has been working herself into exhaustion since the Duchess of Dunway—and half of society—has become an ardent admirer of her masterpieces."

"Tell her she must rest. Take away her files and hammers. Lock her in her bedroom if you must."

Ara smiled. "I already did tell her nearly that very same thing."

Caine reached forward, flipping open the lid of the box. Only placeholder stones sat in the necklace, but he recognized the spirited exuberance of the design. Twirled golden snakes to be draped across a bare chest. Perfect for the *ton's* indulgent proclivities and taste for blood. He, on the other end of the spectrum, liked the simplest of Greta's designs—but he knew he was in the minority.

"This is beautiful. They always are."

"Yes." Ara nodded, staring at the piece.

"Does she have rubies identified from Mr. Flagerton for it? His latest batch of rubies was of exceptional quality, or so I heard."

"That is the genius of Greta—she does not want to use common rubies with the design, she thinks it too ordinary. She is demanding Burmese 'pigeon blood' rubies. Only those will be dark enough, she insists." Ara's lips twitched in a wry smile. "Mr. Flagerton has been throwing his hands up in the air more than usual with Greta, as of late. And while I would like to, I cannot fault her—she does know how to make pieces that are extraordinary."

"That she does." Caine closed the box, placing it on the desk and looking up at Ara. "You are dressed to show more designs today?"

Her mouth tightened, her jaw shifting as she stared at him. Her eyes flickered, the golden rings around her irises scattering into the green of a pure emerald.

Her silence unsettled him.

"Ara?"

She stepped away from him, going to the round mirror on the wall next to the French doors that led to the back gardens. She eyed her hair, tucking a few stray blond strands into her upsweep. An upsweep that was far more elaborate than her usual knot, with twisting braids weaved into an artful display on the crown of her head.

"I have an event I will be attending tonight."

Caine sat up in his chair. "An event? What event? Why do I not know of this event?"

Her eyes veered to him in the mirror. "You do not know everything I do, Caine."

He took her point as intended, and sighed. "I do not want to argue my current situation, nor how I found myself in it, Ara. The whole of it is as distasteful to me as I imagined it would be." He stood from the chair, his thumb rubbing the leather along the top of the chair back. "You know very well why I must go down this path. The estate needs the money."

She nodded, her gaze going back to her own reflection. "I do. And I apologize for my disrespect of your decision. I have been far too involved in your affairs. Affairs I have no right to witness."

Caine bit his tongue. So that was what she had been doing these past three weeks. Withdrawing. Withdrawing from something she didn't want to watch—him finding a rich bride. And if she was withdrawing…

His eyes narrowed on the back of her head. "Ara, just what is this event you are attending tonight?"

"The opera."

He let the slight breath he held slip from his lips. "I am happy you have finally decided to take time to attend one. If I recall, Mrs. Merrywent always enjoyed the opera when she accompanied my sisters. Where will you be sitting?"

Her eyes slid to him in the mirror and then back to her hair as she fiddled with the same strand of hair across her brow again and again, the exact placement she strove for eluding her. "I am not positive. Mr. Flagerton said he has a box, but I am not sure where it is, or even how many there are in the theatre."

"Mr. Flagerton? Our gemstone merchant?"

"Yes. He has invited me on more than one occasion to accompany him—ever since we started purchasing the emeralds through him. I had always declined, but he invited me again a few days past. I said yes. I am excited to go."

"No."

Caine's sudden blurt surprised himself, just as much as her. But he couldn't keep his mouth closed.

Ara whipped around, her forehead inclined downward so she could pin him with the bristling fury in her green eyes. "No?"

"No." Without control, he repeated the damn word.

She took a deep breath, the slope of her chest rising far too enticingly above the cut of her gown. "I know you are not demanding to have control over my time—or are you, Caine?"

What the hell was he saying? He didn't even know. He shook his head.

Her glare deepened. Waiting.

He had to say something—anything. He grasped onto the first thought in his head. "Why? Why now, Ara? Why accept his invitation?"

Her chin tilted up, her gaze leveling, but also softening at him. "I cannot be a burden to you any longer, Caine. That was made clear to me weeks ago. I do believe this house alone can free up tremendous amounts of money for you."

His head snapped back in a quick shake. "What are you even talking about, Ara? This is your home."

"It is your home, Caine. It always has been." She took a step toward him, her voice at the volume she always used when she was speaking nothing but good, common sense. Common sense he wanted no part of.

"I will move in with the other women at the Baker Street house. It only makes sense, as there are four empty bedrooms there right now, five, once Amelia gets married next month." She paused, clearing her throat. "Or I will get married as well, and start my own life. Either way, the Vakkar Line can easily support the running of the Baker Street townhouse, so that need not be a burden on your estate either."

"No." His fist slammed onto the top of the chair. The leather took the blow easily. Of course it did—anything Ara created could withstand a simple blow. "Dammit, Ara, that is not the solution."

Her right eyebrow cocked. "Then what is, Caine?"

"I…I do not know."

"Exactly. But I do." She nodded, smoothing down the silk over her belly. "So I will be pursuing Mr. Flagerton's affections. He is a kind man. Solid. Generous."

With a tight smile and one last quick nod, Ara stepped around him, exiting the study before Caine could respond.

His silent breaths—much closer to heaving than he would have liked to admit—came fast. He stood, fists clenched, staring out the glass of the French doors at the vines running up a trellis along the walk.

Kind. Solid. Generous. That was Ara's blasted list for a mate?

Walking over to the French doors, he glanced at the silver gilded frame Ara had studied her reflection in.

Damn, but she was confident.

He had seen it too many times to count—and he had always been astounded by her abilities. The care Ara took with the girls, how she transformed them from frightened mice into confident women. Women who knew how to create lives of their own making.

Exactly as she had done with herself.

That was what she was doing with Mr. Flagerton—creating a life of her own choosing.

So why did he so brutally want to stop her? Why couldn't he let her have that? Let her have a life of her own?

She was his.

That was why.

She was his, yet he was the one working bloody hard to marry someone else. An ass.

But there were too many people dependent upon him. Lives at stake, food in the bellies of children. The miners, the farmers, every single soul on his lands. His responsibility.

Not to mention the vow he had made long ago to never touch her again.

He had not fought in the war—fought for honor and the way of right—just to abandon his own honor when his strength of character was tested.

And it was tested every time they were in the same room.

For six years, he'd had to live by that vow. Stand by what honor demanded of him. It had been easier in the first years, when he was still grieving Isabella. But Caine had found it harder and harder during the last four years to hold his hand back when he wanted to touch Ara's cheek, brush back the lock of blond hair that always fell to tickle her chin. Harder to hold back the need to slip his fingers around her waist when she stood before him, draw her to him to let the full scent of the sweet lemons she smelled of invade his head.

No. He would live with his vow. Even if it killed him.

Caine ground thoughts of Ara deep into the recess of his brain.

She wasn't his. She never would be. Above everything else, he had ruined that possibility years ago when he had been a bastard to her and treated her like a whore.

He swore he would never touch her again, and he had adhered to his promise. Adhered to the vow he berated himself every single day for making.

But he knew that vow was the only reason Ara stayed in his life. The only reason Ara didn't hate him.

Distance.

He needed distance from her. Maybe with that, the boil of jealousy running through his veins would cool. He hadn't expected it to be so vicious, but he couldn't deny it. Ara in that dress that showed off far too many of her curves placed perfectly on her svelte body. The way her blond hair pulled gently from her face to highlight her high cheekbones, the delicate lines of her nose and chin, and the thin golden rings in her green eyes.

All of that care for another man.

Caine's fist pummeled into his thigh.

Dammit.

He needed to distance himself.

~ ~ ~

The flush steaming Ara's cheeks went hotter, and she tried to still her nervous knee twitch as she eyed Mr. Flagerton out of the corner of her eye. The man was handsome, and fully engrossed in the splendid performance of Rossini's Il Turco in Italia before them.

Or what she assumed was splendid. She didn't understand much of the opera, as she had never been to one. Add that to the fact she didn't speak Italian, and she found herself quite lost trying to follow the story. Ara idly wondered how many languages Mr. Flagerton spoke, as he obviously knew Italian quite well, and the many travels he did for his business of trade sent him to ports far and wide. He had said he was an enthusiastic devotee of Rossini's operas, which was evidenced by his rapt attention on the stage.

That same rapt attention on the performance was not mirrored in the man sitting in the box directly below and across the theatre from Ara.

In obvious contrast to Mr. Flagerton's steadfast concentration on the stage—Caine had stared at no other place in the theatre than at the box she and Mr. Flagerton sat in.

Of all people to see at the opera, Caine was the last person she would have imagined to be at the Italian Opera House. Over the years, Caine's mother had dragged him to a few performances, but he had grumbled about it each and every time.

Surprise did not do justice to her reaction when her eyes had flitted past him, then darted back in recognition. By the time Ara had verified it truly was Caine in the box across from her, it was evident that he had been watching her for some time. Half hidden by the red curtain along the side of the box, he lounged, his body fully directed toward her, not the stage. Fletch, Lord Lockston, sat next to Caine, full smirk on his face as he occasionally let his look wander from the stage, to Caine, and then to Ara.

As hard as Ara had attempted to keep her eyes on the performers, she could not resist ongoing sideward glances in Caine's direction.

Sideward glances that told her Caine's glare had only grown more searing throughout the first act.

Was he irate about their interaction earlier? She had assumed he would be off wooing a potential bride this evening, just as he had been occupied with that goal every other evening for the last three weeks. So why was he at the opera—of all things—on this night? And with Fletch, who clearly had very little interest in the drama unfolding onstage.

Ara exhaled with the last note of the first act, leaning to the side as the note echoed throughout the Haymarket venue. Thank goodness. Her eyes darted about for escape. She had to get to fresh air before her cheeks flamed up and caught the whole blasted theatre on fire.

Ever the gentleman, Mr. Flagerton's hand was to her elbow as she stood, sympathetic to her overheating. They left Mrs. Merrywent in the box, as she wanted to watch the masses below, and Mr. Flagerton steered Ara through the throngs of people to an empty alcove near an open window.

She inhaled the cool evening air, waving the fan attached to her wrist and praying her cheeks weren't as red as they felt. The rush of air felt good, and Ara kept waving her fan steadily, knowing she wasn't gently fluttering it as one normally did. But she guessed the heated splotches on her face were far less attractive than her boorish fan fluttering skills.

"Would you appreciate a glass of punch?" Mr. Flagerton asked, his soft brown eyes worried. "I would hate for you to have to miss the next act, as it is a remarkable showing of Rossini's ability to utilize bold dramatic elements to create a triumph of comedic ingenuity. I would, of course, understand if we must leave. Your comfort is much more important, Miss Detton."

He looked so very hopeful to not have to leave the theatre that Ara managed a smile. "I think I will recover. Punch does sound delightful in helping me to do so."

Mr. Flagerton looked over his shoulder at the crush of bodies, a cringe crossing his face. He braved a smile to Ara with the tilt of his head. "While it appears to be a massive feat, I will persevere and succeed, have no doubt."

Ara chuckled at the bravado, watching him disappear into the crowd. She turned to the window, closing her eyes as she leaned to the window opening to let the night air cool her chest.

"Watching you two is more entertainment than I thought to have this evening."

Eyes flying open, Ara spun from the window to find Fletch trapping her in the alcove. "Whatever do you mean, Fletch? Mr. Flagerton is a perfect gentleman."

"I mean you and Caine." A smirk curled up the right side of Fletch's cheek, creating the look of wry amusement that usually sat upon his face as he observed the world. "Him staring at you. You trying not to stare at him. Him spewing blasphemies under his breath. Your face turning red. Comedy at its finest. Much better than Rossini's attempt at the same."

Ara went to her toes, searching over Fletch's shoulder to make sure Mr. Flagerton wasn't on his way back to her. Catching her chatting with another man would put a damper on their first evening together. Her look went to Fletch. "I am glad we are able to provide such entertainment for your bored disposition. Why are you and Caine here tonight? And why is Caine muttering blasphemies?"

Fletch shrugged. "I thought you knew everything about him, Ara."

"Far from it, Flet—Lord Lockston." Her eyes skirted over his shoulder again, hoping no one within hearing distance overheard her gaffe with his given name. For as much as Fletch was a regular fixture in Caine's study, and for as long as she had known him, Ara couldn't very well call him "Fletch" in a public space such as this. "In truth, I know very little about what goes through Caine's mind. Especially as of late."

"Then maybe you should be looking a little harder for the answers to your questions."

Ara's head tilted. "My questions?"

The smirk on Fletch's face dropped, his grey eyes turning serious. "The questions that are obviously running through your mind, Ara."

Ara sighed. "Are you attempting to be sly, Lord Lockston?"

"I will take that as a compliment, Miss Detton."

"Let us examine your slyness, then—just what questions do you see in my mind?"

Fletch's finger tapped his chin, his eyes going to the gilded plaster frieze detail of a mermaid in the curved wall above the window. His grey eyes dropped to her, unusually solemn. "The first would be—why does he not see you? You take care of almost all of his affairs. You check over all the work his man-of-affairs sends his way. You started the Vakkar Line—which is now the talk of the *ton*. You have done everything and beyond to integrate yourself into his life, to become indispensable, and yet, he does not see you. That is what you think, what you wonder upon. And that is just the first question."

Fletch's words bordered on rudeness—no, they were rude. And the renewed flames in Ara's cheeks told her she was not taking his rudeness with grace.

"I did not stand here so I could listen to insults, Lord Lockston."

"Are they insults, or are they the truth? I merely speak the question, so I can encourage you to search—truly search for the answer."

"Since you know so very much about Caine and me, you must already know the answers as well, so why not just share them?"

"If I must." Fletch leaned in, his voice low next to her ear. "The first answer is that you love Caine, Miss Detton."

Ara jumped back, both away from Fletch's incendiary words and, more damning, the truth that sat within them. Her head shook, her voice hissing. "Too far, Fletch. Much too far."

He shrugged, taking a step backward to afford her space as he gave a quick glance over his shoulder at the crowd. He looked back to her, his grey eyes piercing. "If you search hard enough, Ara, you may just find what you are looking for—but it is not going to be easy. Caine owns his guilt with more vehemence than anyone I know."

With a slight bow, Fletch moved away from her, slipping into the bustle of bodies.

Ara sighed at the riddles Fletch insisted on speaking in.

Guilt? Caine harbored guilt? What on earth did that have to do with anything?

And how in the blasted hell had she made it so obvious she was in love with Caine? She had worked damn hard to cover that fact.

If Fletch knew, then the whole of London probably knew as well.

Except for Caine. No, she was positive Caine had no idea of her feelings.

For if he did and he had still chosen to go forth with his plan to pursue a bride…

Ara whipped back to the window, her hand on her belly, gulping air as she fought back waves of humiliation.

He couldn't know.

Could he?

~ ~ ~

"What are your plans for the day, Ara?"

Ara stilled for a second, her chest rising in a quick breath before looking up from the ledger on her desk. Her fingers twirled the quill Caine had watched her scratching numbers with. "Caine. I would have thought you dedicated solely to preparing for your upcoming trip to Notlund Castle with Miss Silverton's family."

Caine stood in the doorway to Ara's study and took in the annoyance on her face. After torturing himself at the opera weeks ago—watching her with Mr. Flagerton had been brutal—he had forced himself to truly gain distance from Ara. He hadn't talked to her in more than a fortnight.

But those weeks of distance had done very little to clear the consistent sourness that marred her face when she looked at him. Nor had the distance eased the sourness eating away at his own disposition.

The only thing that had changed in the time since the opera was that the weather was now warmer, and Ara's current dress had a decidedly lower cut across her chest.

It had to be the heat. He didn't want to consider it was because of Mr. Flagerton's attentions.

Caine sighed, tapping his riding gloves on his thigh. "So you know of my upcoming visit to Notlund Castle?"

"Yes."

Of course she did. She had far better relations with his staff than he did, even if their loyalty should belong to him. "I am letting my mother and sisters plan the excursion to Notlund. It is only for a few weeks, and not necessarily where I would like to be."

Ara nodded, her eyes going to the ledger in front of her without letting the slightest emotion slip from her green eyes. "Miss Silverton appears to be quite the perfect catch. The papers have been expounding upon what a delightful match you two make—they have deemed you as the most worthy of her suitors. She should suit the Newdale line well."

Ara was right. Miss Silverton was the perfect solution to his problems. Beautiful, an unmatched singing voice, and the woman could handle a decent conversation well enough when she wasn't foxed. Most importantly, her dowry alone would easily support his estate for the next fifty years. His mother was elated that Caine was seriously pursuing Miss Silverton and that the upcoming visit to Notlund Castle with her and her family would hopefully result in an engagement.

His mother was elated. He was not.

Caine stared at Ara sitting behind her rosewood desk.

Because Miss Silverton wasn't Ara. She wasn't a part of him like Ara was. And every moment Caine spent with Miss Silverton, he was keenly aware of that fact.

Caine swallowed hard.

"So my mother keeps reminding me." He stepped into the room. "What are your plans for the remainder of the day?"

Her look rose to him, her mouth a tight line. "I have a previous engagement this evening, Caine."

He knew she did. Knew very well she planned on attending the opera again with Mr. Flagerton that eve. He had known of every single moment Ara had spent with the merchant, and it was driving him nearly mad. Which was exactly why he was here.

Caine walked fully into her study, pulling from his jacket a familiar red card and dropping it onto Ara's desk.

"What is that?" Her posture straightened as her eyes flickered down to rest on the folded card.

"You know exactly what it is."

Ara's mouth clamped shut and she picked up the card, her fingers holding it delicately along the edges, careful not to crimp the paper.

She stared at it for a long moment. With a deep breath, she turned it over, unfolding it to the writing within. Caine's purse was generous, and he had become such a regular at the virgin auctions that the Jolly Vassal made sure he received an invitation to every auction they held.

"Tonight?" She looked up at him, the blood pumping into her cheeks, flushing them.

"Yes. Tonight. Another auction at the Jolly Vassal. I cannot do this alone, Ara. I can ask Mrs. Merrywent to serve your role if you cannot accompany me."

"No. No, this is important." She stood, going over to the bookshelves to pull a sheet of the simple white vellum she preferred for personal correspondence. "And Mrs. Merrywent is gone to sit with her dying aunt. Only I know what it was like to be them—what to expect with them in the carriage. I will cancel my plans with Mr. Flagerton."

Caine exhaled. "Excellent. I already have our usual men in place."

Ara nodded, already sitting with the quill flying fast across on the vellum. Caine could see Mr. Flagerton's name across the top in Ara's neat script.

His fingers tapped along the edge of the desk.

"That goes well—Mr. Flagerton?" Caine regretted the question the second it left his mouth—but not enough to rescind the inquiry.

"Do you really want to know, Caine?" She didn't look up as she finished with her signature and quickly sanded the sheet.

"I want to ensure your happiness, Ara."

She looked up to him, her green eyes wary.

"So yes, I want to know if he is a man worthy of your affections."

Her eyes dropped and she folded the note, sealing it.

Finished, she looked up at him again. "You do not need to worry on me, Caine. As we both know, I am no longer your responsibility."

"You will always be my responsibility, Ara."

She stood, moving around the desk toward him. Caine almost had to step away from the force of the vibrating energy that came with her.

"Do not do this, Caine." She stopped as her voice caught and her gaze dropped to stare at his chin for a long moment. Her eyes crawled back up to his, the gold rings in the green quaking. "Do you not see how hard you are making this for me, Caine?"

"Why, Ara? Why is it hard? You cannot ask me not to care—not after everything we have gone through these past six years."

She licked her lips, and Caine watched as she swallowed hard. She opened her mouth, but then closed it, giving herself a slight shake.

"What time will the carriage be by for me?"

~ ~ ~

Ara rubbed her eyes. Damn, but she was tired.

The earlier scene with Caine in her study had drained her—made her feel like she hadn't slept in a week. Then the auction at the Jolly Vassal had gone deep into the night and given her far too much time to dwell on the man now sitting across from her.

And now the first rays of light were hitting the sky. They had travelled with the windows of the carriage open, as a suffocating wave of heat had descended upon the land. But now she hoped the sunlight wouldn't wake young Nelly, the girl from the brothel now sleeping on her lap, as they still had hours to travel to Nelly's home.

Ara had been trying. Trying to give Caine leave of her daily presence in his life, so he could pursue his ladies of wealth.

He wouldn't want to see her dour face every morning when she read the scandal columns reporting on his latest exploits—who he chatted to, which ladies he danced with—any more than she wanted him to see her reaction.

She was determined to no longer be a hindrance on either his time or his estate.

She had been trying, even as every day passed without seeing Caine cut just a little bit more from her heart. He needed to marry to ensure a secure future for all that depended upon him, she reminded herself. He was doing what his responsibilities demanded of him. She had to respect it, even if, once again, it was something she would never quite fully understand.

Ara looked down at the head in her lap. This girl, Nelly, was unusually pretty and looked even younger than her fifteen years as she slept, her body curled onto the bench and her head bouncing on Ara's lap with every rut. They were getting younger and younger.

Ara tightened her hold across Nelly's chest, holding her from slipping off the bench. The girl was well-spoken and appeared to have brains, even as scared as she had been when Caine dragged her into the carriage. They had escaped the East End without incident, and Nelly was determined to make her way to her home in Suffolk, positive her family would welcome her back in their arms.

Ara hoped she was right.

She looked up at Caine. He was wide awake, staring at her. Staring at her as he had been the entire night. At least in the dark she had been able to pretend his blue eyes weren't searing into her.

But now the rays of light, growing stronger by the second, gave her no shadows to hide within.

She pointed with her free hand to the window, wagging her finger to get Caine to draw the curtains. She didn't want

Nelly to wake. Truly. Plus, it would offer enough dark to continue to avoid him for another stretch.

Caine obliged, and Ara settled her head back against the cushions, closing her eyes.

It was time to feign sleep.

CHAPTER 8

"Tom is securing our rooms." Caine held his hand out, palm up, to assist Ara from the carriage as his eyes swept over her head. "Your hat is not nearly big enough, so you will need to keep your head down in the public spaces. You will be posing as my sister—your hair color is similar enough, were anyone to ever question who was here with me."

Ara nodded. Whereas Mrs. Merrywent always accompanied them when delivering a girl to her home outside of London, her absence on this trip did create a bit of a problem for them traveling together. The last thing Caine needed at the moment was his name attached to a scandal. "Which sister?"

"Rebecca. Her size is closest to yours. Why does it matter which one?"

Ara's boots crunched onto dried mud. The sun had been bright all day, baking the earth. "If I hear someone say her name, I know to bolt in the other direction."

Caine chuckled. "Your gift of thinking ahead rarely takes a rest—even when you are twenty-hours past a proper sleep."

She couldn't help a grin as she shrugged. The last six years had honed her skill at averting possible disasters.

"Just keep your chin on your chest, and we will be fine. We are still six hours from London so should encounter no acquaintances." He pointed across the green grasses leading from the coaching inn. "Come, let us wait over here where there is a fresh breeze."

Her joints cracked, muscles stretching. To move again after the last twenty hours in the carriage was glorious. She had been out of the carriage for just a short period of time at Nelly's home, a quaint, two-story stone cottage with a smattering of red roses growing up trellises flanking the door. It did not take long for Ara to recognize that Nelly was key to the family's upward mobility, and they were relieved to have her back in their arms. Ara guessed the family would never breathe word of Nelly's five-day disappearance again—they would all pretend it never happened.

Ara stepped behind the carriage. If only she had been so lucky. What would her life be like right now had she never been stolen, never been disowned by her father? Married? Children? Content? At peace?

She gave herself an invisible shake.

Never think on what could have been. It was a dangerous game only made more precarious by her current exhaustion.

Mind reset in the present, Ara followed Caine's lead across the grasses to the crest of a hill. For as tired as she had been in the carriage, the warm breeze blew away the sludge in her mind, and her eyes perked open.

The hill rolled downward, where sheep dotting the pasture were busy with the last greenery they could munch before night fell.

The bottom half of the hazy sun dipped below the trees of a far-off forest, and minutes passed, the orange streaks in the sky turning to glorious purples and golds.

Caine stood silent next to her, and Ara took the moment purely for herself, watching the world transform from sparkles to shadows.

The last vestiges of the sun disappeared behind the trees, and Ara exhaled at the beauty. When was the last time she had felt such peace settling her body, fleeting though it was?

"It has been so long." The muttered words slipped out in a whisper, answering her own question.

"So long for what?"

She couldn't peel her eyes away from the wispy clouds scattering the sweeping lines of pinks and purples. "Since I have seen a sunset."

She felt him look down at her, the air crackling as it did every time he stared at her this close.

"I do not see sunsets like this in London—not true sunsets," she said, her voice soft.

Caine was quiet for several breaths, assessing her, but Ara refused to let her attention slide from the vista.

"Ara, are you telling me you have not seen a sunset in six years?"

She stayed silent, her eyes grasping at the streaks across the sky as the dark blue-grey of the night chased the colors down into oblivion. Satisfied she had squeezed every last drop of beauty from the sky, she looked up at Caine.

"It was my favorite thing in childhood—the sunsets off the fields behind our house. It looked like this, the hills, the trees. My mother, when she was alive, would take me to her favorite spot and we would sit there together, just the two of us. I used to dream that when I was grown, I would have my own little cottage where I could set up an easel and paint the wonder that is the end of the day. Birds chirping, the wind sending the rushes into a rustle, the colors in the sky, my five children running, chasing goats in the pasture below."

"Five children?"

"Yes, that seemed to be the proper amount." Her chin jutted sideways. "Yet now that I think on it, I do not know where I would have stuck them—the cottage I imagined was quite small. That was an oversight."

Caine smiled. "And I did not know you painted."

"I do not. I have never even held a paint brush in my fingers. But it did seem like the perfect life when I was little—so adventuresome, the painting. And each and every painting would be a masterpiece, of course."

"Of course." He nodded, the smile holding on his face. "You never told me that story."

She shrugged. "It never occurred to me. I had forgotten myself until seeing this just now."

Caine's brow furrowed. "So I ask again, Ara, you have not seen a sunset since you lived in Marport?"

Ara nodded, a lump forming in her throat. She hadn't heard—hadn't thought of the name of her village in so long. And she thought she had dodged the question. Of course she hadn't. When Caine wanted to know something, he got what he wanted. He always had with her.

Her eyes dropped from him to watch a wobbly lamb trotting after its mother in the field below. She had just wanted to preserve the moment in time, the moment of peace. And there was no sense in looking backward, when backward only filled her head with painful memories.

Pretend it never happened. All of it.

She forced a smile onto her face. "I have not been out of the city, except when we have travelled with the girls to return them to their homes. And there has been scant time to take in a sunset on those trips. So no. No sunsets."

He didn't reply, and Ara was grateful. It was just a sunset, after all. Nothing to dramatize.

"M'lord." Tom paused to cough his arrival. "The rooms have been readied for you and Miss Detton."

Ara looked over her shoulder to the coachman standing a discrete distance away. Tom looked even more tired than she felt, and a pang of guilt ran across her belly. Tom had helped to save her life those many years ago, and his devotion to her and Caine had always gone far beyond what was expected of a normal driver. Caine had already paid him plenty, but when Ara had taken over his household accounts, she had doubled Tom's pay. It still wasn't enough.

"Thank you, Tom." Caine looked down at Ara, the blue in his eyes darkening with the deep greys of the sky. "Let us get you upstairs to your room, and then I will deliver some food. Just remember, head down. If you want to feign an ache of the head, and clutch your forehead, that would also do us well."

Ara turned with him, stretching her shorter legs to match his long stride. "I do believe I can pretend quite admirably, Caine."

She swallowed a sigh.

If he only knew how well.

~ ~ ~

An hour later, Ara's fingers worked down the jade buttons lining the front of her hunter green riding jacket. She had waited patiently for the food Caine had promised, but now she had slipped into exhaustion again and the bed she could see in the spacious adjoining room beckoned to her.

She loosened and pulled off her tall black riding boots, peeled down her stockings, and just as she stripped the jacket from her arms, a knock echoed into the room.

Shoving her arms back into the sleeves of her jacket, she buttoned the front as she opened the door. Caine stood in the hallway balancing a wide covered platter in his arms. He lifted it up slightly, a small twinkle in his eyes. "As promised."

Ara stepped to the side in her bare feet, her hand on the door as Caine moved past her and set the silver platter on the table.

"Since Tom told them you were feeling ill, I could only order for myself, so I have just the one platter—and according to the barkeep downstairs—a gluttony issue, as well."

Ara moved to the table and lifted the silver dome off the oval platter, her eyes going wide at the piles of food—potatoes and thick slices of meat and pies and beans, with sugar plums and ratafia cakes wedged onto the ends of the plate. She glanced at Caine. "You told him all of this was for you?"

"I did."

She chuckled. "Then he judged you accordingly."

"May I eat in here as well, since we just have the one platter? Tom did sneak me an extra fork. I would like to dive into the pies before they go cold."

"By all means." Ara pointed at the extra wooden chair by the marble-lined fireplace as she settled herself down on the chair already at the small round table.

Caine dragged the chair to the table, sitting down opposite Ara. Both silently dug into the food, minutes of silence filling the air as their mouths remained stuffed. Apparently, Ara hadn't been the only one starving.

This wasn't the first time they had eaten together—countless meals they had shared—but this was the first meal they had taken together since Caine had decided to land a rich bride.

She had missed it. Their easy dinners. Chatter about the Vakkar Line, the politics of the day, his sisters' latest antics, what he was concerned about with his lands, the mines, and the families that lived on them, and of course, how each and every one of the Baker Street house girls were doing. The men that were courting some of them, what the younger girls were learning, and debating how best to move each one forth into the world with the confidence to live a happy life.

She had missed it.

And she would miss it.

It was also, most likely, the very last meal they would ever share. Caine was leaving for Notlund Castle in two days.

Chewing a particularly juicy bite of mutton, Ara glanced up at Caine. He poked at one of the sugared plums, his intake of food slowing, and she wondered if she was out-eating him again. She did that. Forgot to eat during the day, and then she would stuff as much food as possible into her mouth when she was sitting across from him.

Luckily, she hadn't ballooned to unusual proportions as of yet, and Caine had always been amused by her appetite.

Was it any wonder she loved the man?

A sneak attack, the reality sliced straight through the middle of her mind, firing tendrils outward until her mind was consumed with the thought.

Dammit. She had sworn to herself she wasn't going to admit to the fact anymore. Wasn't going to let it seep into her brain to ruin her time with Mr. Flagerton. Wasn't going to make her pine away for something so very unattainable.

She had sworn.

But there it was. The plain truth taunting her, as her subconscious liked to attack at the most inopportune times. She needed a better place to lock away unwanted thoughts in her mind.

"What is it, Ara?" Caine looked across the platter at her, the four candles in the room lighting the left side of his face and cutting shadows down across his hard jawline. He leaned back in the chair, finished with the food, and eyed her with concern. "You are pondering something serious."

The morsel of meat in her mouth turned into a rock as her mouth went dry. She swallowed, forcing it down her throat before she could no longer manage the small feat.

A wide smile she had to force set across her face. "This may be the last time we eat together. You are leaving for Notlund Castle in a few days, and after that…who knows?" Ara couldn't bring herself to actually speak the word "marriage." "I just wish…"

"You know exactly why I have to do this, Ara. Money. It is the only reason." Caine moved to grab the one wine glass, filling it from the bottle of wine that was in the room when Ara had entered. He poured the deep red to near full in the glass and then swallowed a third of it.

"I just wish it had never come to this," Ara said. "That you had told me earlier. Years ago. Maybe we could have devised a way to create a new scheme, something that could support the revitalization of the mines. Anything. That it came to this and I can do nothing to help. And now I must disappear."

He set the wine glass down, his eyes moving from it to her face. "A marriage does not mean we have to sever our ties, Ara. I do not know why you continue to insist this is the end of us."

Us? Hell. Did Caine even know what he was saying? Ara's mind raged. There could be no "us" after he married. Did he not understand how this was ripping her apart?

No.

Of course not. How could he? She had never told him—and he would never want to hear it.

She nudged another piece of meat with her fork. "Caine, you know very well no woman with all her faculties about her would dare to allow you leave to spend as much time with another woman as we spend together."

"I will allow exactly what I want to, Ara."

"Yes, but do you want a bitter wife? Do you want a mother to your children that resents you at every turn? There is only room for one woman in a marriage, Caine. And I refuse to be a festering splinter in your marriage."

"You do not know that would happen. I depend on you, Ara, and I am not going to let anyone—anyone—tell me I can no longer do so."

"You depend on me for what? To oversee your numbers? To handle your staff? Your solicitor and your man-of-affairs and your new wife are all you need for those things. The oddity of our relationship…"

She stabbed the piece of meat with her fork, then dropped the silver to the table, folding her arms across her belly. "If it was me—"

She cut herself off. She wasn't going to speak it. Speak the imaginations of a fool.

He leaned forward, his blue eyes piercing her. "If what was you, Ara?"

Ara held his gaze, refusing to cower. He knew exactly how to challenge her in a way she could never back down from.

Her head tilted. "If I was married to you, Caine, I would never let another woman near you. You are…too desirable. I would not want to see another look at you with adoration. With lust. With wanting. I do not think you know how you affect people, Caine, women in particular. They bend to your will without fail—they simper at the slightest glance from you."

"You never bend to my will, Ara."

"That is only because you need me not to." Her jittery leg thumping under the table, Ara stood and moved to the middle of the floor, her eyes locking onto the glowing coals in the fireplace. Just enough heat to stave off the night's chill. But not enough to warm the cold invading her spine.

"You cannot be mad at me, Ara. I must do this for the title. For future generations."

"When have you ever cared about blasted future generations, Caine?" Her words came out in a bitter hiss.

"Do not disregard what you do not understand, Ara."

The reprimand hit her, stinging. But then the floorboards creaked behind her.

Caine moved close, his body stopping near to hers, and his voice softened. "I would not choose this, you know that."

She whipped to him. "Yes, of course I know that. But it is the money. Always the money. My life was ripped apart once for money. All because some bastard wanted to sell me. And now everything I am—everything I do—is being ripped apart again because you need a wife with money and I cannot be in your life once that happens."

"Everything?"

"Yes, everything. I do you, Caine—your life, me in your life. That is what I do best." She sucked in a breath, trying to calm the boil that had overtaken the chill in her body. "So yes, I am mad. I am losing everything once more, and you do not even care enough to acknowledge the truth of what will become of us."

"You have already moved on, Ara—wanting to leave the Gilbert Lane house. Mr. Flagerton."

"I did not have a choice, Caine. I wanted this to be easy for you. To not be a burden."

His hand ran through his hair. "So now you think to not make this easy for me, Ara?"

Her mouth opened, but then clamped shut.

It slammed into her head at that very moment.

She had to tell him everything. Easy for him or not.

If this was the last time she would have him alone, she had to tell him.

She had vowed after the horror of the brothel, the beating from her father, that she would never be a coward again. Yet here she was. Wallowing. Whining. Hiding behind anger because it was easier than admitting the truth to him.

She loved him.

And she not only had to tell him that, she also had to tell him the whole truth—what really happened at the brothel all those years ago with Isabella. If she could tell him everything, then she could be done. Her conscience clean. Come what may.

His cravat long since removed, Ara stared at the base of Caine's neck where his skin disappeared behind the white linen of his shirt. She waited for the pounding in her chest to cease, but it only thumped harder, blood rushing to her ears. Her eyes crept upward. "What am I to you, Caine?"

"What do you want me to say, Ara?" His words came slow, wary.

"Am I your secretary? Your man-of-affairs? Your friend? Your partner in saving the girls? Your confidante? What am I?"

His look dove to the fireplace for long seconds before it lifted to her, the blue in his eyes intense. "You…you are everything, Ara."

"You say that, yet how do you not know I love you?"

He took a step backward, his body stiffening. Exactly as she expected it would.

"Ara—"

Her hand flew up, stopping him before he had to scrape together excuses she didn't want to hear. "I do not need you to love me, Caine. But you need to know why I cannot do this—cannot be in your life when another woman is in your bed—the mother of your children. I cannot watch that. Not if I plan to keep my soul. And there is more—"

"There sure as hell is." He stalked forward, halting a hair before his body touched her chest. "By all that is holy in the world, Ara, I swore I would never touch you again." His hand rose, hovering next to her face, but not making contact. "But I am having a bloody tough time keeping that vow at the moment."

Instant tingles ripped across her scalp and dropped down her spine. Her eyes locked onto his, their breath mingling, twisting the air between them.

She fought to catch her breath, fought to unleash words from deep in her belly. "Never make a vow you have no intention of keeping, Caine."

His hand hung in the hair, frozen except for the slight tremble running through it.

Ara would have none of it. Not after six years of loving this man.

She reached up, her fingers sliding along his knuckles until her hand covered his. She pressed.

His palm landed on her cheek, his fingers curling into her hair as he exhaled. In the next breath, his mouth was on hers, lips attacking, owning her the very second his heat met hers.

She had to tell him everything. She knew it. He needed to know.

But the onslaught on her senses, the sudden pounding pulse between her legs took all thoughts of honesty from her mind.

His hand on her face slid, wrapping around the base of her neck. Caine opened his mouth, his tongue breaching her lips, exploring, adjusting with everything he found, with how she reacted from his touch while his other hand slid down the side of her body.

He had the buttons on her jacket and silk shirt undone, both of them stripped off before she even realized where his hands were.

And when she did realize, she made no motion to stop him, made no effort to halt the dream she had walked into, her mind muddled with six years of longing finally unleashed.

He worked the laces on her short stays, slipping her chemise over her shoulders before loosening her skirts.

Her clothes puddled to the floor in one jumbled mess, covering her feet. Her body bared to him.

Caine broke the kiss, pulling back from her to look at her body. His blue eyes rode along her curves, devouring every piece of her skin. She resisted the instinct to cover herself. This was Caine, and she refused to hide herself from him.

"Hell, Ara. Beautiful." His eyes lifted, the hunger in them blazing.

She met his look, a devil smirk teasing her lips. "And I would like to see how beautiful you are."

Caine laughed and grabbed her behind the neck as he kissed her. His tongue delved deep into her as he worked off his jacket and waistcoat. Her fingers quick onto his skin, she lifted his shirt over his head as he unbuttoned the flap on his trousers.

It only took seconds, but seconds that stretched on far too long for Ara. And then he was naked. Bared to her just the same.

She gasped a breath, shuffling a step away from him so she could see him in the light of the candles.

The first and only time he had touched her, years ago, she hadn't known exactly what was coming—what Caine was doing—only that it felt like bursts of heaven running through her veins.

Countless nights spent waiting—watching and listening—in the East End outside of the brothel had taught her much about anatomy, about the possible acts that a man and woman could do together. Both lewd and imaginative. But aside from a few glimpses of unsavoriness through the crack in the carriage's curtains, she had never seen any of it, not truly.

But this, seeing Caine naked, it made her jaw drop. Every single one of her past imaginations were instantly rewritten.

For all she knew—had heard on the streets, the imaginations in her mind—she had never thought Caine would be so...magnificent. She had seen Greek sculptures in the British Museum and knew what Caine should look like. But this. His shaft long and huge, stretching up to his belly.

Fascinated, she stepped forward and wrapped her hand around it, marveling at the smoothness, how it pulsated with his heartbeat under her fingertips.

Caine's head fell back, a low growl erupting.

Ara slipped her fingers along his shaft, taking in every ridge, every texture, up and down.

"Hell, Ara, yes. Keep it there." His hand lifted, wrapping around the back of her neck.

Unable to tear her eyes away, Ara slid her fingers downward, tightening the pressure with every stroke she made.

"Damn, Ara." In the next breath he grabbed her wrist, stopping the motion.

She could see his muscles straining, demanding something she did not quite understand.

"Not yet, Ara. Not like this. And not until you're ready."

"Ready?"

His hand dragged across her skin, moving downward from her neck, between her breasts, over her belly, until his forefinger slipped into her folds, a magnet to the core of her. The first touch sent Ara gasping, fire running through her flesh, and she grasped his shoulders, leaning into him for support.

Caine chuckled, his breath hot in her ear. "Your body aches for the release, Ara, doesn't it?"

His fingers spread her wide, his thumb circling the nubbin that sent her hips shifting, pressing onto his hand. Begging for him to move harder, faster.

He obliged without her even asking, his forefinger diving into her as his thumb continued the onslaught.

Still, it was not enough. "Caine—please—please."

"Please what, Ara?"

"Please—all of this." She moaned as he flicked his finger over the rock hard core of her, not caring how guttural she sounded. "Just—all of it—this—"

Her voice left her. Air left her. Thought left her. Her head started spinning, control lost from all limbs. She was nothing but hot, demanding need gathered under Caine's fingers. All she could concentrate on was her nails digging into Caine's back. Holding on to this man giving her body life. Riding his hand. Screaming into his shoulder.

It attacked, shattering, stealing every ounce of who she was and leaving nothing in its wake except for rolling waves of pleasure.

Through the blackness, she felt Caine setting her onto her back on the bed, his fingers still coaxing spasm after spasm from her core.

She felt his weight upon her. His shaft nudging through her pulsating folds.

"Ara, do you want this?"

Her release still ravaging her body, she could only crack her eyes to him. His face was strained, his control near breaking, yet still, he asked her.

For all that she couldn't imagine it, she knew she wanted more. Wanted—needed what he was about to do. Her mouth opened, her voice breathless. "You saved this from being stolen from me. It is yours by right, Caine."

The words snapped him backward.

He yanked his hands off of her, jumping from the bed to his feet. "I want no damn rights to your body, Ara. I want an invitation."

Her eyes opened fully, his growled words pulling her from the hazy fog of nerves rolling through her body. The sudden absence of his heat above her sank into her brain, and before she could even sit up on the bed, Caine had shoved his legs into his trousers and was stomping toward the door to the hall.

He stopped for only a mere second, looking back to the floor before the bed. His eyes did not lift to hers. "I touched you when I should not have, Ara. I swear it will not happen again."

Two steps, and he disappeared into the hall, the door slamming shut.

Confusion ravaged her, so thick it clouded her eyesight sent her body into a quiver.

What the hell had just happened? What had he said? She wasn't sure she heard him correctly. He wanted an invitation to her body? She looked down at her naked flesh. If this wasn't an invitation, what was?

Collapsing back onto the bed, her hand covered her eyes, pressing down tears that threatened.

She had been so very high, floating, and in a second, he was gone.

She had no idea what had just happened between the two of them.

Except that she had just watched her heart walk out the door.

She had told him she loved him.

Offered herself to him.

And he had rejected her.

Tears squeezed past her fingers, rolling down her temples.

Not that she deserved him. Or his love. She hadn't gotten a chance to tell him the rest of what she needed to. Maybe he realized, deep down, how she was going to disappoint him—how he would hate her. He must have known it instinctively, and he had left.

Left before there was no turning back.

Ara rolled to her side on the bed, her bare legs sliding up to her belly.

She had bared absolutely everything of her being to him—her body, her soul, her love.

And he had rejected her.

There was only one thing to do.

Curl away. Hide. Survive.

{ CHAPTER 9 }

Flat on his back in his own bed, Caine eyed the bottle of brandy on the table by the fireplace in his room. For three hours he had stared at the damn thing.

He had never needed a drink more in his life. But he wasn't about to chance it—chance he would do something so regrettable with Ara that she would exit his life forever.

There had been that one moment. The moment when she had said she loved him and his entire existence up until that sole second in time hadn't mattered.

That she could love him after how he had violated her those many years ago—impossible. But he had latched on full force to those words, latched on until her clothes were on the floor and she was riding his hand, her nails in his shoulders, her beautiful eyes drugged with his heat, her open mouth begging with each gasp that passed by her lips.

Caine shifted on the bed, adjusting his newly revived rock hard bulge.

But Ara didn't love him.

Why had he not seen that? She was indebted to him—she had been for the last six years. Her words were proof of that. *Her virginity was his to take?* There could be no more brutal proof that she would always be beholden to him.

Always see him as the man that bought her.

His usual solid reasoning should have reminded him there was no way she could love him—truly love him—after the bastard he was to her all those years ago.

She was just reacting—she didn't want her life to change—didn't want him to marry. That was a very different thing than loving him.

It had taken will power he only barely possessed to walk out her door, and he knew if he had even a tumbler of brandy, he'd be back in her room, finishing what they had started. Honor be dammed, he would tangle himself up in her naked limbs and never untwine them.

So no. No brandy.

Not that he couldn't stare at it longingly.

A garbled cry cut through the wall from Ara's room. Caine tensed.

Silence. Then a whimper. Then the word "crow" screeched. Silence. Scream. More garbled words. Silence.

He lay still, praying the silence held.

Agony ripped through her next nonsensical screams. Louder. Horrified.

Dammit. Dammit to the bloody depths of hades and back, and then back again to hell. Dammit. He couldn't let her suffer.

Caine stood from his bed, his legs heavy as he made his way out of his room and turned the knob on her door. Not locked. He gave a growled sigh. She knew she was supposed to lock the door. She knew that.

He opened her door, his eyes adjusting to the low light from the glowing coals in the fireplace. He walked by the table in her first room and looked to the chamber holding the bed. Ara was thrashing, but he couldn't yet make out where her head was on the bed—she was a flopping mess of flesh and bedsheets.

Moving to stand next to the bed, he watched her, cringing with every new scream, every cry. The wolves. The crow. The horrified whimpers that cut into his chest.

The wolves and the crow. Always the wolves and the crow.

He had no idea she still suffered the terrors at night.

Her forehead breached the sheet that had covered her head, and Caine dove, searching through the sheet for her neck.

His fingertips connected to warm skin, and she spun, twisting, her terrified screams a staccato into the room. Caine didn't let her escape, his hand crawling along her neck until his fingers stretched, reaching the very spot behind her ear that Mrs. Merrywent had shown him years ago.

She instantly stilled. Her breath stopped for a long moment. One long exhale, and then her breathing went back to a quiet normal.

She never woke up.

Caine started to pull his hand away, but her head followed him, just like Patch's when the dog nuzzled his head under Caine's hand for a long scratch.

His fingers left her neck, and her breathing sped, her chest starting to heave. The whimpers started again.

Caine set his fingers back into place, his fingers touching the one spot behind her ear. She quieted once more.

He repeated the exact motion again. Ara reacted in the exact same way. Fascinating.

Fascinating and vexing. Caine stood next to the bed, debating about what to do. He couldn't very well stand there all night. Nor could he remove his hand.

Minutes passed, and with no clear path to extract himself from Ara's room, Caine sighed, crawling into bed next to her, his hand never leaving her neck.

She had curled onto her side, and Caine wrapped his length along the back of her. Between the chemise she had put on, the sheet, and his trousers, Caine was fairly assured skin would not touch skin. That didn't stop him from feeling the heat pulsating off of her in waves. Her breathing was normal, but her body and heartbeat were still wild.

He settled his head on the bed, her hair tickling his chin. Lemons. Her hair always smelled of bright lemons. It wasn't until that moment that he realized how much he missed that very scent wafting about in his study.

A shudder ran through her body, and his gut clenched.

The damn wolves and crow. Always those two things. He had never asked her about them—what they meant, why she dreamed of them.

Early in the years when they were delivering virgins back to their homes outside of London, Mrs. Merrywent was always with, and would quickly calm Ara in the middle of the night. Though some of those nights Caine was convinced Mrs. Merrywent's hearing was suspect, for he would listen to Ara mumble and then start to scream. His gut had always curdled at the sound, no matter how fast Mrs. Merrywent was at calming it away.

Caine had believed Ara's terrors had subsided over time. He hadn't heard her screaming in any of the coaching inns during the past year.

But he was wrong. The screams he heard tonight were as intense as they were the first time he had heard them. An instant reminder of how Ara had come into his life.

An instant reminder of how brutally he had failed to protect the last woman he had loved—Isabella had died.

His body tightened instinctively to the curve of Ara's backside. He could not be a failure again. Especially with Ara. He had no right to love her. But every ounce of him needed to protect her.

Caine inhaled deeply, trying to ignore the scent of lemons and calm his own pounding heart. If his body was calm, hers would follow suit. He shifted his arm, trying to position it more comfortably without his fingers breaking contact on her neck.

The wild pulsating of her heartbeat under her skin eased into rhythm, and her muscles relaxed. The tenseness dissipating, her body burrowed into his body wrapping hers.

Caine swore to himself, acutely aware of how hard her wiggling was making him. But he held still, wanting to give her this—safety in her sleep, since he could give her little else.

He closed his eyes and the image of Ara watching the sunset flashed through his mind. The sunlight sending a glow along the edge of her delicate profile, almost magical, if not purely angelic.

How had he never taken her to Villsum House?

When she had told him about not seeing a sunset in years, all he had wanted to do was climb back into the carriage and take her to Villsum House. Show her the beauty that he had at his fingertips—and had never taken the time to share with her.

Because she wasn't his wife. The thought rumbled through his head, crushing any imagination of Ara standing on the western patio, saying goodbye to the day in a bath of ethereal golds and pinks and purples.

She wasn't his wife, only a far removed relation that he was guardian to. That was how he had been able to take care of her. And they needed to stay that way for him to protect her properly.

With distance and a clear head—clarity he hadn't had earlier when she was wrapped in his body, writhing under him. In those few fleeting minutes in her arms, Caine knew he would have given up everything for her—his responsibilities to the title, to the lands, to the people. Given up a certain future for the chance to be with her, come what may.

What could he have possibly been thinking in those moments—that Ara could love him?

She never could, not truly. She would always be beholden to him. Her words were evidence of that fact. She had confused love with gratefulness.

But in those brief minutes—minutes that had felt like a lifetime—she had been in his arms. Accepting him. Knowing the past. Knowing his failures. Yet accepting him.

Loving him.

He could not let her do that.

By whatever honor he had left, he had to leave her alone. Give her freedom to live her life away from him.

His stay at Notlund Castle would be good for that. Good for him. Good for her.

Caine waited until the first light of the day to carefully lift himself from the bed, leaving a still sleeping Ara to her dreams.

~ ~

From the foyer, Caine watched Ara trudge up the stairs, the deep green skirt of her riding habit sweeping the steps. Patch had already run ahead of her, turning and waiting at the top of the steps, his tail wagging. She turned at the top, disappearing with Patch down the hall. Her slow footsteps receded until he heard the click of a door.

"She is frightfully worn out." Mrs. Merrywent turned from watching Ara's exit up the stairs to Caine. "I believe I have you to blame for that. You should have sent someone for me. You two travelling alone is not part of our bargain, my lord."

"Our six-year-old bargain, Mrs. Merrywent?" His eyebrow cocked, inviting her to say something more. He had adhered to the woman's wishes for propriety for the past six years and was not about to let her fixate upon this one misstep.

She crossed her arms over her chest, glaring at him.

Caine glared back. "There was not time, Mrs. Merrywent. I did not know you were unavailable until I came for Ara. And you were too far out of the city to retrieve you in time to accompany us. You know there is no one else we trust to bring with us to last night's situation."

Mrs. Merrywent waved her hand, shaking her head with a sigh. "It is unfortunate. But as you are clearly contrite, I will let it pass."

Caine bit back sniping words, staring down at her audacity. Who paid whom? He was far too tired for this nonsense. Yet for all her bluster, Caine knew Mrs. Merrywent had become a pussycat when it came to him. It had taken half of the last six years, but now the woman at least respected his honor when it concerned Ara.

"Why is Arabella exhausted—did you not stop at a coaching inn on the way back to London?"

"We did." Caine turned from the steps, lowering his voice so it would not carry up the stairs to Ara's bedroom. "The terrors that visit her in the night—they are back—or have they never ceased, Mrs. Merrywent?"

Pity creased the edges of her eyes. "She had the terrors last night, my lord?"

"She did. I stopped them with that spot on her neck you showed me long ago."

Mrs. Merrywent nodded, a frown on her face. To her credit, she kept her mouth shut about Caine being in Ara's room unsupervised. But he could read the disapproval easily enough in her face.

"So she still has them often? I thought they had stopped."

"They have never left her, my lord. I had thought with time they would cease, but they do not."

"So they have continued for these many years? Why did I not know this? I have not heard her scream on any of the journeys in the last year."

"I have always been with, my lord. I always sleep near her and can quiet them before they are too loud. I wake up much faster now when I hear the whimpers start."

Caine nodded, taking a deep breath. So they had never stopped. Mrs. Merrywent had just gotten very, very good at her job, which was taking care of Ara in every way possible. He needed to double her pay.

Caine moved to the front door, but then paused, turning back to Mrs. Merrywent. "Ara has always screamed of wolves and a crow…why?"

Mrs. Merrywent shrugged her shoulders, her meaty lower lip jutting out. "She has never told me, my lord. Don't believe she ever will. The terrors are why she always insists on going to sleep at a right hour. They come too often when she is overly tired—every night she goes out with you…" Mrs. Merrywent cut herself off, apparently realizing she was about to blame him for Ara's terrors.

"Every night she is out late?"

"Yes, my lord."

Caine ran his fingers through his hair, scratching the back of his neck. "For the last six years she has suffered this? Born this burden?"

"Yes, my lord."

"Why did she never tell me? Why continue to go out late into the night?"

Mrs. Merrywent stepped toward him, her own voice dropping to a whisper. "I do not know, my lord. I have wondered the same. But I believe Arabella is more concerned with saving the innocents—with being there to help them the second you bring them from that place— than with her own welfare."

"Worried about everyone but herself." Caine resisted the urge to stalk up the stairs and give Ara a little shake.

"That she is, my lord. It is a fault."

Only a second before, he had wanted to shake Ara for being so damn worried about others that she was a detriment to herself. But at Mrs. Merrywent's words, he instantly wanted to defend her. Ara didn't possess a fault. Her caring was a gift—of course she was worried about the girls—her capacity for compassion knew no bounds.

Instead of defending Ara, he simply nodded. "You have done well by her, Mrs. Merrywent. You have my gratitude for all you have helped her and the other girls over the years."

A gruff smile appeared on Mrs. Merrywent's face. Judging by her awkward smile, Caine had apparently never thanked her before.

He turned back to the door, opening it and stepping out into the hazy London sunlight, even more sure of his actions than he had been that morning.

He not only needed to free Ara from him, he needed to free her from the past.

She had to move on, and in order for her to do that, he needed to leave her alone. He needed to leave for Notlund Castle.

Caine had thought pulling himself from Ara's bed that morning without waking her was the hardest thing he had ever done.

It wasn't.

His chest tightening, ripping him from the inside, the steps he took down Ara's front marble stairs were even more brutal.

But he had to let her go.

If he didn't, eventually, he would fail her, just as he had Isabella.

{ CHAPTER 10 }

Caine leaned back against the smooth squabs in his coach, taking the first easy breath he had had in weeks. Finally, escape.

For three weeks he had played the dutiful suitor to Miss Silverton and the engaging guest of the Duke and Duchess of Letson at Notlund Castle. It had taken more energy than he had imagined it would.

He liked Miss Lily Silverton well enough—she was most certainly the finest match for him of the season, even aside from her sizable dowry. Pretty, shaped quite nicely, flawless voice, and she made him laugh on occasion. The woman would make a fine wife, so why were the last three weeks such a drain upon his spirits? Where was the excitement when she walked into a room?

Caine let his head drop against the cushion, wishing he were already at Villsum House. He closed his eyes just as the door to his carriage opened.

He sat up, his eyes wary on the woman climbing into the carriage.

"What do you want, Mother?"

The countess sat across from him, adjusting the small black hat atop her silver hair. She had aged well, even if she had never abandoned the widow weeds that darkened the shadows on her face. Her hands settled on her lap as she eyed him.

Caine stifled a sigh. His mother almost exclusively rode in her carriage with his two sisters, so for her to jump into

Caine's carriage at the last second meant she had business she didn't want him escaping from.

Ever since taking over the title, Caine had spent much of his time avoiding his mother and sisters. His older brother had been the head of the family since Caine was twelve and their father died, and Caine had never expected to come into the title—and had been treated thusly for the entire first half of his life.

The carriage started to roll, the castle moving out of view. Blast it.

His mother's face went pinched as she saw him eye the carriage door. "Son, I am riding in here because I need to speak with you privately, and you have made yourself scarce these weeks at Notlund Castle. I will remove myself to the other carriage once we are at the nearest crossroad."

"What is it you needed to speak with me about?"

"Your actions here at Notlund. You did not give a good showing to Miss Silverton or her guardians."

Caine's eyebrow arched. "I did not give a good showing? Am I a stud horse in the auction ring?"

"Do not be crass. You know perfectly well you were polite, but not enamored with Miss Silverton. I know young hearts, and that is a woman that needs a man to be enamored with her. At this juncture, I can only pray her upcoming visits from her other suitors, Lord Bepton and Lord Rallager, are disasters of the first order."

"Your goodwill for Miss Silverton making a proper match is overwhelming, Mother."

She waved her gloved hand. "There is no room for goodwill in the marriage market, son."

"Then I do well to have you at my side." Caine didn't bother to hold the acidity from his voice. He looked out the window at the passing trees. The crossroad to Bristol could not come soon enough. "So what would you have me do differently, mother?"

"You need to fully commit to the pursuing of Miss Silverton." She paused, lips pursing. "That must begin with Miss Detton."

Caine's look cut sharply to his mother.

"Miss Detton and whatever purpose she serves in your life—a secretary, a man-of-affairs—whatever it is she does for you, it is man's work, and it should be regulated as such."

"Miss Detton is more intelligent than most of the men I know, Mother, and does her work far better than any I have ever hired, so you would do well to tread lightly in this conversation."

"Then you must hire one of those few men that is a more intelligent creature to fill her place." She wrinkled her nose. "I have allowed this…peculiar relationship between you and Miss Detton these many years, son, but I must insist you end your associations with her. As she is a relative depending upon the estate, we cannot cut her living expenses without sullying the honor of the title, but you can remove her from your daily life."

"You have allowed nothing, Mother." Caine leaned forward, pinning her with his gaze. "You realize you have no say in the matter—who I associate with and who I do not."

"Do not take that tone with me, son. I am not blind to how this woman monopolizes your time. Do you honestly think to extend an invitation of marriage to Miss Silverton

when you already have someone filling the role of wife
in your life? You need to end your association with Miss
Detton—marry her off to be someone else's responsibility.
Lord knows we have enough to worry about at the moment
without another mouth to feed."

"You know very little of my life, Mother, if you do not
understand the role Miss Detton performs in it."

"Do *you* even understand it?" Her blue eyes, a match
to Caine's, went hard. "Honestly, son, I have traded upon
nearly every favor I have been hoarding to get you within
Miss Silverton's realm this season. She is the best catch, by
far, of the girls available to you—not to mention the one
with the largest dowry. It has taken a lot of hard work on
my part, and you do not even seem to care to commit to the
goal of marriage."

"I have just spent the last three weeks at Notlund
Castle pursuing Miss Silverton's affections." His jawline
stretched, Caine strained for control. "I think that alone is
evidence of my commitment to marry."

His mother's hands flew into the air. "Why, then, did
you not extend an invitation of marriage to Miss Silverton?
She is to be visited by the two other suitors at Notlund over
the next month. You just had the perfect opportunity to cut
the others off at the knees."

"It was not the time." Caine leaned back, his mouth
clamped shut.

She watched him, the shrewd cut to her eyes searing
into him. "Not the time? Or was it Miss Detton?"

He met her eyes, returning the glare. "Do not presume
to know my mind, Mother. If you had ever taken an interest
in doing so before this moment, you may have a thread to

balance upon. As it is, you did not, so you do not currently own that right."

He glanced out the window before his gaze landed back upon his mother. "This is the last of the discussion we will have on the matter of Miss Detton."

~ ~ ~

Her boots clicked on the wooden floors, the strange, empty echo of it filling her ears as Ara walked across the wide foyer and back through the hallway into her study.

Her old study, she corrected herself silently. She just needed to pick up the correspondence that Mrs. Merrywent said was here, and then she could make her next appointment with the Dowager Countess of Prewlter on Park Lane.

Stepping into the doorway, her feet skidded to a stop.

A man, his back to her, stood looking out the French doors at the roses in full bloom on the trellises in the garden behind the townhouse.

Not just any man. Caine.

It had been two months since she had seen him. His visit at Notlund Castle was followed by a stay at his estate in Somerset. The longest time they had ever spent apart.

Caine's shoulders snapped back as he straightened, obviously recognizing her presence, but he didn't turn around. He stood, staring out the windowpanes of the door.

"I do not know how you get these to bloom here without much sun, aside from the fact that every other rosebush I have come across in the past week has wilted with the August heat." His voice low, he didn't turn around.

Ara glanced about the room, noting the pile of correspondence on the desk, and then her eyes rested on the back of his dark jacket. "It is Mrs. Merrywent's doing. She has always been the genius with the plants."

He turned slowly, his head trailing his body as his eyes drifted from the scarlet roses. Ara's stomach dropped, her breath catching as his blue eyes settled on her, skewering her from across the room. Anger—lust—indifference—Ara wasn't sure what she was seeing in the hard tilt of Caine's brow.

"Where is everything, Ara?"

So it was anger.

She hadn't written to him of her move while he was at Villsum House during the month after his stay at Notlund. She had taken care of the details of it without his knowledge, just as she had always taken care of much of his business. This house was now empty, the walls echoing the slightest sound.

"I have moved in with the women at the Baker Street townhouse." Her hand swept across the room at the last remaining items in the townhouse, her desk, desk chair, two heavy mahogany inlaid sideboards with cabinets below, and Caine's leather chair. "There is no room for these items. So you will have to sell them with the house. Everything is in order and prepared for the sale."

His eyes narrowed. "These are your things, Ara. This is your home. You should not have moved from here." Fury vibrated under the smooth rumble of his voice.

Ara forced a bright smile onto her face. "I believe we agreed that keeping this house was nothing but a drain upon your estate. I can ensure a much more secure future for all the Baker Street house women if I condense all the expenses down to one household. The Vakkar Line can easily sustain all of the needs at the Baker Street house."

His left hand balled into a fist. "I agreed to no such thing, Ara."

She knew he hadn't, but she also knew this would be the easiest thing. She had planned to have a buyer at the ready by the time he found out she had vacated the house, making it difficult for him to withdraw from the sale. Blast herself for dragging her own feet.

The smile on her face quivered, but she held fast to it. He mustn't know how much it had pained her to leave this place. How she had cried silent tears every night for the last week in her bed at the Baker Street house. Even now, standing in the gaping vacantness of her home, her heart twisted, longing to be back in its comfort.

Her look dove away from him, landing on the desk as her smile finally faltered, her lips drawing in. She could not let him see how much she missed this house—nor that her stomach was having a hard time keeping an even keel when his look scorched into her like that.

Ara pointed at the small stack of papers and envelopes on her old desk. "I am just here to pick up these letters."

He nodded, silent, his eyes not leaving her face.

Ducking his unflinching gaze, she went over to the desk and made a production of flipping through the letters and notes to avoid looking at him. "Your visit to Notlund Castle went well? I understand there was a…hasty… wedding of the elder Silverton sister while you were there?"

"There was."

"It has been all the chatterboxes can talk about—the Earl of Luhaunt and his new wife do well to stay in the country and avoid the sniping of the drawing rooms."

"I have never known you to partake in gossip, Ara."

Was that what she was doing? She had thought she was just attempting to fill the empty air between them. And maybe discover where he stood with the younger Silverton sister. If they had gotten engaged, Ara would have surely read about it in the papers or heard of it in the drawing rooms, and a wedding would already be in the process of planning. Unless Caine and Miss Silverton were keeping their betrothal quiet. That was possible. The thought sent a lump into her throat.

She shook it free, shrugging with another bright smile. "Since the Duchess of Dunway has purchased several Vakkar sets, I have been in demand to show a number of Greta's designs in the past months. It has placed me in numerous drawing rooms, that is all. I nod politely at whatever the ladies would like to talk about, and the main topic has been Lord Luhaunt's unexpected wedding."

She tugged the edges of her white gloves along her wrists, pulling them farther up her bare arms. For how warm it was at the moment outside, the air in her old study seemed oddly chilly. Gathering the small stack of correspondence into her arms, Ara looked to him. "As I said, I am just here for these. Why are you here, Caine? I have been maintaining all of the affairs and accounts as warranted. Did you need something?"

His hand disappeared under the lapel of his dark jacket, and he withdrew a folded red note. A very distinct red note.

Ara jumped a step toward him, fumbling with the letters in her arms as she snatched the note out of his hand. "Where did this come from? I have been keeping up on all of your correspondence—every day. Why did I not see this?"

"I made Wilbert pull any of these envelopes."

Dread settled into her belly. "You what?"

"Mr. Wilbert has been pulling them from the piles for me before he handed the stack over to you." Caine plucked the note out of her hand. "I was not about to chance you coming across one of these without me present."

"But it has been months, Caine. How many did we miss?" She turned to slam the papers in her arm down onto the desk before she lost control and tossed them across the room. Her hand on her hip, she whipped back to him. "How could you do that? There were girls, Caine, innocent girls that you let...that you just let..." Her hand cupped over her mouth, fighting the sudden urge to vomit. Head shaking, she glared at him. "You had no right to do such a thing."

"No?" He tucked the envelope back into his jacket, returning her glare. "I have every right, Ara. I already know I cannot save the world. Something you have never been able to come to terms with. I was not about to leave you with the opportunity to do something stupid, because you still—even after all these years—have no regard for your own safety."

Her head snapped back, struck at the vehemence in his voice. "That is not true."

He closed the gap between them, his breath seething as he looked down at her, his blue eyes set hard. "It is true,

Ara. What would you have done had you seen one of the invitations come through while I was away?"

Her jaw clamped shut, her lips tight as she wedged her arms up between them, crossing them over her chest.

"Exactly. You have no business in the East End, Ara. None. So save your look of outrage for someone it will work upon. I was not about to let one of those envelopes into your view while I was away."

"You do not know what I would have done, Caine."

"I don't?"

"I can keep myself safe."

His eyebrow cocked at her. "You still do not understand this world, do you, Ara? Even after all you have seen. You think you are impervious to the danger."

"I know very well I am not impervious."

"No, you do think that. You escaped the worst once, Ara, so that is where your mind turns. Unfailing optimism. You think that somehow you will escape any danger—that people are inherently good and life will spin well for you. And that makes you very dangerous to yourself, Ara." His gaze went to the ceiling as he shook his head, hissing out an exhale. His eyes settled back on hers. "Tell me, Ara, do you think Mr. Flagerton would look kindly upon your late night activities?"

Her eyes flew wide. "You would not dare do such a thing to me."

"No? You care that much for him?"

"What if I do?"

"Do you not think he should know what you are capable of? How far you will go to save those girls? Why he will wake one night, alone in his bed, and wonder where you disappeared to? How he will eventually come to wonder why he is not enough for you?"

Control lost, Ara's hand whipped up, aiming to slap him. He snatched her wrist in the air before she made contact.

"Caine, I swear—"

"No, I swear, Ara—I swore to keep you safe a long time ago." He forced her arm downward between them. "And I am not about to break that vow. So yes, I will hide the damn notes from you, because you are a menace to yourself."

Red flew in front of her eyes. If only she'd been raised without manners, she would be spitting in his face right now.

Her chest expanding in a breath so deep it hurt her lungs, she stepped backward, ripping her wrist from his grasp.

She shoved the papers from the desk back into the crook of her arm, unable to keep her feet from stomping like a five-year-old's as she went to the door.

"Ara, stop."

Her steps quickened.

"This auction is for tonight. Shall I pick you and Mrs. Merrywent up at the usual time?"

His words stopped her at the door, but she refused to turn back to him. "I will go tonight, but it is for the innocent one. Not for you. For the girl."

~ ~ ~

Caine looked out the carriage window into the darkness at the torchlit gate they approached.

Shit.

This was no ordinary girl they had saved from the brothel tonight.

Every moment they had spent with the girl, Lizzie, in the carriage—her speech, how she held herself—told Caine she reeked of proper breeding. And judging by the size of the gates they were approaching, and the light from the massive torches reflecting off the gold gilding of the crest with a roaring lion in the middle, this was a place of power, of wealth. A place that would not look kindly upon having a precious daughter stolen from them.

That was assuming she was a relative of whoever owned this estate in Kent. She could be a scullery maid for all Caine knew. His eyes ran over the girl's straight posture, shoulders that did not slump, the slight upward tilt of her chin. She even hid her shaking well. Bred to not show emotion. No, she wasn't a maid. This one came from—and lived in—a world of privilege.

Caine turned back to the window, scrutinizing the crest. The double-tailed, three-talon lion had field rose vines wrapped about the hind legs. Vaguely familiar, but he did not recognize it attached to any of the peers he knew. Quite possible the place belonged to new, untitled money. An ancient-looking crest sometimes went far to impress the masses.

He looked from the carriage window to the girl across from him. Per her request, they had stopped after they were out of the East End to get her properly clothed in a brown dress with a high neck and long sleeves, even though it was still warm in the middle of the night. Mrs. Merrywent had combed and braided her hair during the ride only two hours outside of London, and now the girl looked of the innocence she had been sold for.

Guilt sliced through him, Ara's accusing eyes from earlier haunting his mind. How many young ones had they missed while he was away from London? How many were now dead? Or pieces of meat for men to desecrate again and again?

The argument he continually warred with himself over swallowed his mind—was it worse to let his purchases, his money, fuel the trade? Or was it worse to pull his money from the trade and lower the incentive, but in the process, be forced to leave all of the innocent girls to be bought by derelicts? Especially when, just like the girl he had purchased before he left for Notlund Castle, this one was too young—thirteen, maybe fourteen at most. Tiny, especially as she was squeezed between Ara and Mrs. Merrywent.

Despicable.

Caine cleared his throat as he tried to control the shot of rage running up his spine. "This, Lizzie?" He waved his hand at the window of the carriage. "This is your home?"

The girl leaned forward, stretching over Ara's lap to see out the window. "Yes. This is home."

Caine knocked on the roof of the carriage. The wheels immediately started to slow.

Lizzie looked to Ara. "I want you to bring me in, but my brother-in-law—he will not be…pleased. I am afraid for you if you accompany me."

Ara grabbed her hand. "Will he harm you, Lizzie?"

"No. Never. No one would ever hurt me here. My sister will be furious with me for riding off of the estate, but I just wanted to escape to read…" She took a quivering breath that turned into a slight whimper. "That was all. I just wanted to read, nothing more. Somewhere away, and then that man appeared…"

"Shhhhhh." Ara grabbed Lizzie's head, tucking the girl onto her shoulder before Lizzie's words could turn into sobs. "From what you have said about your family, they must be frantic for your return. And it has only been a few days. You are so lucky to have them, Lizzie. That is what you need to concentrate on—being home with them, where you are loved. And if you can make yourself forget this ever happened, you must do so. Let it be a bad memory you never think about, because you are now safe. Home."

The wheels of the carriage came to a stop, and Lizzie nodded as she drew away from Ara's shoulder, instantly calmed.

Caine's heart contracted at the scene. How Ara always managed to calm the girls, the capacity she had for empathy and compassion, when her own experience had been so very harsh, always astounded Caine. Where she drew the strength from, time and again, he did not know.

What he did know was that Mr. Flagerton was not damn good enough for her.

Not that he was any better.

"Here. If you ever need me, this is the address where I can be found at," Ara said, slipping a small card into Lizzie's hand and giving her a quick hug. "Are you sure you do not want anyone of us to accompany you up to the residence? As we told you, we have done this before, and after a few tense moments, once things are explained, the situation becomes quite manageable."

"No, thank you. For everything." She looked back to Mrs. Merrywent and then back to Ara. "But I would like to go up alone. Please."

Ara nodded.

Lizzie looked at Caine. He offered her a slight nod and then leaned to the side to open the carriage door. Tom stood under the mounted lantern on the side of carriage, his hand at the ready to help Lizzie down the carriage steps he had already pulled.

Within seconds, the girl had ducked to the right of the main gates, disappearing through a small doorway in the stone wall.

The ride back to London was made in silence.

Mrs. Merrywent had dozed off almost immediately once the carriage wheels started turning again. Ara's eyes, on the other hand, stayed wide open, moving from corner to corner in the carriage. Everywhere but at Caine.

Yes, he had been harsh with her at the Gilbert Lane house, but he had no other recourse. He knew full well Ara was bound to get herself hurt or killed without his guidance.

Despite the drizzle that had set in, Tom made adequate time back to London. Her foot constantly tapping, Ara managed to avoid eye contact with Caine the entire way.

The coach stopped outside of the Baker Street house. At the turn of the carriage door handle, Mrs. Merrywent's entire body jerked with a start, and she sat up, eyes bleary. "That was quick."

The right side of Ara's mouth lifted in a smirk. "It was."
She motioned her hand for Mrs. Merrywent to exit.

Waiting for Mrs. Merrywent to move down the stairs
in front of her, Ara scooted along the bench, her eyes solidly
on escape.

Caine knew he should let Ara go in silence. It was the
honorable thing to do. He was due back up at Notlund
Castle in a week.

Due there, ready with a marriage proposal.

His mother knew it. Miss Silverton knew it. He knew
it.

Ara probably knew it. Even though she had not spoken
a word of it. She probably knew.

Let her go.

Yet his mouth opened the second Ara stood to exit.
"Ara, wait."

Ara glanced at him and then out to Mrs. Merrywent.
Tom was already bringing Mrs. Merrywent up to the door
under the cover of an umbrella.

Ara sank back to the seat, looking across to Caine.
"What?"

His mouth opened, but no words fell forth. What had
he thought he was going to say?

She nodded, her lips slightly jutting out as her eyes
read his face. "Caine, earlier today…"

"Yes?"

Her hands clasped together on her lap as her heel
started to tap on the floor. "You told me you swore to keep
me safe."

The tone of her voice made his body tighten. "I did."

Her words went soft and slowed, each word said with distinction. "You are absolved, Caine—of everything to do with me. Everything we still need to do, we can do through written correspondence. We can even figure out how you can hand off the girls to me after an auction without interaction. There is no reason we need to ever speak again. I do not know if he told you, but I have already turned over much of the responsibilities of our association to your new man-of-affairs. He appears to be competent. It will do, until you are married and your new wife can decide how much involvement she wants with running the households."

"That was not necessary, Ara."

"It was. It is." Her hands shifted to the right in her lap, pressing on the thigh of her tapping leg. It stilled, forced to the floor. "You care too much about me, Caine. You feel too much responsibility for me. It cannot continue."

"So you are absolving me from your life because I care about you?"

"I am absolving you from my life because I cannot do this any longer, Caine." Her foot overcame her hands, her heel tapping again. She leaned forward, setting the weight of her torso on her thigh. "What happened today…I cannot have you appearing in front of me out of nowhere. I cannot watch you pursue another woman. I cannot watch you get married. It is too hard. Especially after what I told you in that coaching inn…after what we did. How you left me in that room."

"That was for your own good, Ara." Caine's jaw flexed sideways, the memory of that night hitting him hard. *Twice a bastard to her.*

Her hand flew up, touching the corner of her eye. A tear? He couldn't be sure in the low light.

"How, Caine—how was leaving me without a word, after I told you I loved you, for my own good?"

"I did it for you, Ara. You do not know your own mind. You do not love me. You are indebted to me, you always have been—that is what you feel."

"What I feel?" The words turned into a low shriek as the hand at her eye balled into a fist, punching into the cushion next to her leg. "Now you dare to presume you know more about my mind than I do?"

She shook her head, and this time when her fingers reached up to her cheek, it was a definite tear, caught in the flicker of the carriage lamp, that she wiped away.

"Ara—"

"Damn you, Caine. Damn you." Her green eyes, dark with the night, landed on him, blistering with pain. "We are done. I will ensure there is no reason for us to ever have to speak again."

She stood, jumping out and down from the carriage, running through the drizzle to the front door. Tom bumbled, trying to run alongside her up the stairs and protect her from the rain even though he was not nimble enough to keep up with her speed.

Caine slumped back against the cushions.

Did Ara not realize she had no need to damn him?

He already was damned.

There was no arguing that.

{ CHAPTER 11 }

Ara looked down at the calendar in her arms, stopping in the wide hallway to read her tiny scribble. Too many appointments were squished into the next three days. Ruby brooch with Lady Padwall. Matching emerald earrings, necklace, and bracelet with Lady Severson. A set of diamond rings with Lady Ferron. It went on and on.

But it didn't matter. No matter how many appointments she set up. No matter how she tried to fill her mind, she could not forget, not for even one precious second, that Caine was marrying Miss Silverton in three days' time.

He had proposed. Miss Silverton had accepted. Only three days remained until their union.

Ara sucked in a breath, trying to force air farther down into her lungs and past the constant tightness in her chest. She just needed to make it through these last three days.

Three more days, and Caine would be married. Then the pain in her chest would ease. The knot in her stomach would disappear, allowing her to eat again. Three more days.

She lifted a heavy foot, walking down the hallway that cut through the center of the Baker Street house. A lusty, full laugh floated into the hallway, and Ara stopped just outside the doorway to the main drawing room.

She knew Mr. Flagerton was waiting for her. He was going to accompany her on a walk in Vauxhall Gardens before the trees lost their plumpness to the chill of fall.

But before they left, he needed to go through the latest shipment of gemstones with Greta.

Turning the corner, Ara watched them. They sat in the middle of the drawing room, foreheads almost touching as they pored over the jewels spread between them on the round rosewood table. Greta's shoulders were still shaking at whatever she had just been laughing at, and a low chuckle filled the room from Mr. Flagerton.

Ara's head tilted, watching them unnoticed for a few minutes. Why had she never seen this?

Greta glanced up from the table, her eyes catching Ara. Loupe in her fingers, her arm swung, ushering Ara into the room. "Darling, you must see what Mr. Flagerton has brought me with this set of gems."

Ara stepped into the room, eyebrows arched, as both Mr. Flagerton and Greta stood from the table. "Something unusual?"

Greta pointed down at the table. "Gems with the most…peculiar shapes. Mr. Flagerton has always had an eye for the interesting." A devil smirk lit up her face as she looked at Mr. Flagerton. "Perhaps I will create a new line that we can sell specifically to the madams on the other side of Charing Cross."

A quick glance at the table verified the peculiar shapes of some of the stones. Leave it to Greta to go to the outrageous. At least Mr. Flagerton had the good sense to look sheepish at Greta's suggestion. Appropriate, even if Ara had just heard him chuckling over the very thing Greta suggested.

Ara shook her head, her eyes to the ceiling as she set her calendar onto the one clear spot on the small desk in the corner. Space was limited in the Baker Street house. The study had become Greta's working studio, so Ara had attempted to take up only a small corner in the drawing room with her work, but she was quickly losing the battle being waged between her many ledgers and space.

"Do not look the prude, darling Ara." Greta picked up one of the aqua-hued gems, holding it to the light shining in from the window. "If you would only examine them, you would see the potential."

Ara smiled. "That is quite all right, Greta. I believe what you say and do not need to verify." She looked to Mr. Flagerton. "Are you done with Greta for the moment? I can take leave to walk now, or we can delay it, if need be."

Mr. Flagerton looked to Greta, and receiving a nod, he turned to Ara. "Now would be delightful, if it does not take too much of your day. Greta says you have been beyond busy."

Ara shrugged. "It has been manageable. And I would like to fit the walk in. Mable should be down in a moment so we can leave."

Within a half hour, Ara and Mr. Flagerton strolled through an outside path in Vauxhall Gardens, Mable trailing them at a discreet distance.

Ara glanced up at Mr. Flagerton's profile. He was handsome. A traveler with the darkened skin to prove it. Somewhat rugged, even. Quick witted. And while Ara liked him immensely, she now fully realized the truth that had been twitching about in the back of her mind for weeks.

She had been so absorbed in using Mr. Flagerton to forget Caine, that she hadn't even seen what had been in front of her for months.

Beneath all of her flamboyance, Greta was very much in love with Mr. Flagerton. And he was quite enamored with Greta in return.

But he was also far too much of a gentleman to cut things with Ara and turn his attentions to her dearest friend.

It was time Ara set at least one thing right in her life.

Her hands clasping behind her back, Ara focused on a sculpture at the far end of the path. "Mr. Flagerton, you have done me the great honor of giving me your attentions these past few months, but I feel I must ask you something."

Worry instantly spread across Mr. Flagerton's brow. "What is it, Miss Detton? I pray I have not offended you?"

She looked up at him. "No. Not in the slightest. What I need to ask you about, I only just saw today—or more correctly, I only just realized it today."

"What was your realization?"

"Greta."

"Greta?"

"When you talk to her, her eyes glow. Your eyes glow. They do not do so with me."

His foot caught in a slight stumble. "Truly, Miss Detton, I would never—"

"Please, no. There is no need to deny it. Not on account of my feelings. My ego can absorb this. I love Greta like a sister, Mr. Flagerton, and if what I just saw in the drawing room is indicative of what you two could possibly have together, then I want that for you."

Ara paused, taking a deep breath with her next few steps. She smiled as her head turned to him. "Even more so, I want that for Greta. For all of her outlandishness, she is a special soul, Mr. Flagerton, and she deserves every happiness. If you can give her that happiness, I think you should."

His brow still furrowed, Mr. Flagerton continued ten silent steps before turning to Ara, his hazel eyes sincere. "I agree with your thinking on the matter, Miss Detton."

Ara exhaled her held breath with a nod. She would not find happiness with Mr. Flagerton, but Greta would. She could not have asked for more. The smile on her face widened. "I thought you would, Mr. Flagerton."

~ ~ ~

The glow of the swinging lantern sent shadows scurrying in front of him within the cold stone hallway. In the middle of the blasted labyrinth of Notlund Castle, Caine was lost, searching in vain for his betrothed.

The toe of his boot stubbed on an askew stone in the floor of the hallway, jamming his toes. Dammit. It was the night before his wedding, and his fiancée shouldn't be this hard to find.

Caine stopped his long strides at a three-way split in the corridor. Left, right, or forward. And not a bloody clue which way would bring him back to the main guest wing of the castle.

He stood in the split, staring down each of the dark corridors. He needed to find Miss Silverton. Find her and say what?

They were making a mistake?

The bloody wedding was only hours away.

And what would await him if he did break it off?

An estate that would be drowning in debt in another five years? An empty townhouse? A distinct cut from society after breaking the engagement? Two sisters that would be ruined by his scandal, their chances at proper matches scratched?

There was only one thing that he knew for certain wouldn't be awaiting him.

Ara.

That fact he knew without a doubt. She was done with him.

So why was he searching so hard in this blasted castle for his betrothed—who appeared to have gone missing herself? What madness kept him seeking?

Caine set the lantern down on the stone floor, both of his hands going to his face, vigorously rubbing his eyes.

Dammit.

He was holding on. Holding on to what, he couldn't quite name.

Hell. He could name it, even if he wanted to lie to himself and not do so.

Hope. Ara.

But Ara was done with him. He repeated it five, twelve, twenty-two times. Done with him. Her own lips saying the words.

But that damn flicker of Ara would not extinguish itself. It sat in the darkest part of his mind, taunting him, telling him that marrying Miss Silverton would be a massive mistake. Caine tried to grip that ember and crush it.

He had to be pragmatic and not turn into a bloody romantic that let misplaced optimism rule his actions. That trait was reserved for Ara alone, and had no part in his life.

Caine kicked at the stone floor, re-stubbing his toe.
Dammit.

Where in the hell was his fiancée?

And what in hades was he going to tell her once he
found her?

Caine picked up the lantern, veering to the left, his
strides long.

Maybe he would find her down this path.

~ ~ ~

Caine yanked at the end of his cravat, dismantling the
knot that was near choking him. He had wanted to leave
Notlund Castle with the veneer of an unbowed aristocratic
gentleman—a paragon—but now he could get rid of the
stifling thing. The start of fall had done little to cool the air,
and they had a long ride back to London.

"What?" Caine grumbled, his eyes not leaving the
countryside to look at his companion across from him in
the carriage.

"You are handling being left at the altar—well, the
night before the altar—fairly well, considering the erupting
scandal." His tone light, Fletch plucked off invisible flecks
from his trousers, a smirk cavorting along the edges of his
mouth. "I had not taken Miss Silverton as the eloping sort."

Caine sighed, crumpling the white strip of the cravat
onto the cushion. "How in the hell am I supposed to take
the events of the last twelve hours? Do tell what would be
an appropriate reaction."

Fletch shrugged, nonplussed by Caine's tone. "I would
have thought a frown or two would have been appropriate.

Not the look of a man who has just escaped the gallows and cannot believe his good fortune enough to smile about it."

"I am not happy about what just happened, Fletch. I almost just lost everything."

"So you are not happy you did not have to wed Miss Silverton?" Fletch's eyebrow cocked. "Personally, I had placed my bets on you absconding from the estate before the wedding and leaving me behind with your mother and sisters to try and calm the masses. I think Miss Silverton did both of us a favor last night by disappearing to the Scottish border."

"A favor that would not have mattered in the slightest had the duke not had the good grace to show mercy upon my mother and sisters. After finding out I buy virgins from the Jolly Vassal as a pastime, he made it astoundingly clear there would have been no wedding, even if Miss Silverton hadn't eloped with that physician."

"The Duke of Letson is a discreet fellow, as far as I understand." Fletch leaned forward, handing Caine a flask of brandy.

It was early, but since Caine hadn't slept last night, he had no trouble taking a long swallow. It did little to ease his annoyance. "Yes, I am happy for Miss Silverton's elopement. It saved me from the brutal discussion I was seeking her out to have before the duke found me."

"You were going to end it?"

Caine shrugged. "It does not matter now. What does matter is how in the blasted hell did the duke come by the information about my activities in the Jolly Vassal? That is where my fury lies. That knowledge is how I nearly lost everything. I—we, for you have certainly helped through the years—have done everything possible to bury my affairs in that brothel. Not a trace. How the devil did he find out?" Caine's eyes narrowed at Fletch.

"Don't look at me, Caine. I swore long ago I would do whatever I could to help and never breathe a word of it." Fletch grabbed the flask back from Caine's hand. "In fact, I would take offense at your current glare if you didn't already have my sympathy over your recently jilted status. But all secrets find the light eventually, Caine. Your activities in the brothel are no different."

"How in the hell did he find out, then?"

"I do not know. But you are right, you did almost lose everything." His hand came up, forefinger and thumb nearly meeting. "You were this close to becoming a disgrace to everyone you have ever known—but instead, you escaped. Without a wife you did not want, and with half of her dowry. Overly generous of the duke, considering the circumstances."

Caine nodded. "Especially when he heard I was considering ending it."

"You bloody well told him that?"

"I did. I could not in good conscience leave that unsaid." Caine still could not believe the duke had offered such a deal. Yes, Caine had been the jilted party, and yes, it was proper to make compensation from the dowry in these situations. But for the duke to offer the portion of the dowry instead of exposing him and all his nefarious activities to society had gone beyond mercy—even if the duke had done it for the sake of Caine's mother and sisters. The Duke of Letson had more honor in his pinky than any man Caine knew. Or at least the duke wanted it to appear that way.

"You realize you could have told him the truth about your purchases at the brothel—what you actually do with the girls—and he would have likely turned over the entire dowry to you?" Fletch asked.

"And put Ara—or any of the girls—in danger of being found out, ruined because they were victims of greed?" Caine's fist tightened, knuckles cracking. "No. Never. They have lives, Fletch. Those girls, those women now have safe, secure lives—I am not about to jeopardize that. I would have walked away with nothing if it meant protecting their secrets. Let the duke think of me what he will."

Fletch shrugged. "Regardless, I somewhat expected you to be happy on this ride back to London."

"Tell me again, why exactly I should be happy about almost losing everything—about having my life almost dissolve into utter scandal?"

Fletch drew his ankle up, resting it on top of his thigh. "You should be happy you have been given another chance to be the man you want to be."

Damned if Fletch wasn't aiming to get under his skin with every word this morning. Caine needed to just keep his mouth closed and take a much-needed nap. Instead, his voice came out in a growl. "What the hell is that supposed to mean?"

"Easy." Fletch's palm came up, warding off Caine's acrimony. "Let me clarify. Be the man, with the woman you actually want to be with."

Caine's mouth tightened. "Shut your mouth, Fletch."

Fletch's smiled widened, abrupt enthusiasm filling his features. It looked odd, for the harsh lines of his face rarely disappeared. "So it is acceptable for me to start courting Ara when we get back to London? I was going to wait until you were properly wed to your fortune bride. But as the first bride has slipped through your grasp, I only foresee this process of you finding a wife to be dragging onward, and I find myself somewhat impatient to declare my intentions toward Ara."

His teeth grinding, the threat in Caine's voice bordered on livid. "Again, I beg you to shut your mouth, Fletch, before I shut it for you."

"It won't be the first time."

"It will be the most painful."

"So you take offense at my intentions toward Ara?" Fletch leaned casually back against the carriage's thick cushions. "I had never actually considered her as a possibility to pursue until you went on this fool's quest for an heiress bride. I can only assume Ara is now in play and available for my attentions."

"She is not in play, Fletch. Not with the likes of you."

"With the likes of anyone?"

Caine bit his tongue, wanting nothing more than to smack the satisfied smirk off of Fletch's face. He knew Fletch was baiting him. He also was not in the mood to be baited.

Fletch tilted his head toward Caine in deference. "As I can see you are only a second away from making good on your threat to shut my mouth, I admit, I know she is yours."

"She is not mine, Fletch."

"No? Are you sure about that? Is she sure about that?"

"If you are implying that Ara loves me, be assured, she does not."

"Whatever gave you that absurd notion?"

"She is indebted to me, Fletch. Nothing more. Not love."

"And you are not willing to fight her on that score? You do nothing but spar with the woman when you are not looking at her with besotted eyes. Do you not think you would win?"

"You know nothing of what she is thinking."

"And you do?"

Caine heaved a sigh. "You are meddling where you should not, Fletch."

"Maybe so." Fletch uncapped the flask and took a long sip of the brandy. "It seems to me, my friend, you now have absolutely nothing standing in the way between you and Ara. The money from the dowry will allow you to either make new investments or revitalize the mines. So your responsibility to the title is satisfied. There appears to be nothing but your own damn guilty conscience in the way."

"I don't feel guilty."

Fletch snorted a laugh. "Never have I heard such a falsehood."

"You are agonizingly close to getting thrown from this carriage, Fletch."

"Throw me out, or not, but remember, I have been your friend for too many years to count, and the war years count for at least twenty years each."

"Your point?"

"Unbelievable as it may sound, I do look outside of myself on occasion, and I have watched you these past six years. And you have been condemning yourself ever since the day Isabella died—flogging yourself for not saving her. I do believe you have determined that you are not good enough to find happiness with the woman that means the world to you."

Caine bit the inside of his cheek. As much as he wanted to punch Fletch, his words, each and every one of them, rang too truthful. He did fail Isabella. He didn't deserve to love another. And if he was completely honest with himself, Ara did mean the world to him, even if he was determined to let her go. Even if he had to let her go.

Caine rubbed his eyes, wishing he were anywhere but captive with his best friend in this damn carriage. "Ara does not love me, Fletch. She is beholden to me for saving her. It is not love."

"As you said." Fletch nodded, at least trying to appear as though he took in Caine's words with the proper weight. Fletch's lifted foot came down to the carriage floor, and he leaned forward, the lines on his face deepening. "And that is the lie you like to hide behind, Caine. But in as long as I have known Ara, she is not one to misplace her words or her feelings—sure, she is optimistic to a fault. Cares to a fault. But the woman has always known her own mind. Has always made her own destiny happen. Look at where she came from, what happened to her. Yet she sees the good in other people, and she figures out a way to make them shine. She has done it with her girls. Hell, she has done it with you."

Caine's eyes narrowed on his friend, a vicious swipe of jealousy cutting across his chest. "You were not just feigning an interest in Ara, were you? You truly mean to pursue her?"

Fletch shrugged, noncommittal. "Just consider my words, Caine. Ara does not look at you like she is indebted to you. Wherever you got that notion, you need to rethink it. And these last six years, you have paid dues that you never owed, Caine. Isabella's death was an injustice, there is no denying that. But you did not cause it. Evil men did. This wedding that you just escaped from—it is a gift. A gift of the future you actually want—could actually have. Don't be an idiot and waste it."

Caine's head dropped backward, his eyes closing.

Hell, was Fletch right? Could his atonement possibly be fulfilled for failing Isabella?

He had never thought it possible.

But maybe. Maybe.

The tiniest flicker of hope sprang from embers he had thought he had extinguished.

Yet even with hope, there was still the matter of what he had done to Ara over the years. Twice a bastard, violating her, and then he had abandoned her in the worst possible way this summer.

She had wanted him gone from her life, and he let it be so she could move on from him—but he could not put his actions solely upon her. He had made his own choice in the matter as well.

And he was beginning to see what an atrocious choice it had been.

{ CHAPTER 12 }

Ara pulled the dark cobalt hood on her cloak farther down her forehead. What had been a light drizzle when she had set out to the small *House of Vakkar* storefront they were readying for opening on New Bond Street had turned into fat droplets during the past few hours.

Thank goodness she had taken Patch with her and had left Mable at the Baker Street house. Mable despised the rain and grumbled about it endlessly when she was forced to be in it—whereas Patch loved the rain, loved jumping at it, his tongue flapping as he tried to snatch drops out of the sky.

A smile broke wide at watching her dog's antics. If she had anything to be thankful for in the past few months, Caine's absence and her moving into the Baker Street house had freed her from Caine's constant insistence she adhere to the strictest rules of propriety.

Which suited her fine. Patch was good entertainment on a walk such as this. Mable was not.

Ara had only needed to gather a few measurements from the foreman at the site, so the designs for the cabinets that would house the jewellery collections could be complete. But what had been intended as a five-minute conversation had turned into several hours discussing with the foreman, Mr. Littlefoot, a multitude of finishing options he wanted her opinions on.

She liked the man—he and his crew were honest hard-workers—but he openly admitted to knowing very little about selling items, and even less about selling jewellery. Ara especially appreciated that about him—he knew his limitations, but once she explained something, he got it right, down to the most precise detail.

And Ara had been having to explain a lot as of late— Greta had a very specific vision for how her jewellery needed to be presented to the world, and Ara had been the only one able to translate the vision in Greta's mind to Mr. Littlefoot's work-worn hands.

Not that Ara minded the extra work in the slightest. This was her life now. Opening this store. Expanding the coveted Vakkar Line into the even more exclusive *House of Vakkar*. She needed to make a success of it.

But the last few unexpected hours spent at the storefront had seen the drizzle turn into a downpour— much to Ara's disappointment, but Patch's delight.

Cutting through the small park a block away from the Baker Street house, Ara glanced up from watching Patch leap in the air every few steps. The sky was darkening— which meant it had gotten late and the sun was setting far above the grey mass of clouds hovering close to the spires of the rooftops.

A brutal pang cut across her heart at the thought of a sunset and the last one she had seen.

The devil of it.

Without warning, the little memories—the smallest moments in time—would sneak up upon her and slice open wounds she thought were healing.

She took a deep breath. She needed to see a new sunset—one that would replace the last one she had seen with Caine in her mind. She needed a sunset so fantastic that it would be the only one she would ever think about again. Maybe when the shop opened, she could convince Mrs. Merrywent, Greta, and several of the girls to accompany her to the Eastbourne seaside for a stay. It could be something for them all to look forward to. That was, if Greta wasn't already married to Mr. Flagerton by then.

Ara looked down and realized Patch was no longer in front of her. She was only halfway through the park, so she spun, scanning the neat bushes and lawns alongside the gravel paths. No Patch. He never strayed far from her, so Ara hurried, scanning the street they had been walking toward, praying he hadn't darted out into the lane to get trampled by a horse or a carriage.

Reaching the walkway, Ara darted to the right around a carriage stopped in front of her, searching the street in all directions. Patch wouldn't have just moved on to the Baker Street house without her, would he?

A yipping bark caught her attention. Ara spun around, looking under the carriage next to her.

"Miss Detton."

She recognized that voice. Ara lifted the front of her dripping wool hood, looking up to the coachman. "Tom?"

He tipped his hat, pointing behind him to the inside of the black carriage. Ara's eyes dropped, truly seeing the carriage. The door was open, and she hadn't taken much notice of it when she had passed it. Caine's carriage.

Her stomach instantly tightened as she considered fleeing. But then another bark echoed from inside the carriage.

Ara forced herself to shuffle to the opening of the coach and looked inside.

There sat her dog, tongue hanging out to the side and happily panting as the spot behind his left ear was scratched with gusto.

Ara followed the line from the hand, up the arm, to the face.

Caine.

She glanced down to Patch. His foot started thumping, his head leaning hard into the scratch. Traitor.

Droplets fell in front of her eyes from the edge of her hood as she looked up at Caine.

The same as always. His imposing form, swallowing the carriage seat. His dark jacket and waistcoat stretched to perfection over his shoulders. His devilish dark hair curling down to tease the whiteness of his cravat. His clear blue eyes watching her, instantly intense. The only thing that was different about him was the slight flush over the hard lines of his cheekbones, most likely from the damp coolness.

Ara steeled herself.

"You have my dog."

The side of his mouth curled up slightly. "I do."

She looked down at Patch, clicking her fingers through her gloves. The traitor's foot thumping only went faster. Ara whistled, or at least tried to. She had never mastered much more than a faint tweet.

Patch only shifted his head farther back onto Caine's hand, his neck stretched long.

"Can you please stop petting him? He will not come when you are mauling him so."

"I don't think he would consider it mauling."

"What is it you want, Caine? I need to get back to the Baker Street house."

"I need to talk to you, Ara."

"I am standing here, waiting for my dog, so feel free to proceed. He will tire of you eventually."

Caine's hand switched to Patch's other ear. Blast it.

"I would like to speak to you while you are not standing in the rain, dripping, Ara. Where is Mable?"

"She is at the Baker Street house. I was just out for a walk."

Instant censure crossed his face, but he kept his mouth shut.

"You have no right to that, Caine."

"What?"

"Judgement. No. Not anymore."

"I said nothing."

Her head tilted, her eyes pinning him.

"I don't think you truly know what is in my mind at the moment, Ara." He motioned to the bench across from him. "Please. Come with me, just for a short while. I do need to speak with you, and it seems bad form that I sit in here, dry, while you are drowning out there. Patch likes it well enough, and we both know how he loves the rain."

Ara grumbled, lifting her skirts and stepping up into the coach. Caine reached around her and swung the door closed before she gained her seat across from him.

A quick jerk, and the wheels started to roll.

"Wait. I did not agree to go with you anywhere, Caine. Have Tom stop the carriage."

"He is just bringing us to my townhouse, Ara. While I didn't want to watch you standing in the rain, I also know I don't want to have this conversation with you in a carriage."

Her arms crossed under the swath of her cloak as she eyed him warily. What on earth could he take from her now? Did he know about the shop? Of course he did. Of course he would want to involve himself in some fashion. "What conversation is that?"

The half-cocked smile was back on his lips. "It is only a few minutes to wait, Ara. Patience."

She took another big breath, looking down at Patch as she tugged the hood back off her head. Caine had ceased scratching Patch's head, but now her stalwart dog had wrapped himself along Caine's ankles. Her eyes rolled. Double the traitor.

Silence filled the carriage until Ara found the nerve to ask the only thing that had pulsated in her mind since she sat down across from Caine. "Was the wedding all you had hoped for?"

His eyes went wide, shock crossing his face.

Ara wondered at it. Shock that she had dared to speak of the wedding? It had only been five days ago, so why wouldn't she acknowledge it?

"You do not know?"

"Know what?"

"I thought you always read the papers, Ara."

She shrugged, not that he could see that under the draping of her cloak. The truth was, she had buried herself in her work during the past week, her eyes avoiding anything that would even hint of Caine's nuptials. She very well knew he was getting married, and she certainly hadn't wanted to be reminded of it at every turn.

"It seems the papers have escaped my attention as of late."

He nodded, his light blue eyes suddenly serious as he stared at her.

Ara shifted uncomfortably, looking out the window at the droplets sliding down the glass. Why were they not at his townhouse already? She looked to him. "I am sure you have heard from Mr. Peterton of the jewellery shop we are opening for Greta's designs. It is the next logical step, and I am sure you will see the proceeds from it soon, as you are part owner. It has consumed my time as of late."

"It is a great idea. I am sure it will be a success, Ara. But you did not need to name me part owner of it. Everything you and Greta have built has been your own."

"You invested in the idea of a jewellery line, in Greta's skill—"

"I invested in you, Ara."

Her look dove from him, staring out the window. "Regardless, you allowed us to start and grow her work. You will always be part owner, Caine." Her eyes lifted to him, smirk playing on her lips. "As long as you are a silent owner, that is."

He chuckled. "I will strive to remain so."

"Thank you. I have enough to do what with handling Greta's wild whims."

"She is driving you mad?"

"She is genius. Apparently, genius sometimes comes with madness." Ara smiled wide. "But I wouldn't trade her for the world—she is fierce in her loyalty to me—and to you. I suggested she do this on her own, as they are her designs, but she would not hear of it. Almost slapped me when I suggested it."

"She has always been fiery."

"Yes. And I love her dearly, even with her eccentricities."

The carriage stopped and Patch was quick to his feet, his nose nuzzling Caine's knee. Ara's lips pursed. Had her own dog so completely forgotten her existence? She stared at Patch's perked ears, her voice low. "This was a mistake. I never should have gotten into the carriage."

"Please, Ara."

She looked up at Caine, her eyebrows cocked in question.

"Please come in, just for a moment. Just in the study, like we always were."

A lump suddenly lodged in her throat, her head shaking.

"Please."

The one word was strained coming from his lips. Strained, what begging would sound like if the man knew how to do it. But she knew Caine too well for that. He did not beg. He got.

And of course, he got her. He always did.

She nodded.

~ ~ ~

Unclasping the silver catch on her cloak, Ara followed Caine down the hall to his study. She pulled the cloak free from her body, handing it and her wet gloves to Wilbert. If Wilbert noted that she had come in hidden under her cloak, sans Mable, but with Patch at her heels, he offered nary a blink at it.

Caine nudged Patch on the rump with his shin, sending him farther down the hall and back to the kitchens. Ara stifled a sigh. Now she would have to tear Patch away from his begging for scraps in a few minutes. For a man always worried about her keeping her reputation above reproach, Caine was making it quite difficult to exit his house without the entire staff knowing she had come here unchaperoned.

Of course, maybe it was different now that he was married. New rules. Ara's eyes flew to the hallway ceiling as if she could see into the rooms above. Was his new wife here? Of course she was.

Ara's heart flew into a frenzy, battering against her chest. Caine did not mean to introduce her to his new wife, did he? Why had she not figured this out in the carriage?

She spun in the hallway, panicked, taking one step first toward the kitchens to retrieve Patch, and then she flipped her motion, aiming to retrieve her cloak back from Wilbert first. Cloak, dog, back door. That order.

"Ara." Caine snatched her forearm before she made it even two steps from him.

She yanked on her arm. Damn his strong clamp. "I need to go, Caine. I didn't realize your wife would be here and I cannot—"

"Stop, Ara." A smile cut across his features. That he found her panic amusing was cruel.

"No, you stop," she hissed. "I am not going to meet your wife today, Caine, not ever, if I can help it."

With one swift motion, he pulled her into his study, slamming the door behind her. "Dammit, Ara, you need to stop for just one blasted second and look at me. Listen to me."

Her mouth agape, she looked up at him.

"I did not get married, Ara. I thought you knew. I thought you would have read about it—heard about it."

"You…you did not get married?" She twisted her arm free, taking a step away from him into the center of the room. "But you were up at Notlund Castle—the wedding was days ago."

"The wedding was supposed to be days ago. I was jilted."

"You were *what*?"

"I was jilted. Cast off. Left at the altar. Miss Silverton discovered I have a penchant for buying virgins in a brothel and then eloped to Scotland with a past love to avoid me."

Her feet shuffled backward as her right palm landed on her chest. The back of her calves hit wood and she sank, landing in a chair, her left hand clutching the armrest. Ara stared at the floor for a long moment before her look crept up to Caine. He remained standing by the door, a mixture of concern and amusement playing along his features.

"You did not marry her?" As much as she would have liked her voice to be solid, it came out as a squeak.

"No. No marriage."

Ara closed her eyes, shaking her head as the news settled into her consciousness. She opened her eyes, noticing her fingers gripping the chair.

"The devil—this is my chair." She bolted upright to her feet as her eyes flew around his study. "This is my desk. And your chair from the Gilbert Lane house."

She turned on her heel to him. "What is going on, Caine?"

He walked across the room and stopped at her rosewood desk, running his fingers along the gleaming edge of it. Her desk now sat at an angle to his desk and still his enormous study had room to spare. "I had the furniture brought here. I could not part with them—they are a part of you, Ara. Plus, I have always been quite fond of the chair you had made for me. I did not know what to do with it all at first, but then I arrived back here in London yesterday, and I knew, without a doubt, what to do with them."

His knuckles rapped on the desk as he looked up to her. "I do not know if this is the proper placement of them, I thought you could decide."

Ara dragged her fingertips across her forehead. "How have I landed in this bedlam?" Her eyes locked onto his face, skewering him. "What are you doing, Caine? You have been jilted and now you have gone slightly mad? We cannot just go back to the way things were. You absolutely know that fact and you are being nothing but rude to me. Disrespectful. You still need to find a wife and I still cannot watch that transpire."

The look on his face quieted, his blue eyes sobering against her glare. "I hope—no I beg—that I am looking at her."

She stared at him blankly, hearing the words but not able to process them, much less believe them. "You are looking at her?" The words slipped out in a stunned whisper, as Ara collapsed back down onto her chair.

Caine advanced on her, gently, but with stealth, lodging himself right before her, the tips of his toes touching hers. Her eyes dropped from his face to stare at a black onyx button on his waistcoat.

"I am horrified that what I put you through would draw such a reaction from you, Ara—I did not realize that you possessed this much anger at me. So much so that you obviously cannot believe the words I say. But know that while I cannot rewrite the last four months, Ara—the hurt I caused—I do apologize for it."

Ara shook her head, his words only reaching the outer edges of her mind. Craning her neck, she looked up at him. "What about the money? Your responsibilities?"

Caine shrugged. "To be jilted is a scandal of humiliation, but it also created a nice opportunity. The Duke of Letson has given me half of the dowry."

"But why?"

"It is expected. The marriage was a contract. He is not about to tamper with the honor of his family and his charges. It normally would have been the full amount of the dowry, but I believe he was more than generous after discovering my virgin-buying depravity. As I did not defend myself against the allegations, I do commend the duke for his honor. This exchange of money is common in these situations."

"But is it enough to right your estate?"

A smile reached the corners of his mouth. "Ara, you sound as if you are reaching for excuses for me to go out and troll the marriage market again."

"No." She blurted the word and instantly wished she could pop it back into her mouth. "It is just after everything this summer…"

He reached down, clasping both of her hands in his own. Taking a step back, he pulled her to her feet, but didn't let her fingers slip from his. "I do not care if it is enough. And I finally realized that fact. There was nothing I wanted more in that castle than to leave those stone walls and come and find you. Find you and take you in my arms. For days before the wedding I warred with myself—so much so that Fletch had a horse saddled and ready for me to escape on, consequences be damned. But then the choice was quite neatly taken from me, and I was nothing but relieved."

"But all of your responsibilities."

His hand came up, gripping her chin. "Damn my responsibilities, Ara. I will figure out a way. I am seeing quite clearly for the first time in forever. I am not willing to give you up."

"But you cannot just cast your responsibilities aside for me."

"Cease, Ara. I refuse to be worried about the future if it is to cost me the most important thing in my life." He shrugged. "I still have the responsibilities of the title—I know I do—but I have been given another chance to do what I should have done months ago—no—years ago. And damn if I am going to be scared of it any longer."

"Scared of what?"

"To tell you I love you." Both of his hands cupped her face. "I love you, Ara. And I know what I have done to you this summer. I also know I never want to fail you again. I have been so damn concerned about our past, what I did to you, and about failing you in some imaginary way in the future—concerned that I wasn't a man that deserved to walk beside you—that I did not recognize that I have been failing you every day for the last six years."

Her hands came up, gripping his wrists to steady herself against her legs that threatened to collapse. "You have not failed me, Caine."

"No, I did." His hands tightened around her face, his thumbs running along her cheekbones, his blue eyes vehement in their intent. "Every single moment I did not take you in my arms. Every single moment I thought I knew better for the two of us. Every single moment I did not kiss you, when it was all I could think about. Every one of those moments I failed you."

He drew a deep breath. "No more, Ara. Not after today. As selfish as it may be, I don't care. I need you, Ara."

Her soul shaking, she tried to steady her mind. How she wanted to believe him. How she'd wanted this for years. So much so, she could not comprehend it even happening.

And then a thought, another reason why it could not be happening set darkness into her mind.

Eyes closing, she fought the thought, fought the question. What did it matter? She had tossed everything away for pride once—could she truly live with herself if she did it again?

"Ara, what are you hiding from? I tell you I love you and worry appears in your eyes."

Damn him. Damn that he knew her too well. Damn him because he was going to force her to tell him what was in her mind.

Pride forced her eyes open. "You left me, Caine. I told you I loved you and you left. You chose another woman and then were jilted by her. I am merely consolation to soothe your wounded ego."

A chuckle erupted from deep in his chest. "That absurdity is the worry marring your beautiful green eyes?"

"Do not laugh at me."

"I only laugh because I am relieved. I thought you had manifested another reason why I should not want you." He leaned in, his forehead touching hers. "You were always the one I wanted, Ara. Always the one I needed. I knew it every step of the way, but I could not bring myself to believe…"

"Believe what?"

"Believe you could truly love me after our past. After all I did to you." He pulled his forehead away from hers, but left his hands in place lining her jaw. "Maybe still, you cannot."

"No—do not think that, but…"

"But what?"

Ara swallowed hard. Pride be damned. "I needed you to choose me, Caine. Not another woman. I know it is silly, but I do not want to be what you settle for."

"I was at Notlund Castle because I was settling for being half the man I want to be, Ara. You are the one that makes me whole. You are the one I would—and always will—imagine my life with. So I beg of you, please do not let your pride and my stupidity get in the way of this."

He bent, his lips touching hers in the gentlest of kisses. "Or this."

His hands moved downward, his right fingers curling around her neck as his lips dropped to her chin, her neck, his hot breath trailing along her skin. Her head tilted back, unable to resist the shivers running along her skin from his touch.

"Or this."

His lips reached the juncture of her neck and shoulder, pausing as he dragged his knuckles past the short sleeve of her dress and agonizingly slow down her bare arm. His hand wrapped along her neck moved up, searching through her hair, plucking pins one by one until her simple chignon fell, her hair dropping down her back.

"Tell me I can touch you, Ara." The words were a low rumble in her ear, his lips teasing her earlobe.

"You already are." Her eyes closed as the shivers expanded across her body, rippling her skin. Ara moved her left hand over his shoulder, her fingers stretching into the back of his hair, the thickness of it curling under her touch.

Caine did not move his lips from the spot on her neck just below her ear, every word a fresh caress. "I have sworn twice in my life I would no longer touch you, Ara. And I have attempted it twice. But I am not a man that can stand by that particular vow."

He lifted his head, his eyes level with hers. "Unless… unless you make me."

{ CHAPTER 13 }

Ara stared at the clear blue in his eyes, the raw honesty. Her chest rose with a deep breath, brushing the front of him. "I told you once you should never make a vow you have no intention of keeping, Caine. It gives honor far too much rein to wreak havoc. And honor is your weakness."

A smile played on Ara's lips as she reached up, her thumb running across the crown of his forehead and slipping into the hair at his temples. "I release you from your vow, Caine. Again."

An exhaled growl filled the room as his arms collapsed about her, his hands wrapping down to the curve of her backside. He picked her up and took five steps. The back of her thighs hit the front of his massive desk, and he set her down on the edge, wedging his thighs between her legs.

His lips met hers again, not gentle, not soft. Unyielding and demanding, his mouth attacked hers, his tongue slipping past her lips, aching to explore every depth within. His hands flurried between them, stripping himself of his cravat, jacket and waistcoat.

When Ara realized his intention, her hands circled his waist, pushing up on his linen shirt. Her fingers dragged along his skin, along the hard, taut lines of his back as he pulled away to shrug out of his shirt.

She stared at his chest, the rise of muscles with every ragged breath he took. His body was beauty—art—in living, breathing form. Her palms went flat onto the small of his back. Instant heat under her hands.

This. Her skin on his. This was what she needed. The throbbing in her core intensified. Every single moment he had touched her in the past flooded her mind, her senses, and her body shuddered at the memory of what his skin, what his hands could do to her.

She looked up at him, her breath catching as his eyes sliced into her soul. The throbbing between her legs turned into pounding.

His gaze unflinching, Caine's hand curled around the side of her neck. "The devil take me to hades, Ara, I do not want to ask this. But I do not want you beholden to love me. I could not have you like that. And the last time I touched you like this, you said you were mine by rights. But I have no rights to your body, Ara. Only permission."

A bolt of understanding washed over Ara. "What? That was what happened? That was why you left me? Dammit, Caine."

She slapped his stomach, and he caught her wrist, holding her hand flat against his belly, her fingers splayed to the inner curves of his ribcage. She looked up, her eyes pinning him. "You have rights to my body because I love you. No other reason. I am not beholden to you, Caine." She paused, her head tilting. "Well, yes, I am—you saved me from the brothel, from dying in that pasture—and I will always love you for those acts. But I love you even more for every single minute we have spent together since then."

His eyes closed, his chest visibly exhaling in a long breath.

She lifted her left hand, spreading it flat across his chest above her other hand. His blue eyes opened to her. "That you respect me, my mind. You trust me. You are courageous and you care so damn much about what is right and what is wrong that you go out time and again and put yourself in danger to save the girls."

With the look of pure predator, he leaned down, kissing her.

Ara jerked to the side, breaking his lips on hers. "But wait, I am not done. I do not want you to ever again doubt why I am yours. So you will listen to this."

A guttural groan shook his body, but he paused his attack.

She smiled, not hiding from the power she realized she held. "You make me laugh and challenge me, but you also listen to me. You are an entirely unique man, Caine—one that I know does not exist elsewhere in this world. The only one."

"I damn well better be the only one." His hand on her wrist lifted to grab her chin, stopping her next words. "Are you done yet? Because I am about to burst I need so badly to take that bottom lip of yours in my mouth, suck it. Slip my tongue down the front of you and stop at your breasts. Tease my hands up your thighs."

Ara's gaping mouth clamped shut, and she swallowed hard at his words. "Yes, I am done. All of that, please."

He smiled, wicked, but his words were serious, weighted with the world. "But I am not going to do any of that until you promise me, Ara."

"Can I just say yes?"

"No. I can see you squirming, wanting everything I said and more. But I want you to know exactly what you are promising me."

"Speak quickly then." Damn him for stealing the power and making her want with no relief in sight. She glanced at her hand on his belly. With her own wickedness curving her eyebrow, she slid her hand downward, fully clasping onto the straining bulge in his trousers.

"Hell, Ara." He grabbed her wrist, stilling her. But he didn't remove her hand. Telling.

"Listen to me now, Ara."

She looked up at him, stilled by the fierceness in his voice.

"I want you without memory of the past, Ara. Without thinking of how we met. I want you because of who you are. Who I am. Now. In this moment. I want you because you love me. I want you to marry me, Ara."

His words hit her, shaking every fiber of her being. Everything. Everything she had ever dreamed about.

Her lips shaking, she opened her mouth. "Heaven help me, I still love you, Caine—there will never be a time when I do not—for that fact alone, it is a yes. But I—"

"It is a yes?"

The words had almost slipped out. Words that would take away how he looked at her in this moment. He wanted her as she was today, he wanted to be done with the past. But he did not know everything he needed to of the past. Things that would void all of those words he had just said to her.

Ara bit back the story he must never know. She nodded. "Yes."

His mouth crashed onto hers before she could rethink the decision, before she could confess everything that had haunted her heart, put a stain on her love for him. A stain that she had tried to wash out a thousand times, but never could.

But then his tongue was deep into her, probing, demanding she react to him. His lips moved downward, his hands wrangling buttons and laces and freeing her breasts to the air. The wetness of his mouth captured her nipple, his teeth clamping with just enough pressure to make her nipple taut, make her lean back against his hand holding her up.

She finished unbuttoning the front flap of his trousers before her body arched into him, out of control, demanding more.

"Lift yourself, Ara." The demand came from Caine's mouth, muffled by the breast he was adoring.

An order she did not think she could manage, but Ara set her palms along the sides of her legs on the desk and pushed. Her dress, stays, and chemise disappeared down past her waist and legs. He stopped at her shins, dragging off her boots and stockings.

Bared to him, memory of the last time she was naked before him sent her arms flailing, but Caine would have none of it, capturing both of her wrists to hold her hands at her sides on the desk.

"You are beautiful, Ara, and I have waited too damn long to tell you that. To take your body like I need to." He looked up at her, the wicked gleam back in his blue eyes. "Like your body needs me to."

His head dove back to her chest, trailing kisses, his tongue slipping along her skin. Downward, between her ribs, along her belly. He was to her abdomen before Ara realized where he intended to go—where his chin already was.

She gasped, squirming, but his grip on her wrists clamped tighter, forcing her still. Ara could not shift, could not breathe for the wretched pounding he had just created in her core with that one movement.

His elbows shifted to her thighs, spreading her legs before him. He dipped downward before she could resist, his mouth slipping to her folds, parting her to his teeth, his tongue plunging, circling.

Ara could only gasp, jerking forward, her body held in place by his clamps on her wrists and her curling around him.

The begging happened instantly—nonsensical words, his name, and curses she could only utter again and again— the raging build attacking her body from every nerve. He tugged, sucking harder at her words, and then shifted her hands behind her backside, locking her in place and forcing her core to meet the lash of his tongue with every uncontrolled rock of her body.

The onslaught continued until she gripped him with her legs, her body arching backward as the thousand tiny explosions turned into a raging ball that erupted, ravaging as it spun through her body.

He pulled away from her core as the rolling waves consumed her body, his grip on her wrists loosening as he brought her hands above her head. Shoving papers off the desk, he eased her backward and flat onto the wide expanse of wood. He released his grip on her wrists, leaving her hands stretched high above her head, and grabbed her hips, angling her on the desk so her legs had support.

Every spec of her body vibrating, Caine followed his earlier trail upward until his face was hovering over hers. She cracked her eyelids to find his blue eyes searching her face, his brow creased and straining.

His lips delved down to hers, consuming her senses. She could taste herself on his lips, on his tongue as it slid next to hers. Unusual. But not bad. It tasted exactly the way this moment should.

His lips moved against hers, his breathing fast. "Ara, are you mine?"

She couldn't talk, only nod, her eyes half closed.

"Speak it, Ara."

Battling against the surges still rushing her body and stealing her ability to move, she pulled one weak arm down, grabbing his shaft fully, the silk of his skin sliding along her palm. She opened her eyes fully to him, only to find the strain had etched even deeper into his features.

"I am yours, Caine. And you are mine."

A growl clawed from his chest as he covered her mouth, the sound vibrating on her lips, and he slid into her. Pain. And then only him. Him filling her.

"Hell, Ara, are you adjusted? Tell me I can move."

"Move."

And then the odd, glorious sensation of him sliding in and out of her, his breath on her neck. He pulled out, and his fingers went between them, his thumb plying her folds once more. He matched his thrusts with strokes of his fingers, and Ara felt it again, building deeper within her this time. So deep and so out of reach she nearly wished for her own grave.

"Ara."

The thick word filled her ear and his body expanded deep within her, the swells from his shaft pushing her over the last barrier and sending her to a scream only partially muffled by Caine's mouth.

He collapsed on her for a heavy breath, almost crushing her, but holding himself aloft. With an exhale that shook his whole body, Caine wrapped her in one arm and spun them on the desk, balancing the length of her on top of him.

He adjusted so his back was fully on the desk, one leg straight, one leg hanging off the side edge, and then he wrapped his other arm around Ara's waist.

Their panting evened out, and Caine tightened his hold around her. "Damn, Ara. If we had just done that six years ago, I could have saved myself years of cold baths and a number of bottles of good brandy. Honor be damned, I think I honestly do not care how you're in my arms, just that you are. Selfish man that I am."

Ara shifted her arms that she had tucked onto his chest, her forefinger moving up to play with the line of his jaw. "I am here because I want to be—because you are still my everything, Caine. That has never changed."

He kissed the top of her head, his head clunking on the desk as he set it back down. "Then I must confess, I already have the special license in-hand. It was the first thing I did when I arrived back in town."

"You already have the marriage license?" Her eyebrows flew up as she craned her neck to look at him. "Your confidence astounds me sometimes. Am I that easy to manipulate?"

He chuckled. "You know very well I have never been able to manipulate you. No, I just decided to borrow some of your unfailing optimism. It is a trait of yours I am trying to emulate."

"So that is where all my optimism went. My well of positivity has been sorely lacking as of late."

"Impossible—I do not think you capable of losing your optimism." His hand went to her hair, twisting a lock around his palm. "Do you know how I always tell you that you do not understand the world I live in?"

She shifted, resting her chin on his chest so she could watch him without cricking her neck. She tapped her finger on his chin. "Yes. And you know it drives me to bedlam."

"Well, I guess I can join you in the madness, Ara, because the optimism flowed easily once I came to the conclusion that I want to be in your world. It is a much better place to live in. You do not dwell on what others think is right and wrong, you just make your world as right as it can be. You don't hide behind facades and gates and propriety. You go forth and live your life, respecting, but not bowing to the confines of society. From the moment I met you, you have always found a way to rise above the horrors that man can create."

"You do the exact same, Caine—you have enabled every step I have taken since we met."

He shrugged, noncommittal at her words. "Possibly, but it is how you live. It is genuine. I knew it the day my brother died. You found me broken, and that was the very first time in my life when someone had cared enough to touch me in comfort."

His fingers trailed down her back, gently swerving along her spine. "And you barely knew me. You didn't care that it was not proper to touch me, to hold me. That world—your world—where it is acceptable to love someone—to have compassion. To live your life with open optimism. I am none of those things by birth and rearing, but with you…with you I am."

Dread seeped into her chest. "You are not turning your back on your title, Caine, are you? Because I will not be the cause of you losing who you are. I love you no matter what happens in the future—but the title, your mother and your sisters, and all of the people who depend on you—it is who you are."

"Yes, the title is a part of me, but it has driven me for too long. No more. I will not turn my back on it, but it is far past time that I decide how the title is used. And I will devise a way to keep the estate solvent." He looked at her, a smile crossing his face. "Or we will devise a way. I would be daft not to expound every good idea from that magnificent brain of yours. Just look at what you have built with the Baker Street house girls in the last six years, Ara."

"It is Greta's genius." Her mouth stretched in a humble grin. "But I will concede that I am adept at recognizing an opportunity."

He smirked. "Thank goodness. I do not want to have to start our life together trying to convince you of your own brilliance."

"No? I think that is the perfect way to start our life together."

He squeezed her, a shriek of laughter his reward.

"Speaking of starting our life together, will you be ready to marry me in two days? One day to prepare and then we will wed the next morning. I will leave you alone tomorrow so you can prepare anything you need to, but I want you in my bed, Ara. I want to be done with this dance where I have to curb myself from touching you—wanting you and never having you."

She stared at his blue eyes glowing in excitement. "I would marry you this instant, Caine, if there were a clergyman in the room."

"He might frown upon our lack of clothes." Caine tucked a lock of hair that had fallen across her brow behind her ear. "I only allow the one full day because I want you to find a dress you adore and gather up Mrs. Merrywent, Greta, and the rest of your lovely Baker Street house brood. It will give me a chance to find and pin down Fletch—a wedding is the last place he would like to be, but as it is not his own, I imagine I can drag him along. Actually, if you will accompany me to the Halton's party this evening, I think he will be in attendance. You will have to bring along Mrs. Merrywent, of course. I can arrange for an invitation."

Her eyebrows cocked. "Right into the fire for me, then?"

"You would like to wait until you are officially the Countess of Newdale?"

Ara sighed. She wasn't afraid—no, if she was honest with herself, she was afraid. Theirs was not a common match amongst the ton, and aside from the many drawing rooms she had been in with the ladies of society, she had never been exposed in a social situation with them.

She swallowed down escalating fears. One issue at a time. And the most important issue she needed to deal with at the moment was to marry this man.

Her cheek lifted in apology. "Is it wrong of me to want to wait until after the wedding?"

"No. I think it is smart of you. You rarely step somewhere without thinking of possible consequences."

Ara pushed herself up, her limbs creaking from the hard angles they had been stuck in. "What about your mother, your sisters?"

"They are hiding at Villsum House. My mother was quite mortified that her son was jilted, and she is avoiding all of her London chatterboxes at the moment. And I am not about to wait for her presence to make you my wife." His eyes flashed dark for a moment. "You realize it will take her a while to accept you. You are not exactly the match she had in mind for me."

"I do." Ara untangled her legs from his and sat on the edge of the desk, suddenly quite aware of her nudity in the middle of the study. Looking at Caine's desk would never be the same, and she doubted she would ever be able to add up another column of numbers in here without being driven to distraction. "But as long as you do not take issue with that fact, I do not either. She cannot dislike me forever, correct? Especially if we hurry along in producing some heirs to the Newdale line?"

Caine sat up, slipping his hand behind her neck and pressing his lips onto her forehead. "And that is why I love you, my heart. You have your optimism back."

"It is hard not to be idealistic when I am looking at your naked body." She grinned, hopping off the desk and noting for the first time the wide-ranging mess they had made on the floor. Papers, envelopes, and cards from Caine's desk had scattered far and wide. "Look at all of this—has your man-of-affairs not been keeping up on your correspondence? He was instructed to hire a secretary for you. Especially since you were away at Notlund Castle—that man is not terribly detailed."

Ara bent, starting to gather the papers.

"Yet I cannot help but be woefully grateful for the man's lack of detail right now," Caine said, smirk in his voice.

She glanced up over her shoulder at him. He stood behind her, his arms crossed in front of his chest, a statue of glory in his manhood. "Grateful?"

"His oversight has produced a view right now that is beyond extraordinary." Caine's blue eyes slipped down, ogling her backside high in the air. He slapped her buttocks.

Even though it sent a tingle firing through her core, Ara's eyes narrowed on him. But then she couldn't contain her own smirk. "Crass bugger."

Ara dropped the papers in her hand, leaning to the side to reach her chemise and then pulling it over her head. She picked the papers back up, continuing to collect them in her arm.

With a chuckle, Caine knelt next to her, shuffling papers together in a pile. Ara lifted a few sheets of crisp vellum with Caine's monogram emblazoned along the top, and a red note appeared from underneath.

Ara dropped to her knees, falling back on her heels as she silently set down the pile in her arm and picked up the note. She broke the seal, opening the card before Caine glanced up at her.

"Blast it." He scooted to her side, grabbing the edge of the note.

Ara wouldn't let him tear it from her fingers, her eyes flying over the words.

He yanked at it, the edge of the cardstock slicing along her forefinger.

Her eyes flew up to him as she clutched her finger, rubbing the thin line of blood the paper drew. "It is in two days, Caine."

His jaw instantly set hard. "No. Absolutely not. We are done with that business, Ara."

"No, we are not, Caine." She grabbed his forearm, her fingertips sliding along the silky hair on his skin. "We will never be done—we have to save the innocent ones."

"I am not spending my wedding night buying a virgin in a brothel."

"Then we will get married the day after."

His head shaking, his eyes pinned her. "We have to end it, Ara. It is too dangerous. Going to that brothel, buying the virgins—it almost ruined me at Notlund Castle. I could have lost everything in a flame of scandal had the Duke of Letson not acted with discretion. He could have let my actions be known to all, and that would have been the end of me."

"But you could have just told him what you were truly doing. That you were saving the girls instead of using them."

"When I say I could have lost everything, Ara, I did not mean the estate. I meant the girls I have bought. I meant you, Ara. I could have lost you. That is what I could not bear."

Her right cheek scrunched in confusion. "What? How?"

Caine shook his head, his fingers dragging across his eyes. "Hell, Ara, how can you still be so naïve about this? Anyone who cares to find out could discover I own the Baker Street house. Discover I underwrite the *House of Vakkar*. If I confess why I really buy the virgins, it does not take a genius to determine where many of them have ended up. It will be the end of any respectability the Baker Street house girls have. Any respectability you have."

"Us? But why?"

"You were all sold at the brothel, Ara. There is no greater scandal than that." His voice dipped lower, suppressed rage lacing his words. "What happens to each of them if all respectability is taken from them? From you?"

Her arms folded across her ribs as her shoulders sank. "Utter ruin."

"Exactly."

Head dropping, her fingers rubbed her forehead. Her eyes flipped up to him. "But—"

"No—look at how much this already nearly cost me, Ara. We cannot continue this madness, and I regret that we have let it go on this long." His hand landed on her shoulder, sliding inward to rest at the base of her neck. "We will never win this battle, Ara. There are too many girls. And there will always be more. It is an immortal evil, Ara."

Her eyes cut into him. "Are you suddenly a coward, Caine?"

His hand dropped from her neck, his fingers curling into a fist. "Take care with your words, Ara."

She pushed herself up to balance on her knees, rounding him so her face was directly in front of him. "I am taking care, Caine—it is you that is speaking blasphemy by abandoning those innocent girls."

Caine heaved a sigh, his eyes travelling to the ceiling, and she could see he was holding himself back from throttling her for calling him a coward. But she didn't care—she would call him anything she needed to in order to get him to change his mind. To help the innocent ones.

Another sigh, and his look dropped to her, his blue eyes darkening. "So we are locked in the past, Ara—the same place as we were six years ago?"

"Locked in the past? Do not try to change the subject, Caine."

His hands whipped out, vises around her upper arms. "The past is the current subject, Ara. And I am done with the past. I will no longer allow you to be anywhere remotely near the line of danger. I have finally figured out exactly what the most important thing in the world to me is, Ara, and that is you, dammit. And you are not going to be injured. And you are not going to be ruined. And you are not going anywhere where I cannot protect you."

She jerked back, stung at the roar rolling through his body, at the ferocity in his face.

His chest vibrating with each heaving breath, he dropped his hands from her arms.

Fingers shaking, Ara pushed herself to her feet, silently grabbing her dress and stepping into it. It sat awkwardly around her chest without her short stays, but she wasn't about to take the time to put that layer on.

She needed to leave. Leave before she said something she would regret. Promise something she had no right to promise.

Tugging her boots on, she stuffed the laces next to her calves without tying them.

Out. She needed out.

Going to the door, her hand stilled on the knob as her head dropped, her forehead resting on the thick oak.

She could not fight Caine on this, but he needed to know. Needed to know what he was demanding of her.

Her head bowed, Ara opened her mouth, her voice a raw whisper. "Do you know it is me, Caine? Every time we save one of them…we are saving me. The me from six years ago. The terrified girl that wanted nothing more than to die, that wanted to sink into that earth and disappear and stop everything. To just die and…" Her voice cut off, a silent sob swelling from her belly and stealing her words.

Her eyes closed, squeezing back tears.

Out. She had to leave. Turning the knob, she shuffled backward as she pulled the door open.

It slammed shut, the knob ripping from her hand.

Caine's hand stretched flat on the wood in front of her eyes, his arm brushing her ear.

His other arm wrapped around her belly, and then his hand on the door dropped, capturing her fully, pulling her into the length of him. The harbor of him.

His breath invaded her skin, hot on her cheek. "I will go, Ara." He drew in a deep sigh, his chest hard against her back as his voice ached. "Heaven help me, we will both go as usual."

{ CHAPTER 14 }

Finally, solace. As the door closed to Lord Halton's library, Caine leaned back against the tall dark panels of wainscoting, attempting to loosen his furiously tight shoulders.

Damn his fool promise to Ara that they would go again to the Jolly Vassal. He needed to end this—end this unholy obsession that they both had with attempting to change the past. He could now see with clarity that the past was an unyielding mistress—always provoking and never bending to attempts of appeasement.

A mistress that had its claws far too deep into his love.

Hell. He was starting to question his own belief that he could get Ara to change her mind. Saving the innocents from the brothel was her lifeblood—the thing she had held onto for the last six years. And he had assisted her with that obsession every step of the way in an attempt to assuage his own demons.

Demons he was done with.

Caine considered again on having the current owner disposed of, but when he had done that six years ago to the man responsible for Isabella's death, the brothel hadn't even closed for a day. He had learned an important lesson—there was always another snake ready to gorge on the innocent. And the girls coming through the brothel had been getting younger and younger in recent years—he often wondered if he had replaced one bastard with a shred of integrity, with another bastard devoid of any sense of decency.

So who would be the next monster to take over the brothel?

That very question haunted him every time he sat in the stench of the Jolly Vassal, watching the derelict depths of humanity mill about. Continue the dance as it was, saving the ones they could—or upend the game completely and hope that half of the rotten apples decayed into nothingness?

The door of Lord Halton's library opened, and Fletch walked in. Caine's eyebrow arched as he pushed himself from the wall. "So you did show."

"I was waylaid," Fletch said, walking over to the port and pouring a glass.

"Waylaid in one of Halton's dark corners? This place was built for clandestine trysts, with its maze of halls."

"If I get lost, I get lost." Fletch shrugged, turning from the sideboard with a devious smirk. "What I want to know is why you disappeared into here and are not stumbling your way about this monstrosity of architecture. There are plenty of young chits here that would froth at the mouth to get near the most recently reminted bachelor of the ton."

Caine's lips contorted, his head shaking.

"At the very least, will you be joining us in the music room? I understand Halton's middle daughter is delightful on the pianoforte."

"The devil save me." Caine moved to the sideboard to refill his tumbler of brandy. "I am only present because you have disappeared since we arrived back in London and I needed to talk to you. Why are you even here?"

"Halton invited me."

Caine cleared his throat, giving Fletch a side glance.

"And possibly because the Widow Josten urged me to attend."

"She is over her late husband's death?"

"Has been for months. She is enjoying her newfound freedom." With a wink, Fletch settled himself next to Caine, leaning on the sideboard. "So what was so important that you had to drag yourself out into public only days after your jilting?"

Caine took a sip of brandy, turning to his friend. "I needed to thank you."

Fletch nearly sputtered out half-swallowed port. "Th— thank me?" He managed to get the words out between coughs.

"Do not make a mockery out of my gratitude, my friend." Caine watched Fletch double over in hacking spasms, calmly sipping his drink as he waited for his friend to catch air.

Taking another sip of port, Fletch finally gained control of his breathing. "Do tell what has you thanking me."

"Your words about Ara on the way back from Notlund Castle. They inspired me to evaluate my life."

"And?"

"And we are to marry the day after next."

A rollicking laugh echoed in the room as Fletch pounded Caine's back. "Well done, man. I assume I am invited to—"

The door to the library crashed open, cutting Fletch's words.

Both Caine and Fletch spun to the doorway to find a livid man storming into the room. A trailing second man slammed the door shut.

"You." The first man strode across the room, finger jabbing in the air at Caine. "You bastard."

Caine's stance instantly widened, bracing himself for whatever onslaught this man was coming at him with. The man was large, just as tall as Caine, and seething, his elbow already high and pulling back to attack.

The second man caught the arm of the first and yanked him to a stop only a step before his fist flew at Caine. "Devin, hold it. Not here. This is not the place."

Caine stared at the two, fists clenching. Both were dressed well enough to partake in Lord Halton's party, but Caine didn't recognize either one.

Yanking from his friend, the raging man kept advancing, his eyes not leaving Caine even as his friend struggled to pull him backward. "You bastard, I will kill you."

Fletch stepped slightly in front of Caine, glaring at the two men. He looked to the second man. "Lord Southfork, what in the hell is your man about?"

Southfork yanked the man's arm once more, twisting it behind his back and stopping his motion. Southfork looked to Fletch. "I have every right to unleash the Duke of Dunway onto your bastard friend, Lockston. But I am not going to allow him to do so in Halton's home."

Caine tried to sidestep around Fletch to meet the duke head-on. No one—duke or not—threatened him. But Fletch was too quick, blocking Caine before he could take a full step.

Fletch's hands flew up, calming as much as he could the raging currents in the room. "Hold one moment,

Southfork, your grace. What the hell has happened that you are set on attacking a stranger, and might I add, my friend?"

"You are worthless at choosing friends," Southfork said, grimacing at the strength it was taking to hold back the duke.

The duke shook, trying to free his arm, shooting Caine with venom in his eyes. "You are a dead man, Newdale."

"Will someone please enlighten us as to why you continue to make these threats?" Fletch asked, hands still up and attempting to calm the room.

"I will resist killing him here, Killian." The duke jerked again, and Southfork let his arm drop. The duke's steel look burrowed into Caine. "You were at my estate in Kent several weeks ago, Newdale, and I only have just tracked you down. You delivered something—someone to my estate. Someone that is very dear to me, and what you did to her is going to cost you your life." Each word was wrapped with icy death.

Caine's mind raced. Kent? When in the blasted hell had he last been in Kent? He rarely went that direction out of London, so what the devil? Only with Ara had he—shit.

It came to him in one gut-punch. Of course. The girl they had delivered to the estate in Kent. A huge estate. The duke's estate. Of course. What was her name?

"Lizzie." Her name fell from Caine's lips in recognition, and it damned him.

"You fucking bastard." The duke flew at him, his fist clipping Caine's chin before Southfork latched onto the duke's shoulders and yanked him back once more. This time, it was clear Southfork wasn't about to let the duke go. "You stole her and used her, you bastard, and you will pay."

Caine gained back the two steps the duke's fist had sent him staggering, crunching the shattered glass from his dropped tumbler on the floor. He shoved Fletch to the side. "What do you know, your grace?"

"Here is what I know, you bloody bastard. Lizzie is my wife's little sister, who I regard as my very own flesh and blood," the duke said, breath seething. "She was taken—gone for days, and I only just found the card with the address of the house you own on it. She was delivered back to my home by your carriage. My groundskeeper verified it was you yesterday—he saw you in the carriage when you left her at my estate. And she refuses to say a word about where she was. Do I need to know more?"

Shit.

Caine could only shake his head, praying the duke hadn't figured out why there were scores of women living at the Baker Street house. "No."

"Then I give you a day to get your affairs in order, you fucking worm. I will see you at dawn in Hyde Park the day after next."

Caine inclined his head, his voice frosty. "Until then."

With a nod, Southfork dragged the duke out of the library, the echoing of the slammed door vibrating across the silence of the room.

The silence sat, heavy, until Fletch turned to Caine. "What the bloody devil are you doing, Caine? Why did you not tell him?"

Caine rubbed his jaw, the fury that he had muzzled in front of the duke exploding. "Tell him what, Fletch? That I buy virgins to save them? That I was just delivering her home, unsullied and safe and sound with nary a scratch on her? She had been gone for days—the man is not going to believe that."

"But it is the truth. You have proof."

"No. Shut your mouth, Fletch."

"If the girl won't talk, you have proof, Caine. Ara was with you—and any one of those Baker Street house women will vouch for you—for what you did for them. Ara will be the first in line for that."

"I did not save all of them only to bring ruin upon them. To have what they have built their lives to be get ruined by scandal—to have them spit upon by the lowest of the low on the street. Where do you think they would end up?"

"Well, just Ara, then. Surely—"

"Do not even utter it. Ara, most of all." Caine's right hand folded into a fist. "She is not to be tainted by this. Do you hear me?"

"Uncurl your fist. This is your life, Caine. The duke is a fine shot."

"You are right, Fletch, it is my life. And I will damn well do with it what I please."

~ ~ ~

Her fingers tapping on the sleek wooden box next to her on the settee, Ara looked out the window in the Pearl drawing room at the Duke of Dunway's townhouse, so named, she assumed, because of the layers of cream and white fashioning the room. Ara guessed the duchess's three young children were strictly prohibited from the room, but then again, maybe not. The duchess did not seem the type to put avoiding stains before her children's happiness.

Rays from the late morning sun cut into the room, sending to sparkle the crystals lining the top of the oil lamp by the window. It was unusual to be meeting with the duchess this early, but also one of the reasons Ara so liked the woman. Much like Ara, the duchess did not like to piddle the day away, and she had insisted on meeting with Ara before the normal calling hours.

Ara heard light footsteps outside the door and stood just as the duchess walked into the drawing room.

"Miss Detton, good day. Thank you for coming." While her dark indigo silk dress and elegant chignon were flawless, the duchess's green eyes were red-rimmed, her cheeks a bit puffy. She motioned to the cream settee Ara had been waiting on. "Please, sit."

Ara started to sit, but then paused. "Your grace, forgive me for suggesting, but you seem distraught. We do not need to do this now and can certainly find another time to meet."

The duchess waved her hand. "No. Let us continue. I have been entirely anxious to see the design, and it will take my mind in a better direction than where it is currently at."

Instant worry overtook Ara's usual polite restraint. "There is something of grave concern?"

With a deep frown weighing upon her pretty features, the duchess sat on a delicate side chair. "It is something I have been told by my husband I have no control over, so I can only hope for the best outcome with it."

Ara nodded, knowing all too well how the duchess felt. Far too often in her own life, control that only belonged to a man had brought her despair. She sat, drawing the wooden box into her lap.

"Well, I hope this can give your mind a respite from your worry. I truly think Greta has outdone herself for you on this creation, your grace." Ara handed the box to the duchess. "She took your crest, and I think did a lovely replication of the lion with some inspired uses of diamonds and emeralds on the brooch."

The duchess opened the simple box, staring at the brooch on the swath of velvet. "It is exquisite."

Ara exhaled with a nod, looking over the tip of the box at the diamonds gaining a sparkle from the sun. The first moments she unveiled a design to the buyer were always the most nerve-racking, even if the duchess had never been anything but enthusiastic about Greta's designs.

"Greta crafted both the lion and filigree on this one, as she so adores making designs for you. She set the hidden pin on the back as a loop, so it can double as a necklace. She said, very specifically, it would do well with the simple line of emeralds she created several months ago for you."

"Ingenious." The duchess smiled, fingering the piece. "Greta does have an astute eye for detail that I admire."

Ara nodded. "Yes. And she is working on the watch fob with the matching crest for your husband as well. She has yet to find the specific emerald she wants for the eye, so she is currently badgering our gemstone merchant."

A frown set onto the duchess's face at the mention of her husband.

"Your grace?"

The duchess shook her head, holding back obvious tears. "I apologize, it would seem I am not the best company today." She closed the cover of the box, setting it on the white marble top of the side table.

Ara stood. "No, I should have insisted upon leaving. I did not want this to be a bother for you."

"No—it is not a bother. It has cheered me—at least partially." The duchess stood, walking Ara across the room.

Glancing at the long case clock near the hearth, Ara noted it was still two hours before her next appointment at Lady Gowden's townhouse. Her stomach did an excited flip. She had thought there wouldn't be time between the appointments she had previously committed to that day, but now there would be time to stop at Caine's townhouse. Maybe seeing him would stop her mind from wandering everywhere but on the jewellery.

She had told Mrs. Merrywent about the wedding, and Mrs. Merrywent had gone into a flurry of planning early this morning. Ara needed to warn Caine that their very small, very sedate wedding the next day was quickly spiraling into an elaborate event under Mrs. Merrywent's watch.

The duchess stopped at the doorway to the drawing room, her fingers uncharacteristically wringing each other. "Before you leave, Miss Detton, has Greta ever designed anything appropriate for someone younger? A fourteen-year-old? My sister has been terribly withdrawn as of late, and I cannot cheer her no matter what I have tried. Even her nephews and niece do not bring smiles from her. And they are capable of fantastic antics. So maybe something new and pretty for her to look upon may draw a smile? I know it seems silly, but I will try anything at this point."

Ara mentally scanned what she knew was being created on the goldsmith benches in what had become the workshop in the study of the Baker Street house. "Greta has some delightful new designs for jewelled parasol handles that the goldsmiths have started upon. She is having them use an innovative weave with the gold strands against the enamel of the handle. The first ones are almost complete, and I imagine they will create a frenzy, as they look young and flirty. Do you think that may be suitable?"

The duchess offered a worried smile. "I do. That would be wonderful. Thank you."

"Then I shall see that you are the first to choose amongst the designs when they are finished."

The duchess nodded. "Do give my regards to Greta, as well. She has truly outdone herself with this piece—it captures the spirit of the crest perfectly. I am grateful, even if my current countenance does not do my reaction justice."

Ara smiled warmly. "Be assured I will repeat your praise, and Greta will revel in it."

Stepping out into the sunlight, Ara smiled, looking up at the blue sky as she let her thoughts run to the one thing she was desperate to concentrate on.

By this time tomorrow, she would be married to Caine.

All she had ever truly wanted in life.

With a skip down the stairs of the duke's townhouse, Ara hurried in the direction of Caine's home, hoping he wasn't too busy planning the wedding himself that she would have to referee between him and Mrs. Merrywent.

She chuckled to herself.

There were worse problems to have.

{ CHAPTER 15 }

"You need to tell Ara, Caine."

Caine looked up to watch Fletch stroll into his study. Fletch's fingers dragged along the edge of Ara's desk before he plopped into a leather chair opposite Caine. Caine set the quill in his fingers onto the desk, sighing as he cocked his eyebrow at his friend. Wilbert hadn't announced Fletch—probably because Fletch had just walked right by the man, not giving Wilbert the chance to enforce Caine's strict instructions he be left alone. He had enough to do today without going another round with Fletch.

"She thinks to marry you on the morrow, man," Fletch said, his fingernails digging into the leather at the end of the armrest. "What do you think it will do to her if you do not appear at the church? If you leave her standing there alone? She deserves better, Caine."

With a sigh, Caine pushed back from his desk. "She won't be alone. You will be there, and you will tell her, and she will hate me, and that is a good thing."

Fletch leaned forward, his fingers threading together as he pinned Caine with a glare. "Do not do this to her."

"I do not have a choice, Fletch. Either I die tomorrow, or my life will go down in the flames of scandal after the duel. Tell me you are not naïve enough to think the duke will keep the reason for the duel a secret? If he—by some scarce chance—misses me and I escape alive, you can be sure he will still ruin me in every way possible."

Fletch shrugged. "You ruined or not, Ara will not care. She is made of sterner stuff than you are giving her credit for."

"I know exactly what she is made of, and that is exactly why she must remain ignorant of everything that happens between now and tomorrow morning. This is the only way I can make this easy for her."

"By giving her up?" Fletch jumped to his feet, leaning over the desk at Caine. "Now I know you are made of sterner stuff than that. This idiocy and what you think to do to protect her has gone on long enough. I had thought with some distance from last night's incident with the duke you would have thought the better of your plan. You can stop this, Caine. Up until you take those twelve paces, you can stop this."

Caine's head bowed, his stare on the desk. "It is to be twelve, then? You have met with the duke's second—Southfork, I assume? I would have preferred less."

"Blast it, Caine, I am attempting to save your hide. For little gratitude, I might add. Twelve is as high as Southfork would allow." Fletch shook his head. "But you can still stop all of this with the truth."

Caine's eyes, but not his head, lifted to his friend. "The truth? The truth is what I allow it to be. If I survive, my penchant for purchasing young virgins will be leaked, and it is me who will suffer the scandal of it—there is no way I am letting Ara suffer my fate. Nor will I allow her to put herself in scandal's way by admitting the truth to the duke—that she was once sold at the brothel. The man is too unpredictable and out for blood to chance him with that secret. I refuse to let Ara be destroyed, one sneer, one cut at a time, until her life is ground into shambles. The scandal will be mine. That is the truth I allow."

"I know Southfork, Caine. And he is not an unreasonable man—surely he would not be the duke's second if the duke wasn't worthy of respect. I tell you, the duke will listen to reason."

Caine's palm slammed onto the desk. "I will not chance, Ara, Fletch, so you best stop that talk before I put a dent in that skull of yours."

"Now you are threatening me to get your way?"

"Yes." Caine sighed, his fingers rubbing his eyes. He looked up to his friend, tempering his voice. "But threats aside, I do need to know that you will continue to be my second."

"I beg you, Caine, one last time to reconsider. This need not happen."

"Be a man about it, Fletch, and have my bloody back. If I go down in a duel, I need to know that you will clean up the mess behind me."

"A duel?" Quick footsteps pounded into the study, Ara running, her hand flat on her chest, her face contorted in worry. "Caine, a duel—a mess? What are you two talking about?"

Dammit.

She skidded to a stop at the side of his desk, her green eyes flickering between Caine and Fletch.

Caine stood, moving to her side. "You were eavesdropping?"

She stared up at him, the gold rings in her eyes on fire. "I damn well was—what is happening, Caine? A duel? What madness is this?"

"I will exit at this juncture." Fletch gave a quick bow to Ara. He looked to Caine. "I will do as you ask, of course."

Lips tight, Caine gave him a curt nod.

Fletch walked out of the study without another word, closing the door behind him.

"What do you think to do, Caine?" Ara grabbed his forearm, her words starting before the click of the door.

"What did you hear?"

"I heard the words threats and duel and I was not about to stay in the hall waiting for you to finish your conversation." Her fingernails dug into his muscle through his linen shirt. "Tell me this instant what is happening, Caine."

His teeth clamped tight. He didn't want to tell her. He had planned to give her just one more day of bliss—of everything in her life being perfect.

She glared up at him, waiting. Lips tight, eyes narrowed at him. She wasn't going to move from her spot until she got answers.

He exhaled, shaking his head against the injustice of the spitfire staring at him. "A duel, Ara. I am to be in a duel."

She blinked, struck. "You cannot. I will not allow it."

"You will not allow it?" Caine's eyebrow cocked. "You can do nothing to control it, Ara."

"But no—not a duel." Heavy fear crept into her voice. "Why? Is this because of your broken engagement?"

"No. It is because of the girl we saved weeks ago—Lizzie. She is the little sister of a powerful man's wife, and that man is now out for blood—my blood. He found me—he knows I delivered her to the estate."

"So he thinks you…" She gulped, her eyes wide. "And Lizzie did not tell him you were the one to save her—that she wasn't hurt?"

"No. She refuses to talk about where she was missing to for those days. I do not blame her."

"But you can tell him."

"He will not believe me, Ara. You know that."

"Caine, do not be obtuse. You need to go to him, tell him the truth."

"And what is the truth, Ara? That I purchase virgins? That I do it to save them, rather than use them?"

"Yes. Exactly. You must go and tell him that."

"Even saying the words out loud is ridiculous. He will not believe it, Ara, not without proof."

"So I am the proof." She grabbed his other arm, shaking him. "I will tell him. I was there. I will tell him everything. Everything we have done for the past years. He cannot refute me—or Mrs. Merrywent—or any score of the girls we have saved. Tell me who he is, I will go right now."

Caine grabbed her shoulders, putting distance between them by forcing her to take several steps backwards. "No. I absolutely will not tell you who the man is, Ara. You will not interfere in this business."

"I will very well interfere, Caine. This is your life." She tried to twist out of his grip, but he held tight.

She ceased her contorting, her eyes turning to ice as she stilled and looked at him. "I will stalk you every minute, Caine, follow you when you think to leave for your damn duel, and I will stop this—no matter what."

The frigid resolve in her voice turned Caine's blood cold.

Of course she would.

She would stop at nothing to protect what was hers.

That thought—that reality—terrified him like nothing else.

Ara would sacrifice herself to save him. Sacrifice her respectability, her future.

Blast it. If she appeared in the park—or God forbid, she got in the way of the duke or a stray bullet. The mere possibility slammed into Caine's gut, blanching his face.

If Ara was hurt—or worse—in any way, he couldn't handle it. He had almost been destroyed when Isabella died—and he knew he would suffer that fate fully—a thousand times over—if anything ever happened to Ara.

Caine's eyes settled onto Ara. Her beautiful green eyes that demanded he cede to her. Her full, cherry lips that were parted slightly, heaving breaths slipping between them. The delicate cut of her cheekbones that spoke of gentleness but belied the lioness within.

He had not been able to save Isabella. But he damn well could save Ara.

He needed to get rid of her. He would be dead or ruined by morning. He needed to get her to leave him, leave his side. It was the only way he could ensure she did not become entangled in the scandal that will become his death—or his life if he survived the duel.

The last day of bliss he had hoped to give her dissolved into wispy nothingness.

His chest in a vise, squeezing his breath, Caine hardened himself.

His hands dropped from her shoulders, and he turned from her, going to the back window of his study. He stared out at the elaborately coifed rear gardens of his home. "This is not your place, Ara."

Not letting him escape her space, she moved to his side, looking up at him as her shoulder dragged across the glass. "What do you mean, 'this is not my place'?"

Caine kept his eyes on the crisp boxwood hedges. "I had not realized you would determine you could interfere so in my life, Ara, and I am reconsidering."

She exhaled an audible breath, her hand flattening on her chest. "Reconsidering the duel—thank the heavens. I do not know what you were thinking about in the first place, Caine, and I—"

"No, Ara. I am reconsidering you."

Her head snapped back. "What?"

Caine turned to her, conjuring tired apathy in his eyes. "You, Ara. This is a very clear example. I do not think you fit within the confines of my life. I believed, for a moment in time, that you would. But I was wrong—I was reacting to what happened at Notlund Castle. As much as it pains me to say it, you were right about how the title is my life. There is no place for you within my world, Ara. You don't understand it, and you never will."

Her face crumpled, and as much as it pained him to see it, relief flooded through Caine. But then her face straightened, her eyes narrowing at him.

Of course she would battle it. Her spine was fight to the core.

"You are only saying this because I am mad at you, Caine. But I am not going to stop just because you threaten me, you oaf."

He sighed with indifference. "This was a mistake, Ara. I was wrong to take you. Wrong to extend the offer of marriage. You will be…compensated for your time, just as you always have been."

"Compensated?" The cruelty of the word hit her, taking the aplomb from her stance. "This is madness, Caine. You love me."

"I do not."

"No. You are lying."

"I do not wish to continue this, Ara. I have reconsidered everything since yesterday. You were a mistake."

"No, you are just trying to drive me away. Even a fool such as me, who does not understand your blasted world, can see what you are doing."

Caine's head tilted. "It is true that I am attempting to protect you from my current situation. But not for the reason you think. Not because I love you. I am grateful for your assistance throughout the years, and wish you nothing but happiness, Ara. But if I have loved you, that sentiment has passed to where I no longer own it."

She grabbed his arm, her voice wavering. "Caine, I beg of you, do not do this."

He looked down to her hand clutching his upper arm. It took him a long moment to steel his resolve. His eyes travelled coldly up to her. "You will always be the wrong girl, Ara. The one I bought by accident."

"Bella." The word slipped from her lips, flat, dull. She dropped her hand, her feet shuffling backward.

He nodded, folding his arms across his chest. "I thought I had overcome it, Ara, but I have not. You are not the one I have always wanted. The one I still want." The words ripped from his throat, gagging him. But there was no other way. She needed to hate him.

"You still love Isabella?"

Caine froze, unable to open his mouth. He needed Ara to hate him, but he also couldn't repeat the lie. Couldn't force the words out of his mouth.

So he stared at her. Stared at her in silence, offering no indication his words were false.

Her head shook, swinging wide as her face contorted to disbelief. Moments passed before she stilled, her green eyes landing on him, pain ripping so fully into her, her body shook.

Yet she pulled herself up straight, her chin tall.

Caine expected no less.

Ara opened her mouth, her voice a harsh whisper.

"Then you will always be in love with a false dream, Caine."

She spun, walking silently to the door. He could see she fought for every step. Fought not to turn back to him.

And then she was gone.

Caine waited until he heard her footsteps recede down the hall and the front door open and close, before he sank against the window.

Gone.

She was gone from his life, just like he needed. He was lower than the dung that filled the Thames. There was no denying that truth. But it didn't matter. Ara was safely away from him. That was all—the only thing—that mattered.

Minutes passed before her last words filtered into his mind.

False dream.

He was in love with a false dream? What the hell had that meant?

Caine ran through their conversation again.

He had said he was still in love with Isabella, and then she had said he would always love a false dream.

Hell.

Caine was out the door in three strides.

~ ~ ~

"Ara. Stop."

The bastard was always telling her to stop, and she was damn well tired of it. She refused to turn around at Caine's yell. If he didn't want her—then she damn well didn't want him. She was done with his games. Done.

Six years. Too long. Done.

Her steps quickened down the sidewalk.

"Ara."

She glanced over her shoulder. Caine was running at full speed and only a block behind her.

Glimpsing forward, her frantic eyes searched the street in front of her. Straight, and he would catch up to her in no time. To her left, at least, was a smattering of people strolling and then the park that led to her old residence. Maybe she could lose him amongst the people, if not the park.

Ducking to her left, she hurried as fast as she could without making a spectacle of herself.

"Stop, Ara. Wait."

Caine's bellow sounded farther away, which was good. Jumping across the muck on the street, she dashed into the park, cutting across the swathes of grass rather than taking the meandering pathway.

She looked behind. She couldn't spot him through the trees and people, but she wasn't about to chance him finding her, so she ran the last few feet to her old Gilbert Lane house, slipping in alongside the building and letting herself in through the French doors leading to her old study.

The home was still empty—she knew from Caine's new man of affairs that the place had yet to be sold or rented. Panting, she leaned forward against one of the white painted bookcases, her hands flat on an empty shelf to support herself. She guessed she just needed to wait fifteen minutes or so and Caine would give up on trying to find her.

What could he possibly even want with her now?

To give her a tidy sum?

To *compensate* her?

The word rattled around in her brain, her stomach curdling at the thought. Impossible that he thought he could compensate her for loving him.

"What did you mean, 'false dream'?"

Ara jumped, a yelp squeaking out her throat.

Caine filled the doorway to the study, his chest heaving. Damn him. He must have slipped in the back door. The man had never moved silently in his life—he was too big—and this was the moment he managed to be stealthy?

His fingers curled and uncurled at his sides. "I repeat, Ara. False dream—what did you mean? You said those very specific words for a reason, and I want to know what that reason is."

Dammit. Those words had just flown from her mouth before she could catch them. She had hoped by leaving it would be as if she never spoke them.

She shook her head. He would never hear this story from her. "I have never told you, Caine. And I do not intend to do so now."

"Never told me what?" He stepped into the room, staying a distance away, but he could easily trap her if he wanted. She recognized that.

Of course, what would he do to her if he did trap her? Hurt her? No, he would never hurt a woman—that much she was sure of.

She waved her hand, disregarding him. "Let us just leave what was said in your study, in that room. You clearly have no need for me, Caine, and I will move on. There is no need for us to ever speak again."

He took another step toward her, his hands up, pleading. "In all that I have done for you throughout the years, Ara—tell me. You owe me that."

A scoffed chuckle ripped from her chest as she jumped forward. "All you have done for me? What about all I have done for you?"

His hands dropped to his sides again, folding into fists. Fists that did not unclench. His blue eyes went cold, piercing her.

The look alone stole all the air from the room.

Caine's mouth curled on the left side, his voice chilling. "You were a scared little waif on the side of the road, Ara. Nothing. Dirt. So yes, you owe me. On all that is holy. Tell me."

"I am…I am dirt?" Her feet staggered backward on their own accord, and her backside bumped into the bookcase. She gripped the edge of a shelf, trying to steady herself and met his glare. "I am nothing?"

His mouth set hard, his jaw did not give the slightest twinge.

She cackled, her head falling back as she stared at the ceiling, not caring that she sounded deranged. "I am so stupid. A stupid dirt girl. A stupid, nothing, dirt girl." Her chin dropped, her eyes finding his. "You are right, Caine. So absolutely right. You do need to know. And I am done protecting you."

"Protecting me?"

"Protecting you from your own ignorance. Your own idiocy. You have been in love with a woman for years that never deserved one tiny bit of your affection."

His chin tilted down, his eyebrows lifting. "You are talking about Isabella?"

"Of course I am talking about Isabella." Her head shook as her eyes seared into his. "Do you know I understand exactly why you love her?"

His forehead crinkled, but he didn't say a word.

Ara drew a breath that shook on the exhale. "I sat with her for days in that coach after they took me. I clutched her hand and she clutched mine. And I loved her for that very thing. She was a lifeline for me. The last thing I could grasp that seemed normal in those wicked days. She would see me worry or cry, and she would smile. And she would make me believe that everything would be right in the end. Just with her smile. I did not realize then how very good she was at lying. I just accepted her smile. Accepted her perseverance as if it was my own. I loved her for that smile."

Her words halted, a hard lump forming in her throat. She had started the tale she had vowed to never tell him. She needed to stop.

"What happened, Ara?" Caine's voice had taken a hard edge. Harder than she had ever heard it. "Speak it, Ara."

She swallowed with a shake of her head, her eyes dropping to the floor. She was dirt. Dirt. So what did it matter now, her vow? "It had been days that we had been tied together in that coach, and then they dragged us into that whorehouse. They put both of us in a room with a tub. The water was freezing, but a maid came in and jabbed at us with a fire poker until we both suffered the water. I scrubbed Isabella's hair. She scrubbed mine."

The memory filled Ara's mind, taking over all thoughts of the present and sending her knees weak.

Ara sank, her back sliding down the edge of the bookcase until she was sitting on the planks of the empty floor. "Isabella was combing my hair when the crow came in."

"The crow?"

Ara nodded, her hand rubbing her forehead as her eyes shut tight at the scene flashing, seizing her mind. "The crow grabbed me first. An old, wretched lady. Her back so stooped she was half as tall as she should have been. Her nose was long, curved, like a beak. Black hair. She had the men that came in with her push me onto the bed and yank my legs apart. I was only in a wet chemise. I thought it was the end—why I was there. But then the crow asked me if I was virgin. I said yes, and then she…she stooped over me, verifying that very fact. Her beak nose was all I could stare at, I was so scared—so mortified at her fingers and where they were."

"Ara—"

"No." Her hand flew up, stopping Caine as she looked up to him. "You wanted to hear this, Caine, so do not dare to stop me now."

His mouth closed, and Ara's gaze dropped from the hard lines of Caine's face to settle on the peach muslin that covered her knees as she drew them to her chest. Her voice went low, slow, each word having to be dragged from the depths of memories she had denied for so long. "Once the crow was satisfied with me, she pointed to Isabella. The men dropped my legs and shoved me off the bed. I was still so scared I could only crawl along that filthy floor into the corner. The crow did the very same thing to Isabella—the men grabbed her and held her down on the bed, pulled her legs apart. The crow asked her the same question, Isabella said she was a virgin, and the crow bent over her, checking her the same as she did to me. Except…"

"Except, what, Ara?"

"Except she pulled away and looked at Isabella. Her crow face—so mean, pinched. 'Ye ain't a virgin,' she said. Isabella was shaking then. She kept swearing she was. The crow caught Isabella's forehead, brushing back her hair. And then her voice went so damn soft. 'Admit it, girl. No harm will come to you if you admit to the truth. Are you a virgin, girl?' she asked."

Closing her eyes, Ara tried to swallow, but her dry mouth offered no moisture. "It took forever, and the crow waited. And then…then Isabella shook her head. The crow asked how many times, and Isabella was crying. I barely heard her say, 'Six. Six times.' And then the crow cackled, vicious. She set her face right in front of Isabella's and spit out, 'Ye lied to me boys, wench.'"

Ara's eyelids cracked open, looking up to search Caine's face, horrified that she had just admitted the secret she had harbored for the past six years. A secret she had thought she would keep to her grave. Caine did not need to know he had been betrayed by the woman he loved. He had left Isabella a virgin when he went to war, and she had been unfaithful to him while he was away.

Ara could read nothing in his face. Not shock. Not despair. Nothing.

"What happened next, Ara?"

Ara dragged a deep breath into her lungs, her eyes shutting to the present once more. "The crow stood up from Isabella and opened the door. There were two other men—different than the ones that had us in the carriage—waiting just outside. She pointed back at me and said, 'That one is clean—we need her—she stays untouched.'"

A sob deep in her chest gave hiccup to her words, but Ara pushed on. "But then she pointed to Isabella, and said, 'That one be a liar. She ain't no virgin. And ye know what we do to liars.'"

Ara tightened her hold around her own body, her eyes opening to focus on Caine's boots in hopes the vicious images in her head would stop. "And they laughed, Caine. They laughed and it was a frenzy, and they turned into wolves. They attacked. Wolves on her. Right in front of me. One and then another and another. The wolves they… they…" The savage memory choked off her words.

Caine swayed, Ara saw it in his legs—she didn't need to look up to witness it. She curled tighter around her belly, her forehead touching her knees as she tried to stay the bile that was quickly rising in her throat.

It was one thing to live through that nightmare in her dreams. It was a very different thing to speak the words out loud. Speak them to the man that had loved the woman torn to shreds in front of Ara.

Especially when she had told him Isabella had died peacefully.

She had thought she was being kind when she lied to Caine those many years ago about Isabella's death. But when she had lied, she had believed she would never see Caine again. Instead, that kindness had done nothing but haunt her every day since.

Blood pounding in her ears, Ara almost didn't hear Caine's voice floating down to her.

"Long ago, Ara, you said Isabella did not die alone. Was that also a lie?"

Her head stayed bowed. She couldn't look at him, couldn't face the judgement in his eyes. "I was in the room the whole time. In the corner. I cowered, Caine. Cowered. Terrified. I did nothing to stop them. By the time they were done with her…"

Ara's body went into trembles, her voice shaking, but she forced the words to the air. "Blood everywhere—sheets, walls, me. Her body was limp when the wolves left. It took me so long…I was so scared and it took me so long to move to her, to touch her hand. But it was already cold. Dead."

Ara crumpled into herself, a sob gagging her words. "I only cowered. Weak. In the corner. Nothing against the wolves. A coward. I am so sorry, Caine. I could not help her."

Only silence above.

Desperate shame erupted in Ara's gut, flooding her body. Shame at the past—shame at Caine knowing the truth of her cowardice. Her arm flung up, gripping a shelf and she scrambled to her feet. She kept her head down, her body folded to hide from his eyes.

"I lied to you and I am so sorry, Caine. You just… you just loved her so much, and I did nothing to help her. Nothing." Tears blinding her, Ara staggered toward the French doors. "You love her and I am so ashamed of my failure—my cowardice."

She managed to fumble open the door, stumbling down the few stairs to the ground. Her feet sped, running. Running back between the townhouses. Running through the mews. Running until she collapsed on the back metal steps of a random townhouse.

Caine did not follow her.

It took an inordinate amount of time before she could catch her breath and right herself enough to stand again.

When she finally gained her feet, the sky was slipping into darkness.

She walked to the end of the mews, looking around the main thoroughfare to place herself in the streets. For a moment, Ara considered walking to the right, straight to the docks where she could get on a ship and leave this country. Run away from every blasted memory, everything she had suffered, including her own failure.

Leave everything and start anew.

But then her feet started moving to the left. To Baker Street. To her girls.

For all her failures, Ara knew she had done one thing right in the past six years. Her girls. Her girls she had not failed. And her girls needed her.

{ Chapter 16 }

Ara shot straight up in bed. Her eyes whipped to her window, ignoring the cold sweat covering her entire body.

Still dark.

Thank the heavens.

But hell. Her mind flew in a whirlwind.

The duchess. The depressed little sister. The lion brooch with the vines. The golden lion crest over the thick gates at the estate in Kent. All one and the same. They had to be.

The whole of it fell together perfectly in Ara's mind, speeding from her subconscious to her conscious mind.

The Duke of Dunway. Caine was about to duel the bloody Duke of Dunway.

She had thought she could do nothing, could not force Caine from his course, did not even know where he was at, but now…

Her thoughts flew into hysteria. What did she know about duels? They were at dawn. Caine could get shot. He could die. That was what she knew.

Her gaze darted to the window again. Dark. There was still time.

Flying about the room, she was dressed and out the door of the Baker Street house within minutes. She ran, praying that the harlots and drunks were long gone from the night, and she would only encounter the very early respectable workers on the streets.

Gasping for breath, she gripped the front wrought iron fence of the duke's townhouse, sliding to a stop. Darkness still filled the sky and Ara knew she was well beyond propriety, but she would wake the devil himself if it meant saving Caine.

Even if he was an ass—even if he now hated her for the coward she was—she was not about to let him get hurt—or die—because he had an absurd need to save the girls from scandal. Each one of the girls they had saved—including herself—had already weathered the worst in that brothel, and each of them would survive any scandal life brought.

Ara's eyes rushed across the exterior of the townhouse. Lights burned brightly on the main level of the home, unusual for this time of the early morning.

Hope flickered in her chest.

She ran up the front stairs, slamming the door knocker as hard as she could. If she was wrong about this, she would be putting everything with the *House of Vakkar* at jeopardy, demanding to see the duchess at this unholy hour. The duchess could easily reward the rudeness by disavowing Greta's creations, and the rest of society would follow suit.

That fact, though sobering, didn't stop Ara's hand from its mission on the knocker. She slammed it again.

The door yanked open, the disheveled—and furious—butler peering out at her.

"The duchess, I need to see her."

"I do not need to tell you, Miss Detton, that the duchess does not take visitors at this hour." He started to close the door.

Ara stuck her boot between the door and the jamb, her hand pushing back against the door.

"Please, sir, I beg you. Only a moment. It is a matter of saving a life, and only the duchess can help me."

"Wilford, who is there?" The duchess appeared behind the butler, pulling her robe tight about her body. She went to her tiptoes, spying over her butler's shoulder to Ara. "Miss Detton? Why are you here?"

Ara shoved at the door, gaining a wider angle. "Please, your grace, I need your help. I am desperate." She paused for a second, blinking back caution, but then took a breath—damn the consequences, she needed to do this. "The duel. I need to stop it."

With a gasp the duchess pushed the butler to the side and grabbed Ara's hand, dragging her into the house. "Miss Detton, good heavens, what do you know on that?"

The duchess didn't release her hand, pulling Ara as she scurried into the well-lit Pearl drawing room.

"Your sister is Lizzie, your grace?"

The duchess dropped Ara's hand, spinning back to her with narrowed eyes. Ara knew that look—she had often worn it herself. Defenses drawn, the duchess's visage fortified in fierce protection of her loved one. "Yes. What do you know of her?"

"I know that your husband is making a terrible mistake this morning. He is very wrong about the man he means to kill. Very wrong about what happened with Lizzie."

"How do you know all of this, Miss Detton?"

"I know because I was there. I was with Lizzie when we brought her to your estate in Kent." Ara leaned toward the duchess, her voice going to a whisper. "I was with her when Lord Newdale saved her from the brothel."

The duchess's hand flew to flatten over her mouth. "A brothel?"

"I will tell you everything, your grace, but please, where is your husband?"

"He is already gone." The duchess shook her head, her wide eyes terrified, the color nonexistent in her cheeks.

Ara snatched her hand. "I pray you know where to, because I need your help, Duchess, and I need it right now."

~ ~ ~

Twelve paces, marked by Southfork's counting, and Caine spun, his arm extended, pistol high.

He fired before fully turned, his aim high at the tree over the duke's shoulder. The delope went wide enough to avoid the duke, but close enough to not cause further offense.

Unarmed, a target, a slice of cowardice shot up from Caine's belly that he fought. His instinct was to dive, save himself. But Ara's face filled his mind and he banished the cowardice.

His spine straightened, steadying him. Ara was what was most important. She always had been.

And there was no way now—especially after what she had told him the previous day, after all that she had suffered—that he was going to let the slightest breach happen upon her impeccable reputation.

For her, he would do this with honor. If he was to be felled, he would go down with integrity, knowing Ara was safe from ruin. Safe from him.

His arm dropping to his side, he stared at the barrel of the duke's pistol in the dusty light. Waiting. The aim was square on Caine's chest. There wasn't a doubt that the duke would hit his target. Caine hadn't even bothered to turn his body to make himself thin.

Funny, that for as many bullets as he had dodged during the war, now he stood, impatient for that very thing.

He waited. A second passed that lasted five lifetimes.

And then Caine saw the duke's arm flex, his forefinger slowly squeezing the trigger.

Time to kiss death. What Fletch had always said during the war. It had always made Caine chuckle in a wry, I-would-prefer-to-avoid-death manner, but Fletch had it right. Time to make death his mistress.

The shot fired at the exact second a peach ball of fury flew out of nowhere, ramming into the duke.

Pain seared through Caine's shoulder, sending him flying backward. Falling…falling…falling. His head hit the ground.

Darkness.

Nothing.

⁓⁓⁓

Ara watched, stunned, as the duchess flew across the field, barreling into her husband just as he fired. The woman hadn't even taken the time to change from her robe, or to put proper shoes on.

The shot echoed across the park, and the duke and duchess landed, tumbling. Ara's eyes darted to Caine. Except there was no Caine.

He had been standing there. And now he wasn't.

She ran to the dueling field, searching the ground.

No. Please no.

His body deep in the grass. Blood splattered on the side of his head.

She raced to his side, skidding onto her knees beside him. There was screaming going on behind her. The duchess. The duke. The other man. Fletch. All of them yelling.

But all she could see, all she could hear, all she could feel was Caine before her. Prone. Still. Bloody.

Her hands found his face, gripping it. No reaction.

She dropped her ear to his chest, pressing her head hard against his jacket, straining to hear a heartbeat. His body jerked.

Ara lifted her head, realizing her cheek was now wet. Her fingertips ran alongside her face, and then she looked at her hand. Bright red. Blood.

Her eyes scoured Caine's body. In panic, she had thought the blood on his face was from a bullet to the head, but she had been wrong.

She found it almost instantly, the hole in his black jacket on his shoulder—the fabric hiding the red color, but becoming darker with the wetness seeping from the hole. She smeared the wetness onto her clean hand, proving to herself that was where the blood came from. Scooting around his body, she hefted his shoulder up, searching for another hole in the fabric. Yes. Another tear. The bullet passed through.

"Caine," she yelled in his face. Blast it. If he was shot in the shoulder, why was he unconscious?

Ara grabbed his face again, giving him a little shake. No response.

His head lolled to the side, and that was when Ara saw it. A jagged rock—wide—sat just above the surface of the ground. Blood tainted the light grey ridge of the rock's surface.

Quickly wiping her hand clean, she sent her fingers into the dark hair on the back of Caine's head. She felt the tear along his skin, the blood re-soaking her fingers, and she rocked back on her heels.

"Dammit, Caine." Ara twisted, searching for Fletch in the mayhem of flailing arms and bellowing behind her. "Fletch, dammit. Get over here, Fletch."

Fletch heard her and was by her side in a second, dropping to his knees. "I was attempting to make sure the duke didn't come over here and finish Caine."

"The duchess will take care of that." Ara didn't spare one glance in the duke's direction. "Help me get him to your carriage, Fletch. You grab him by the shoulders and I will take his feet. That bullet just went through his shoulder, but the rock cracked his skull."

"Shit."

"Yes. And I am not about to lose him to a bloody rock, Fletch."

Fletch looked at her, gravity in his smile. "No. I don't imagine you are, Ara."

{ CHAPTER 17 }

Caine cracked his eyes open.

Ara.

Ara staring at him. Watching him.

Heaven.

That was where he landed. By some grace, he had landed in heaven.

She moved, her mouth drawing into a tight line, her green eyes blazing.

She was irate. As furious as he had ever seen her, the air crackling around her, and she hadn't even spoken a word.

Damn. Maybe this wasn't heaven.

And why did his feet feel like they were weighed down by twenty stones?

His eyes shifted to his feet. A furry monster.

He squinted. No. That was Patch curled on top of his feet. The dog lifted his head at Caine's movement, then resettled himself, his snout curling over Caine's shin. He gave one lick onto the coverlet above Caine's leg.

So he was in bed with a mutt holding him captive. And his head was pounding. And his shoulder hurt like hell.

Definitely not heaven.

Caine looked back to Ara. Her rage hadn't quelled.

"The bullet went through your left shoulder, and you fell and cracked your head open on a rock, you bloody fool." Her words shook in fury.

Caine lifted his right hand, slipping his fingers behind his head. He found the cut, the thread holding his skin together.

"The surgeon stitched your head and looked to that hole in your shoulder. The bullet made a clean pass through, and he stitched those as well."

Caine's hand fell down along his side, heavy. "How long have I been asleep?"

She smoothed back an errant lock of hair into her chignon. "The entire day. I have been waiting for you to awaken."

"To castigate me?"

"Yes." Ara leaned forward in the wide leather chair someone must have dragged over from the fireplace in his room. "Do you realize that the bullet was only this far from your heart?"

She held up her fingers almost pinched—a clear exaggeration of how close the bullet could have been to his heart. "This far from death, Caine. Dead. In the middle of a blasted field." Her voice softened slightly at her last words, worry eating into her anger.

"So you are mad at me?"

"Mad does not even begin to describe it. Furious. Livid. Enraged. Frantic. Incensed. I could go retrieve your thesaurus from the library and continue on, if you would like."

His hand flew up. "No. Not necessary. I completely understand your state of mind. What I said to you yesterday was—"

"No, Caine. You understand absolutely nothing about my state of mind. This has nothing to do with what you said to me."

"No?"

Her forearms balancing on her thighs, her head dropped, shaking for a moment.

She looked up at him, her green eyes pinning him. "No. I am furious because you gave up. You gave up on me, on the girls. I saw you there in that field. Standing. Waiting for death. A long time ago you said you would never give up on me. But you did exactly that when you gave up on yourself, Caine."

His head rolled away from Ara, avoiding her eyes. Avoiding the truth he didn't care to acknowledge. "Leave, Ara. You cannot be here. Not with my ruin. You have to distance yourself."

"And now you dare to want me to leave?" Her hands flew up.

He flopped his face back toward her. "Yes. For all that you are acquainted with the evils of the world, Ara, you are still so incredibly innocent. I am now nothing but scandal and ruin—the failed duel, my inclinations to acquiring virgins. All of it is now known—common fodder for the masses. You must not associate yourself with my ruin for the security of your own reputation."

"It is far too late for that, Caine." Her chest rose in an exasperated sigh. "That you insist on letting people believe these lies about you infuriates me to no end. The lies are not who you are."

His hand slammed flat down on the bed. "I will not taint you with this, Ara. I will not taint the girls we have saved. This is my ruin to bear. I take what we have done to my grave. I will never let anyone harm you, or them."

"Oh." She nodded, standing up, her eyes narrowing as she stared down at him from the side of the bed. "You still think to give up."

"Just because I want you removed from harm—"

"No, you are giving up again, Caine. And I am damn well sick of it."

She spun on her heel, going to the door. Her head disappeared into the hallway, and a moment later, she opened the door wide, walking back over to the bed to stand next to him.

"For some reason, you have it in your thick skull that my life, and the lives of the girls, would be better off without you, Caine."

Ara turned to the door. "Greta."

Greta peeked her head into the doorway. Ara gave her a nod. With a smile, Greta came into the room, leading a line of women. Silently, they filed into the room, woman after woman, thirty-eight total, standing in rows along the far side of Caine's bedroom.

Ara looked down at Caine. "As unseemly as it is that you have the lot of them in your bedroom, you needed to see this." Ara's eyes lifted to the rows, her hand sweeping over the crowd of women. "There is no greater proof of how you matter. These women, every single one of them, would either be dead or in a much harsher world without you, Caine. You have made a difference you cannot possibly comprehend. But they can. At the news that you were injured, all of them came here to keep vigil. Each of them has a loyalty to you that you cannot imagine. And each would willingly speak of what happened to her, if it meant restoring your name."

Ara looked down at Caine. "But them doing so is not necessary."

"Ara…"

She looked up from him, finding Greta and giving her a nod. As silently as they had entered the room, the long line of women left.

Ara waited until Greta closed the door behind her before she looked down to him. "You will not give up on what we have built, Caine. You will not give up on me. And you will not get rid of me with a few harsh words. Even though I think you the worst ass for trying."

Caine stared at the closed door, humbled, and more scared than he had ever been in his life. But not scared for himself. Scared for Ara.

He reached out, grabbing her left hand. "You brought the duchess to save me from the duke's bullet, but it came at a price, didn't it, Ara?"

A slight flinch. She tried to hide it, but he saw it. Ara nodded. "I told her what happened to Lizzie. I told her what happened to me. I told her what you have done to save all of the girls, but I did not name any of them."

"You should not have put yourself at risk, Ara."

"I trust the duchess, Caine. She will not tell a soul what I told her, and she will ensure her husband keeps the secret as well. You have to trust that there are some people with integrity in this world."

"Yet you have seen the depravity I have, Ara. I do not know how you manage to believe in the good."

She smiled, genuine. "While I have witnessed the depravity firsthand, I have also seen you nearly every day for the last six years. You—who you are as a man—tends to make me believe in the inherent good, Caine."

He closed his eyes, beyond grateful this woman was standing before him. Still believing in him. Especially after what he had said to her, lies though they were. His eyes opened to her. "So you are less mad at me?"

Her head cocked, her mouth slipping to the side, scolding. "On my way. But you are still in trouble."

"I expect so."

Ara squeezed his hand. "Fletch is waiting to see you. He is a loyal friend to you, Caine."

Caine's lips drew in with a nod that sent a shock of pain vibrating around his head. It took him several breaths before he could reply with a weak smile. "We sometimes get what we do not deserve."

She saw the pain and worry set into her eyes. "I will send him up. And then you need to sleep. Both the surgeon and your physician insisted." She released his hand and went to the foot of the bed, scratching the center white stripe on Patch's head. "Patch wants to stay with you. I have tried too many times today to chase him from the bed and get him to leave the room, but he insists on holding his own vigil."

"Or could it be he is weary of being the only male in a house of females and he recognizes his possible escape?"

She chuckled. "One should be so lucky to be in the Baker Street house. We are delightful." She patted Patch's back, the sound thumping. "But he does miss you, I give you that. Remember—Fletch, and then sleep. Nothing more. Tomorrow you can get out of bed."

She walked to the door, her hand going to the doorknob.

"Ara, stop."

She glanced over her shoulder at him. "That particular order again?"

Caine offered a pained smile. "Ara, please stop. Do not leave me, not yet."

She sighed, turning back to him, but her hand remained on the knob. "What is it?"

She kept her patience, even if Caine could still see the current of anger running under her skin. But he needed to tell her before it faded into one of the many things in life that became unsaid.

"What you told me at the Gilbert Lane house, about Isabella—it was not your fault, Ara. You were not responsible for the madness that you were thrust into in that brothel."

She cringed, her eyes diving to a deep corner of the room. "No, but I did nothing to stop the madness. I cowered, Caine."

"You were young."

"Do not make excuses for my lack of character, Caine. I have been down that path far too many times, and I always end up where I belong. A coward. I hid. I watched. I prayed they would not turn to me. I did nothing."

"You do not deserve this burden you put upon yourself, Ara."

She looked at him, the crux of her palm wiping the corners of her eyes. "Yet it is mine, just the same."

"Ara."

She spun to leave.

"I know, Ara. I know the guilt."

She froze and it took three long breaths for her to turn back to him.

"I know what it is to live with the guilt, Ara. I did not save Isabella, and I was the one that should have. I will always feel that guilt. I left her before marrying her. I abandoned her. I thought I was only leaving her for a short while, but it was too long—an abandonment. It does not matter what she chose to do after I was gone, that she had betrayed me—I had already failed her. And how do I beg a dead person for forgiveness?"

"One cannot."

"Exactly." His head shook, his eyes drifting to the dark blue canopy over his head. With a deep breath, he looked to Ara. "So maybe we beg it of the living."

"I do not know how that would work, Caine."

"Neither do I, except that I am quite sure, in this very moment, what I need to be doing is begging you for your forgiveness, Ara. Everything that I said yesterday, every blasphemous lie I uttered, I did it so you would not be involved in the scandal, in my death. You do not know how I died inside watching you leave from the Gilbert Lane house. How I wanted to grab you. Hold you. It was all I could do to keep you at a safe distance."

A crooked smile reached her lips as her hand behind her back fiddled with the doorknob. "Daft man, I know that. I know what you were doing. But that does not excuse your words. How you tried to rid yourself of me. You should have let me make my own choice about what scandal I was willing to endure."

"Except that your choice would not have been my choice for you."

"Therein, festers the problem."

They stared at each other.

Caine accepted her stare, knowing exactly what she said, what she demanded of him.

Her own mind. Her own choices.

But heaven help him, he did not know if he was man enough to allow it. Life would be so much simpler if she would just listen to his guidance. Bow to his wishes without questioning him at every turn.

But that wouldn't be Ara.

Not the Ara he loved. He loved her for the very spirit he wanted to control.

He sighed. Maybe he wasn't man enough to allow it, but he had to believe he could be, for he sure as hell wasn't going to let any other man try.

"Ara, there was one other choice you made long ago that should have guided my actions—that should have forced me to respect the integrity of your choices, of what you could handle."

Her eyebrow quirked at him. "That I let you save me from that field?"

"No. But that was also an admirable choice." A quick smile crossed his lips before fading. "It was the choice you made in that brothel, to stay in the corner, to do nothing."

Her face crumpled like he had slapped her.

"No, Ara. It was the right choice. It was survival. Isabella was already gone, and you did the right thing by making yourself invisible." Caine shifted, drawing himself up slightly onto his right arm. "But if you need to hear me say I forgive you for that act, Ara, I will not do it. I will not do it because I never blamed you for Isabella, and I certainly will not forgive you for being a coward, because you are not. You are the furthest thing from a coward, Ara. You are a survivor. You are strong. And there is absolutely nothing for me to forgive."

Her face went white, her head shaking against his words.

"And there is no reason for me not to trust your choices."

Her mouth cracked, but no sound came forth. In a blink, she offered a quick nod, spinning and disappearing out the door before Caine could stop her.

Before he knew if she believed him.

He sank down into the bed.

Heaven help him, she needed to believe him.

~ ~ ~

Ara closed the door behind her, collapsing against it.

All those many years she had held her secret, terrified Caine would not forgive her for her cowardice. All those years wasted, holding her love for him at arm's length because she didn't want to see it destroyed when he knew the truth.

He knew it now, knew everything. He didn't blame her. Felt no need to forgive her.

So why had the weight of guilt not lifted from her shoulders with his words?

Why did her heart feel like a rock in her chest, struggling for every beat?

The reality in the back of her mind fought forward, even though she tried to keep it at bay. The fact she had always known but never given credence to.

It was her own damn self.

She was the one not willing to forgive her own cowardice.

So what in the hell was she to do with that fact? There was no hiding behind the secret anymore. No hiding behind what Caine might think of her.

It was her alone that could not lift this burden from her heart.

A glance out the window at the far end of the hallway told Ara it was now past dusk—night settling. A night that needed attending to. She shoved thoughts of forgiveness from her mind.

Taking a deep breath, she pushed herself from the door, tiptoeing away from Caine's room. She didn't want him to hear her footsteps and call her back into his room. She didn't have time for that—not with everything she had to arrange.

Ara turned at the stairs, her feet quick. She needed to get Fletch and send him up and then rush to the Baker Street house.

She fingered the card in her pocket. Ara had intended to remind Caine of the note, but he could not help. Not in his current condition.

But that didn't mean there wasn't a girl to save.

~ ~ ~

The rescue was not going as intended.

Even with the six guards she had with. Even with the solid plan. Mayhem.

And Ara had only moments to right the rescue.

Turk, one of the guards, was supposed to snatch the virgin girl the moment she exited the side door of the brothel with whoever purchased her. It was how it was always done at the Jolly Vassal. The men purchased the girls inside and then exited with them through the side door to avoid the front door bustle of bodies.

The plan had been for Turk to shove the man who bought the virgin aside, throw the girl over his shoulder, and then toss her into the carriage with Ara and Mrs. Merrywent.

Pushing the man to the ground had been easy for Turk. Getting jumped by three cutthroats before he could pick up the girl was not.

And now the girl was running, screaming down the street in her see-through chemise with her hands still bound in front of her, her veil covering half of her head.

The devil in hades.

Ara glanced back to the front of the brothel.

Wolves.

She recognized two of the men instantly—the wolves in the brothel from years ago. Wolves that had torn apart Isabella. They were already pointing, rushing after the girl.

Ara surged out of the carriage, fingernails ripping along her arm as she freed herself from Mrs. Merrywent who was trying to hold her back.

Running, Ara sped down the street after the girl. Just behind her, Franklin and Gordon, two of her six guards were at her heels. A third guard, Lewis, caught up to her speed, his arm brushing hers as he kept pace.

A scuffle broke out behind them, and Ara ventured a glance back to see fists flying—Gordon and Franklin fending off the wolves from the brothel in the middle of the street.

Lewis and Ara caught up to the girl within two blocks, the girl's progress hindered by her bare feet. She flailed wildly when Ara grabbed her shoulder, stopping her escape, and smacked Ara across the face.

The sting of it sent Ara stumbling, and by the time she gained her footing, Lewis had already tossed the girl over his shoulder.

Ara hated to see the terror in the girl as she tried to fight her way from being captured again, her bound fists pounding on Lewis's back. But he had her secure and now was not the time for explanations. Now was the time to get her into the carriage and to safety.

They ran back toward the side street where the carriage waited, though Lewis's speed faltered with the extra weight of the girl. They turned the corner, the carriage in sight.

A sudden grunt sounded behind her, but Ara didn't look back. The safety of the carriage was only a few feet away, Felix high in the driver's seat yelling at her. She could hear him, but she couldn't make out his words.

She should have looked back. She knew it.

If she had, maybe she could have dodged.

Instead, her feet went flying out from under her, a thick body tackling her into the muck of the street.

Ara hit the cobblestones hard, her ribs crunching, but she managed to fight her head upward. Lewis skidded to a halt, turning back to her.

"Go. Get her to the carriage." Ara squeaked out through stolen breath. "Get the girl away, then come back."

Lewis moved, taking the order and reaching the carriage just as the mass of man on top of Ara lurched, his belly landing on her head, smothering her face into the sludge of the street.

All she could see was darkness.

But she could hear the carriage. Feel the pounding of the hooves, the wheels crunching over the cobblestones.

The girl was safe.

It was all that mattered.

{ CHAPTER 18 }

He was going to kill Ara.

There was no question on that fact.

He was going to kill her. But first, he had to get her back.

Caine set his face to indifference, stepping to the side as a painted harlot with only a cherry-red skirt on slipped past him in the narrow hallway.

He tilted his head to her as though they were passing acquaintances riding Rotten Row. If there was one thing he had learned in life, it was to be respectful of women, no matter their circumstances.

Except that particular standard would be lifted the second he got his hands on Ara. He was now thinking to throttle her before he killed her. And to think he had bloody well told her he respected her decision-making abilities.

More idiot words had never been spoken.

Caine glanced down the hallway, stifling the urge to tear every door open. He wouldn't get through three—especially with his left arm bound to his body from the bullet wound—before the two thugs by the stairs tossed him out, probably through a second-story window.

Though he had never been to the upper floors of this brothel, it was just like every other cheap whorehouse he had passed through in his life. Skinny hallway. The suffocating scent of heavy perfume. A distinct cigar haze. Door after door of tiny rooms—the better for volume and speed—as no man was encouraged to lounge about in this establishment.

Disgusting. As was this entire world.

The door to Caine's left opened, a brute standing in the doorway, eyeing Caine.

"In." The one-worded brute stepped to the side.

Caine moved past him, finding the man he was here to see sitting behind a beaten board that served as a desk. The morning light shone through a wispy red curtain pulled in front of the window behind the brothel owner, highlighting the grease on his mousy hair. Wrinkles ran deep along his forehead, drawing attention to the birthmark that covered most of his left temple. Apparently, running a brothel came with a fair amount of worry.

This owner, Mr. Topley, usually had his splotchy red birthmark covered with a purple-dyed top hat—courtesy of the last owner of the brothel. While Topley wasn't as flamboyant as the man that had sold Ara years ago, he was not bashful in how he ran his auctions. This one was thick, a rough brute, yet his speech was impeccably smooth, and it made sense he took over the brothel six years ago.

Scratching a quill across paper with a wide flourish, Topley paused, looking up at Caine. He waved his hand at the brute behind Caine, and the cutthroat exited the room, closing the door. A pistol sat on the desk, conspicuously aimed in Caine's direction.

"I was curious how long it would take before someone came for her." Topley's finger twirled around the feather of the quill. "Though I did not suspect it would be you, Lord Newdale. Not as one of my most prolific customers. What matter is she to you?"

"She is my secretary, Mr. Topley."

Topley laughed, tossing the quill onto the scarred board. "That is rich." He leaned back in his chair, his wide eyes narrowing on Caine. "No one comes into these streets, into a brothel, to retrieve a mere secretary."

"I do. She is valuable to me."

Topley shrugged, threading his hands together behind his head. "Well, as you only appear to need her for her intelligence, you will not mind if I keep her for a few days. I must insist she pay off what she cost me in business last night with that debacle in the street."

Rage flooded Caine's chest. He swallowed, trying to control the twitch along his jaw. "The price? I will pay it."

"Yet there is no price, Lord Newdale. I lost much more than just the sale of a virgin last night. I lost the integrity of my auctions. Word has already spread—the discrete haven I have created for satisfying peculiarities has been breached by your little paladin. It will be some time until I can hold another auction and recoup my losses."

"In all our dealings, Mr. Topley, I have never taken you for a fool." Caine motioned about the space, fingers pointing to the many surrounding rooms. "You are a man that understands well the value of a body."

"Yes."

Caine took a step closer to the desk. "So this body is very valuable to me. I will give you anything for her."

Mr. Topley's left eyebrow arched high, cutting into the lines on his forehead.

Dammit.

Caine hadn't meant to offer up anything and everything right away. There was supposed to be patience involved on his part. Patience that had vanished the second Topley mentioned putting Ara to work for him.

Caine stared at the man, waiting. He couldn't take back his words now, he could only wait to see where Topley drove this.

"I see." Topley nodded. "Except that I now have what is an even bigger problem. You have been buying up my virgins for years, Lord Newdale."

"Yes."

Topley leaned forward, resting his thick arms on the table, his fingers playing with the butt end of the pistol. "So what have you done with all of them? There have been so many throughout the years, and usually, the other men deliver the girls back to my establishment after their use is complete."

"I dispose of them."

"Hmmm." Topley nodded, then looked up at Caine, his beady eyes piercing. "You must not think me a smart man, Lord Newdale. I recognized her. The moment she was dragged in front of me last night. I recognized her. One does not forget beauty like that. I was the one that spotted her first in that field years ago, and I looked at her for days as we came into town. Granted, back then I was only a hired brute, so I had to keep my hands off of her. But now—"

"You bastard." Caine could take no more. He dove at the desk, but Topley had the pistol in hand, pointed, a second before Caine could reach him.

Caine froze, seething, his nose only inches from the dark metal of the barrel.

Topley stood, the pistol trained at Caine. "My business, as you know, Lord Newdale, thrives upon my ability to remain discrete. And an earl purchasing virgins to save them from depravity does not bode well for my discrete operations. If what you have been doing for the past six years becomes known, I do believe it will destroy the most lucrative part of my business."

Topley started to move from behind the desk. "While I do owe you a debt of gratitude—as I believe it was you that disposed of my predecessor here and allowed me to take over the establishment—I am afraid I must put a stop to you, as I cannot have the gentlemen of your caliber going elsewhere for their wares."

"Wares?" Caine drew himself to his full height. "They are living, breathing women, you bastard."

"They are disposable." Topley waved his pistol. "Just as you are. What is to stop me from killing you right now?"

"Nothing." Caine shook his head. "Nothing except for me killing you."

Topley charged, his heavy steps sending Caine back several feet to avoid having the pistol jammed directly into his chest.

Spittle flew from Topley's mouth. "You come into my house, you pompous ass, and dare to threaten me? Threats you can't back—"

His words cut short as the door flung open, knocking Topley hard in the side and sending his pistol arm flailing.

Caine lunged, grabbing Topley's wrist with his right hand and clamping it so Topley couldn't aim the gun.

A barrage of bodies filled the room, and then the click of another pistol silenced everything.

The hulking forms of the Duke of Dunway and Lord Southfork swallowed the office. The duke had the barrel of his pistol on Topley's temple in an instant, shoving him deeper into the room.

Southfork walked around the man to rip the gun from Topley's hand, and Caine released the bastard's wrist.

"She is found?" Caine asked, his eyes not veering from Topley half splayed on the desk.

"Yes," Southfork said. "Your friend, Lockston, found her on the top floor. He already has her in the carriage."

"And the guards?" Caine asked.

"Taken care of."

Caine nodded. "Well done."

The duke shoved his pistol harder into Topley's temple. "This is the one?"

"Yes." Caine moved toward the doorway, popping his head into the hallway. Bodies on the floor by the stairs, but no other activity. He looked over his shoulder into the room.

"There will always be another monster to fill my place, you imbecile." Topley was foaming, his face splotching red under the duke's pistol. "We are the Hydra—you cannot cut off the head of the fucking Hydra."

"No. But we can cut off yours, Topley," Caine said, disgust thickening his words. "You stole the wrong girl long ago. And that alone would have gotten you killed today." Caine pointed to the duke. "But then you threatened his family. Even bigger mistake."

Caine gave a curt nod to the duke and Southfork, and pulled the door shut.

He had a carriage to get to.

~~~

They passed Charing Cross, and Caine finally managed to tear his eyes away from the carriage window, relaxing against the possibility of being followed or attacked.

They were safe.

Ara was safe.

He looked at her, and another wave of nearly uncontrollable anger surged.

His gaze shifted back to the window, as he tried to quell the pounding in his chest.

Ara was here, across from him, and for the most part, unscathed as far as he could tell. She had said in the brothel that she had not been harmed.

While he believed her, he didn't care for the swath of dried mud that ran up her cheek to her temple and then disappeared into her hair, muddying the blond strands. Her dark blue muslin dress was intact, though she held her palm tenderly along her ribcage as the carriage jolted over the cobblestones, which told him she had suffered some bruises.

According to the story Lewis had told him, she had been tackled from behind, slammed onto the street. Which had to have stung. Regardless, she wasn't in enough pain to complain vocally about it.

After verifying the girl from the previous night was safe at the Baker Street house, Ara had not said one word since he climbed into the carriage—not that he had been able to speak himself.

But she had stared at him.

He felt that the whole time. She wasn't about to speak, to poke his anger, but she stared at him, waiting for him to calm. Waiting for a crack in his fury.

She would be waiting a long time.

Well into the West End, the coach slowed as Caine had directed Tom to do so.

Ara leaned forward, scanning the passing buildings. Her eyes went wide as the carriage came to a full stop. Her face swung to Caine.

"A church? You are not taking me home?"

"I am taking you home, Ara. My home. So we need to complete our business inside before that can happen."

She leaned back against the squabs of the seat. "But you have not said a word to me and now this…" Her voice trailed off as her hand lifted, pointing at the tall spire of the church.

"We have much to discuss, Ara, but we are not going to do so until you become my wife."

"But we have to—"

"No. We do not have to do a thing. There is only one thing we need to resolve at the moment, and that is that we are unwed. I am going to marry you, Ara, drag you in there if I have to."

She shook her head, her voice small. "You do not have to drag me."

"No?"

"It is just…you are so angry."

"Yes, I am." Caine leaned forward, pulling forth the voice that had sent grown men scurrying in the war. "Do I need to drag you in there, Ara?"

She shook her head, motioning for him to exit the carriage and then she stood, taking his hand as she stepped down the carriage stairs.

"I am a mess, Caine. Can I at least right my hair?"

"No." He started to the door.

"Five minutes? I have mud on my face." She stopped, pulling on the crook of his arm.

He glanced down at her, his fingers tightening around the hefty gilded handle of the ancient church door. "Three minutes. But I am watching, not letting you out of my sight."

She gave him an annoyed smile. "Do you honestly think I would abscond and dare to leave you at the altar?"

"You do not want to know what I am thinking at the moment, Ara."

Her eyes flickered to the door. "But Fletch is not here. He should be here."

"Fletch stayed behind to clean up the mess you made, Ara. So no, he will unfortunately miss our nuptials. I am sure he will understand."

Her hand dropped from his arm, stung. "You do not need to be so callous about it."

Caine stared down at her. He was being a brute. But he was also forming coherent words at the moment instead of throttling her, so it would have to do.

He attempted and only moderately succeeded in softening his voice. "Mrs. Merrywent is inside, along with my man-of-affairs that you have suspected of being worthless time and again. They have arranged everything."

Ara shrugged, a small smile lifting the corner of her mouth as she wrinkled her nose. "Maybe he is not so worthless." She nodded to the door. "Do you think he brought me flowers?"

Caine bit his tongue, pulling open the thick door.
Flowers.
She was worried about bloody flowers.

Unfailing optimism.

Caine sighed, ushering her into the building.

And damned if he didn't look over his shoulder to the church's side garden, noting blooms he could easily pluck, should his man fail his soon-to-be wife.

{ CHAPTER 19 }

The ceremony was quick.

The quickest one in existence, Ara imagined.

Not that she minded. Or had the right to mind after the debacle she had caused.

Nor could she mind when the succinctness of the ceremony rewarded her with being in Caine's home at the moment, sinking into the steamy waters filling the wide copper tub in his dressing room.

When they had arrived at his townhouse, he had immediately sent her to his chambers to scrub off the muck from the street and the dinginess of the brothel that had hung onto her skin.

As much as she needed to talk to Caine, Ara had not fought his insistence.

She just hoped he was taking the current moment to pour himself a full glass of brandy to help dull his anger.

She scrubbed her toes with the lemon-scented soap—where the maid had procured it from, Ara did not know. She had never once known Caine to smell like lemons. A knock on the door made her head perk up, sending a ripple across the water.

"What is it?" She hoped the maid had not returned so soon. She needed this time alone to gather her thoughts, not to mention she wasn't accustomed to being waited upon so fully—much less by a stranger.

Without a reply, the door opened.

"Fabulous, my darling." Greta swooped in, closing the door behind her and settling herself onto the upholstered stool near the foot of the tub. Patch got up from his spot by the hearth to set his chin on Greta's lap. Greta scratched his nose with her left pinky. "Mrs. Merrywent just returned from the church, and now that I have witnessed with my own eyes that you are fine and well, I can berate you appropriately. Believe me, I have waited years for this opportunity, my darling Ara."

Ara choked back a giggle, every sweeping motion Greta made with her hand exaggerated. Greta did not lack for confidence as of late. But she was Ara's prize—one of the first girls they had rescued, and one that had transformed herself so fully from the terrified girl they had first met. Ara flipped her fingers toward her own face. "You may unleash yourself."

Greta leaned to the side, her forearm resting on the lip of the tub as she dangled her fingers into the water. "Excellent. I will start with how I always believed you were the smartest person I knew, but as it happens, you are an idiot, Ara."

Ara sank a little in the tub, her chin dipping below the surface of the water. "I am becoming aware of that fact."

"What drove you to create this mayhem? Going to the brothel on your own accord? Without the earl? Madness, my darling. And such a poor example."

"I will say, in my defense, that the scene outside the brothel last night could have just as easily happened with Caine there."

"But it did not—that is why you are an idiot. Not because you went there on your own—I expect nothing less from you as a girl was in need—but because you knowingly went without the earl. There is no greater cut to a man's pride, than what you did—leaving the earl behind because he was in a weakened state."

"He was recovering from a bullet wound and a head injury, Greta. I could not ask him to gain his feet and attend the auction—that would have been madness."

"Yet he was well enough to save you?"

"Yes." Ara's voice went small, Greta's words sinking in.

"So instead you belittled him by leaving him in the dark. Yet you say you love him. But this—this was not respect of him."

Ara sighed. She had not considered that. Considered how insulting her sneaking out and leaving Caine at home would be to him.

She had thought she was taking care of what needed to be taken care of. Instead, she had demeaned the one thing above all others she needed to be attending to—Caine.

Her bottom lip jutted out, peeved at her own blunder.

Greta flicked a few droplets of water at Ara's face. "Magnificent. I can see you are contrite. So I will move on now to your next offense—the wedding that took place without me. I must scold you on how terribly offended I am that you married without me or the Baker Street house girls."

Ara sat up slightly in the tub. "I am sorry—you must know I would have wanted all of you there. Caine insisted we stop immediately to take care of it."

"No, my darling. One does not 'take care' of a wedding. It is not done. Now we must hold a celebration—a much larger one than we would have, had you done it properly—to compensate for your earl's hastiness. That is the only thing I will accept in this situation. Mrs. Merrywent agrees with me."

Ara swallowed a groan. "Just who will be planning this celebration?"

"Why you, my darling. Mrs. Merrywent will help as well, I imagine. I am much too busy with the designs for the Countess of Deggard to be drawn away by details at the moment."

Or ever. Ara nodded, hiding a bemused smile. If they didn't pertain to her creations, Greta would avoid details until the day she died. "Of course. And just when will this celebration take place?"

"Soon. It must be before my wedding to Mr. Flagerton, which you will need to afford yourself time for planning as well. As I am the epitome of magnanimous, I have decided you may still attend to the details of my wedding."

"Your generosity does astound."

"It does. Plus, I am also working on a very special design for you, my darling." Her hands clasped, Greta winked at Ara. "One that will need to be ready by your celebration. And, if I may say, if what is in my mind becomes true with the metals and jewels, it will be my finest work yet."

"You do not need to create me anything, Greta, but you do me an honor."

"You deserve it, Ara. I only create what I see in one's spirit. And your spirit—it is the finest." Greta's look slipped into serious. "You are the heart of all of us, Ara, and you must never forget that. And you must never do another fool act like you did last night. We cannot lose our heart."

Her chest tightening, tears swelled in Ara's eyes at Greta's sudden sincerity, her words.

Greta waved her hand in the air. "But enough of the sentiment. You must finish your bath and mollify your new husband. He was in a mood when I arrived."

"You talked with him?"

"I am not such a fool as to draw the attention of a frothing mad dog, my darling. No, he was clanking things about with force in the study, muttering to himself. I could hear him quite clearly as Mr. Wilbert ushered me up the stairs."

Ara cringed. "Clanking or throwing?"

Greta shrugged, gaining her feet and stepping around Patch. "One and the same." She walked to the head of the tub and leaned down to kiss Ara's cheek. "Stop by the Baker Street house when you have settled your earl. The girls will want to see you."

"I will."

Greta walked out the door.

Ara exhaled, dropping her head back against the rounded edge of the copper tub. She had erred quite neatly with Caine. Even though he would have tried to stop her, she should have told him what she was going to do last night. She had owed him that honesty—regardless of the consequences.

She just hadn't imagined that it could have gone so terribly awry. And that was where Caine's strength shined. He recognized danger far before it even occurred to her something was amiss.

A knock echoed into the dressing room, and Patch jumped to his feet, looking at the door, tail wagging. Greta must have forgotten an additional request she wanted to add onto Ara's list.

"Yes?"

The door cracked open, but no one appeared. Patch went to the door, disappearing into Caine's bedroom.

"Are you dressed?" Caine's voice came into the room.

"Far from it," Ara said. "But do come in."

Caine stuck his head into the room, keeping his eyes leveled on hers. "I can wait."

"Please?" Ara extended her arm over the side of the tub, holding her hand out to him. "When I said come in, I meant it."

He walked into the room, stopping next to the tub. Gone were his jacket and waistcoat. His eyes stayed well above the water line, refusing to drift down past her chin.

She smiled, her eyes diving downward to the water. "I was hoping my nudity would help your mood."

She could see him resist for a moment, and then his eyes flickered to the water, pausing for much longer than she thought they would.

He looked at her face, his mouth a grim line. "It does not hurt it."

"But it does not erase your surliness?"

Caine moved behind Ara to the head of the tub. Bending down, he reached over her shoulder, grabbing the washcloth floating in the water, and then balanced on his heels. "Lean forward."

She did so, and silently, he draped her hair over her shoulder and started to wash her back. His thumb dragged along her skin, pressing into the muscles and sending tingles up her spine and down the back of her arms. Delicious and wicked. But not wicked, because he was her husband. Finally, her husband.

She closed her eyes, letting the sensation take over.

As much as she wanted to revel in nothing but his hands sliding over her slick back, words slipped from her mouth. "My optimism got me into trouble, Caine. I did not imagine anything like what happened, could have happened. You were not there to balance me."

His hand on the back of her shoulder stilled, warm water from the cloth rolling down her skin.

"I did not let you be there, and I am sorry, Caine. I should have told you what I was about to do. I did not want you to worry, nor did I want you to aggravate your injuries. Yet I should have told you."

Her words were met with silence.

Ara's mouth closed, her chin dropping to her chest. She didn't know what else to say.

They both sat, still, for several long breaths.

"I only want to know one thing, Ara." Caine's voice, gruff, broke through the silence.

"Yes?"

"When will the atonement end? When will it be enough for you?"

His words sliced into her, cutting to her core.

Only honesty would do now. She opened her mouth, the word almost choking on her tongue. "Never?"

Caine leaned forward, setting his lips next to her ear. She expected him to yell, but his voice was soft. "That cannot be the answer, Ara. You will do this until you are killed? You will die, become a martyr for the cause? Because that is where this is destined to end if you do not stop."

"I do not think I can, Caine."

He shifted to the side of the tub, his clear blue eyes riveted on her. "You have to forgive yourself for Isabella, Ara. You did nothing wrong. Surviving was not wrong."

"But Isabella was innocent. No matter her transgressions, she did not deserve what happened to her—the horror of it. And that girl last night, she was an innocent. I could not leave her to the darkness when I could stop it."

"Blast it, Ara. I don't care about the girl. I care about you." His hand slid along her neck, gripping her skin under her wet hair. "Why in the hell do you think I have supported this for the last six years?"

She blinked hard. "You do not care about the girls?"

"Of course I do. But I do this for you, Ara. To keep you safe. And then you went off, a fool, thinking you could deal with the most depraved of society and win." His fingertips dug into the back of her neck, pulling her toward him. "You cannot win this battle, Ara. They are snakes. The owner said it himself—they are Hydras—you cut off a snake head and two will grow back for every one."

He leaned forward, his forehead touching hers. "There will never be an end to this—there will always be men preying upon these girls. There will always be men—or women—willing to snatch them and make money off of them. Always. It will never end, Ara."

"But it can end—at least for the ones that we save. We have proven that, Caine, time and again."

He drew back slightly, his head shaking. "But even that is not your burden to bear, Ara. It never should have been."

"Yet it is."

Caine sighed, his eyes to the ceiling. His look dropped to her. "You have always said you never understood the depravity of humanity, Ara, so this is me releasing you from that burden you are determined to carry. I will come up with an alternative. We will save the ones we can. But only in a way that does not entail you ever stepping foot across Charing Cross again."

"It is not that easy, Caine. You cannot just make this demand of me."

His left hand moved up to fully capture her neck, his face cringing as it tore at his shoulder wound. "I can. And it is that easy. It is. You are more than busy taking care of the *House of Vakkar*, keeping care and tabs upon the eighty-seven girls you have saved throughout the years."

"You know the number?"

"Of course I know the number, Ara. They are mine to watch over as well." His blue eyes seared into her. "But please, I am begging of you, Ara, please let this—let today be a new beginning for you. For us. I love you and it is not too much to ask of you."

His right hand dove into the water, holding flat against her belly, the water soaking his white linen shirt. "What about when you become pregnant—hell, Ara, you already could be pregnant. You would put our baby at risk?"

That one thought slammed into Ara's mind, into her chest, sobering her like no words ever could. Instant tears welled in her eyes.

Caine loved her. Had married her. She could very well be carrying his baby in that moment.

What was she fighting against? Why would she put any of that—ever—in danger?

Her chin dropped, tears falling to create ripples in the water.

She truly was a fool.

Slowly, she lifted her arm, her hand landing on top of Caine's grip on her belly.

She looked up to him, finding strength in his blue eyes. Eyes that wanted nothing more than peace for her. Nothing more than to love her.

She had to do this. For Caine. For the children they would have. For her own soul.

Her voice shaking, she forced herself to give leave to the years of self-imposed penance. "I am done, Caine. I trust you to find a way."

He was on her in an instant, dragging her to her knees with his right arm, her wet body pressing into him. Words alone not enough, his mouth found hers, parting her lips, demanding her soul answer him as well. She opened everything to him, every ounce of her being, resolute in her words, and needing him to know that.

There wasn't anything more important to her in this world than this man right in front of her. This life with him.

Water sloshing over the edge of the tub, she stood, tugging him to his feet as well. She pushed his shirt up, dragging it over his head, and her mouth went onto his neck, tasting the sweet salt of him. Her fingers slid down his chest, riding the curves of his muscles, the hard lines along his belly, and landing at his black trousers.

She made quick work of the front flap, shoving the top of his trousers downward to expose him fully as her lips followed the trail down his chest.

His hardness jutted out, the smooth skin insistent on her body as she moved downward—silk upon her belly, her ribs, her breasts, and onto the flatness of her upper chest. She moved farther down, sinking to her knees in the water, only pausing when the tip of him touched her chin.

"Hell, Ara." He tried to pull up on her upper arms, his fingers sliding along her slick skin.

"I have been aching to do this for days, Caine, so you are going to let me," she said, her mouth not lifting from his skin.

His slippery grip on her arms relaxed, his fingers moving inward to burrow into her wet hair as she pulled back, intent on studying the wonder of his shaft.

At first, she slid just her forefinger and thumb along the smooth length of it, taking in the ridges, the smallest flickers reacting to her touch.

Slipping her mouth around the tip, she sucked. A guttural groan, and Caine's legs twitched, his knees bending. She took more of him into her mouth, her fingers slipping to the base of him, moving down to cup his bollocks.

The groan intensified, and Ara thought she heard a hissed vulgarity in the middle of it.

Amazing. It was amazing she could make him quiver so.

Her head moved back, then dove forward, her tongue running in circles as she descended along his shaft.

The hands in her hair gripped harder. "Dammit, Ara."

Repeating the motion, again and again, sent his knees to sway, and Ara's own core swelled, aching and ready for him. She pulled away, her tongue flickering on the tip of him, and inhaled, ready to dive again, this time with her teeth scraping ever so slightly. But Caine shifted suddenly, blocking her, holding her off of him.

His hands moved to her upper arms and he yanked her up onto his chest, water splashing.

She looked up, eyes wide. "I thought—can you not finish with me doing that?"

A chuckle rumbled through his chest, shaking her. "Yes, but I am not about to allow our first time as man and wife be without me deep inside of you. Without you clenching around me. Without you feeling how you are everything to me—every breath, every thought, every heartbeat—it is you."

Ara exhaled, her blood pounding. "You are a wise man."

His hands slid down her backside and he lifted her from the water, her legs bending to clear the lip of the copper tub. Taking a step back, he wrapped her legs around his bare waist, his hands under her thighs.

He pulled her upward, his mouth searching for hers. Finding it, he seared her with his tongue, with his soul. His mouth encompassed her senses so fully she could only half grasp that he was sliding into her below.

Before she could react, he was deep within her, pulsating, filling her more than she thought her body could handle. But then Caine lifted her slightly, driving farther into her, shattering all doubts Ara had about her body's ability to accommodate him.

He raised her again, and she saw a grimace flash across his eyes as he watched her.

She pulled away, her lips swollen. "Your shoulder—you should not carry me."

"Damn my shoulder, Ara. I sure as hell am lifting you." To prove the point, he moved her upward, letting her body slide slowly back onto him.

Ara smirked. Damned if he was going to do all the work. She shifted, pushing her inner thighs to rest on his hip bones and wrapping her calves tightly down around his thighs.

Perfect leverage.

Her hips gyrated. Caine's groan was immediate, his good arm clasping around her back. "The devil, Ara, I cannot stand this." His lips found her neck. "You need to come now. Now, Ara."

"Then—"Ara gasped, finding her rhythm on his body, the instinct of the rising swell taking over her motion. She arched back against his arm, exhaling as her hips moved against the hardness of him. "Then free me to do so."

With a growl, his right arm loosened around her back, still supporting, but giving her free rein to move as she needed to against him.

Ara took advantage, letting her body pound against his, the deep thrusts reaching something primal deep within her. The thrusts peaked, near to completion, and she felt it the instant Caine exploded deep in her, the vibration of his body sending her over the edge. Blinding—the moment held complete loss of everything except for the sphere of pleasure, pain, and deliverance pulsating through her body.

Freedom.

Complete and unequivocal freedom.

{ Chapter 20 }

Ara clutched Caine's shoulders, holding herself up, yet frozen in place, unable to move as their bodies vibrated together, his breath heavy on her neck. She could tell he was struggling for control just as much as she.

With a deep exhale, he turned, their bodies still joined, and went through the door to his bedroom. He made it to the bed, collapsing back onto it and not letting Ara escape from the grasp of his right arm.

For minutes they didn't move, and Ara reveled in the simple pleasure of her skin on his, on his chest lifting and settling below her with every breath.

When her thoughts had straightened, making sense in her mind once more, she shifted her head on his chest, looking up at him.

"I liked that."

"Standing?"

"All of it. Anyway I can have it."

He laughed, the sound low and warm, heating her heart. "I will work diligently to make sure you do."

She tapped his chin. "So tell me what you imagined when you mentioned an alternative to getting the girls out of the auctions unscathed."

"Already back to that?"

"Yes. My mind can only stop working for short time periods."

His eyes flew upward, staring at the bed canopy. "You do not need to know the details, Ara."

She cleared her throat.

Caine's eyes dropped to sweep over her pout, and he chuckled. "I thought it was worth an honest attempt." His right hand moved down, resting on the curve of her tailbone. "We can use all our same men—they all survived last night—injured, but no deaths."

"Thank the heavens."

"Indeed. But they all know the risks. We will have to determine someone who can serve in your capacity— someone to calm the girls once they are safe in the carriage. Maybe one of the Baker Street house women? I know you have gone to great lengths to protect them from their past, but doing something like this—helping others in the same situation—some of them may welcome the opportunity to help another."

Ara nodded. "I can understand the thought. I will inquire to find if any of them are interested. Janet in particular has a tender heart and would be wonderful at helping the girls if she could stomach the business of it. Plus, for all Greta has tried to teach her, Janet is not a goldsmith artist—though not for lack of trying. And I believe Mrs. Merrywent will continue to help, though I feel she would not mind some rest from the business of saving virgins."

"I agree. And as for who will purchase them in the actual brothels, I have someone in mind."

Ara popped up, her face hovering over Caine. "Who?"

"The less you know, the better for me."

"How has that worked for you in the past?"

He laughed. "True. But I do not want you involved, Ara. Give me that."

"Are his initials F.W.?"

"Possibly."

"Excellent." Her smile went wide. "Fletch made quite the dashing creature when he was rescuing me from that room at the brothel. He disposed of two guards right in front of me."

Caine's eyes narrowed. "Dashing?"

"Green in your eyes does not suit you, love." She pushed up to nip the tip of his nose and hovered above him, her hand diving into his dark hair. "Besides, you must have forgotten that I was once saved by the best, the handsomest, the most dashing man that ever was."

She kissed his chin, the rough stubble dragging across her lips. "Fletch could not hold a candle to your daring courageousness. And I was well aware you were the one saving me at the Jolly Vassal—he was just the trusted muscle you needed at the moment."

Her fingers went to the scabbed stitches on the front of his shoulder. "It was smart to not tear this open, or to go woozy from your head and fall on your feet."

"Woozy?"

"I saw you swaying by the tub."

"That swaying had not a thing to do with the cut on my head." Smirking, his hand came up, thumb tracing her bottom lip. "And everything to do with these perfect—and amazingly strong—lips."

"You enjoyed?"

"Almost too much so."

She smiled, inordinately proud of herself that she had bestowed that much pleasure on Caine. "So Fletch? Do you truly think so?"

"As you duly noted, he is good with his hands—he can protect himself enough to get out of scrapes. He has the wealth, the connections, and he is a known rake, so his expanding peculiarities into purchasing virgins would not be questioned. Which is why he would be perfect for continuing our work."

"Does he know it yet?"

Caine smirked. "No. But I have decided he needs something more fulfilling in his life past gambling and women."

Ara's eyes rolled. "So thoughtful of you. I would be ashamed of your pomposity if I did not want him to do it as well. I hope he agrees."

"As do I. I believe we will have some time to convince him, though."

"Why?"

"There will be a new owner at the Jolly Vassal, no doubt, so it is possible any auctions will move to another brothel nearby. I will have Fletch investigate that matter, at the very least."

Ara frowned. "What happened to the current owner—that burly man?"

"I did not see. While I wanted to personally end Mr. Topley, I was more concerned about getting to you. I left the Duke of Dunway and Lord Southfork with him. The duke still had murder in his eyes after what happened to his sister-in-law."

Ara nodded. While she didn't take death lightly, she could conjure no remorse over Mr. Topley being wiped from the earth. She settled back down on Caine's chest. "I did not know the duke and Lord Southfork were with you this morning."

"Reinforcements, thanks to Fletch. He was right when he said we needed extra force on our side. And he picked the right two."

Tracing his collarbone with her forefinger, Ara pressed her cheek into the warmth of Caine's chest. She never would have guessed lying leisurely on top of him would feel so delicious. "I know you were trying to shield me from anyone knowing my secret—what happened to me—and what happened to all the Baker Street house girls, but I am actually a bit relieved that the duke and duchess and Lord Southfork know the truth."

Caine stiffened under her. "We differ on that opinion, Ara."

"Yes, well, I trust the duchess. In all our interactions, she has shown nothing but the utmost integrity. I trust her with the secret, so I must trust the men as well. And I am relieved because someone other than Fletch and the girls now knows what I am well aware of."

"Which is?"

She tilted her head on his chest so she could see his blue eyes. "That you are the most humble champion of innocents, and not a sordid lecher. You never asked for this responsibility, yet you took it upon your shoulders without complaint, only steadfast determination. You are a noble man, Caine—the finest, and I am happy that I am not the only one that knows that fact."

"Your secret be-damned?"

"Well, I do hope they can keep disclosure on it. Especially now that I am your wife." She snuggled her cheek into the crook in his chest, her fingertips playing along his upper arm. "I would be devastated if my past brought shame upon the Newdale line because it became known I was in a brothel, sold like so much goods."

"You have nothing to be ashamed of, Ara. Never." He kissed the top of her head, his hand stroking the partially dry strands of her hair. "And if it ever comes to light, we will handle it together—with nothing but impeccable grace."

His palm cupped her head, his fingertips landing on the spot behind her right ear. Instinctively, she pressed her head into his hand.

"This spot, Ara. Why does it have such power over you?"

Instant red ran up her neck, flushing her face. "You know Mrs. Merrywent's secret? That means…"

"I have had to quell the terrors? Yes."

She curled on his chest, mortified. "When?"

"The night we were together before I left for Notlund Castle. They came on after I left your room. I had to hold the spot on your neck the rest of the night."

"You came back into the room? I never knew."

"I was gone before you awoke. And I could never understand why you screamed of the wolves and crow until you told me the story of you and Isabella in the brothel."

Ara nodded, her heart thudding hard at the thought of Isabella.

"So why this spot on your neck? It is most bizarre that it stops the terrors."

A soft smile spread across her face, replacing the embarrassment that Caine had witnessed her terrors. "It was my mother. You know she died when I was five. But of the memories I have of her—that is the one that is a part of me to my soul. That spot was where her fingers would always land on me when she held me in her lap. I do not know why, but that is what I remember, the pads of her soft fingers on that spot. And when Mrs. Merrywent touched that spot—and you, I now know—my mother comes to me in my dreams and she fights off the crow and the wolves. She is very good at it."

"A warrior?"

"And then some." Ara drew a deep breath. "Mrs. Merrywent says it is terrifying to hear me."

"It is. I thought someone was murdering you."

"I am sorry—I did not mean to alarm you."

"I am just happy I knew what to do."

Ara shifted, lifting her head from his chest to see him fully. "But I think, after all this time, all I really needed was you to banish the wolves, Caine."

"I will fight as many as you have, for as long as you have them, Ara." He smiled, warm, protective. "Gladly, optimistically, and with immense pride that you have chosen me to do so."

Her throat choked.

Never had she felt so cherished. So pure in her own skin. So treasured in Caine's arms.

It took her long seconds to realize what exactly it was she felt.

Peace. This was what peace was.

Peace with Caine. Peace with her own soul.

Home. She was finally home. Safe.

{ Epilogue }

Ara tightened her wool cloak about her neck, staving off the brisk breeze. The sunlight was a farce—giving no heat to the land, to the snow-laden hills rolling before her.

Patch appeared at her feet, nudging her leg through her skirts. But her eyes stayed on the horizon, entranced by the sparkling world, the last rays of sunlight forging diamonds in the snow.

Hearing footsteps, she smiled, and then warm hands wrapped around her waist from behind.

Silent, Caine tucked her head under his chin, instant shelter from the wind.

Minutes passed, the sun leaving the sky in a hasty winter retreat. Ara exhaled, her voice a whisper. "A new favorite."

Caine chuckled, his chest rumbling on her back. "You say that every day we are blessed with sun and you are out here."

"They keep getting better." Ara spun in his arms, unbuttoning his coat and slipping her hands inside the warmth to wrap around his waist. She looked up at him, watching the blue in his eyes catch the glitter of the last light reflected off the snow. "Especially when you sneak up upon me and keep me warm."

"You should have gotten me before you left. You never would have gotten cold."

"The sunset happens so early in the eve these days. I did not want to interrupt your meeting with Mr. Peterton and the mine foreman."

He leaned down, his lips brushing hers in the most gentle of kisses. Even with the innocence of it, Ara's belly tightened, her core stirring. He pulled to the side, his mouth next to her ear. "You will always be more important than whatever business needs tending to, Ara. Always."

She smirked in a light scold, squeezing his waist. "And that is why I did not interrupt you. I know how important this meeting was. It went well? Good news?"

Caine straightened with a shrug. "Possibly. A seam of copper was discovered."

"Copper—that is good?"

"It will be worth a good deal if it holds as much as Mr. Belltom believes it does. It is still early in the exploration, though." He gave a hesitant smile, a fat strand of his dark hair blowing across his brow. "Between that and the new investments with Dunway and Southfork's shipping company, my mind is beginning to be eased in regards to the vitality of the estate. Your scheming, love, with the duchess to make that happen was wise."

"Thank you. And thank you for not being angry with me for encouraging it to happen. Plus, I have a thousand more ideas. But truly, between the shipping, the mines, and the *House of Vakkar*, tell me you are optimistic."

"Cautiously so. But everything does not have to happen today, this month, this year—we have years to right the estate for our children."

His hand dropped to her belly, rubbing it through her cloak.

"Exactly." She laughed, her hand clasping over his. "But let us concentrate on getting this first one out, first."

His fingers tightened on her belly. "Speaking of our first one, there was a package from Greta for you."

"Did you peek in it?"

"I did. And I dread the day she finds out this babe is a boy and all the miniature jewellery she has been sending will go to waste."

"Or the babe will be a girl, and the most bejeweled one ever. The envy of all the nurseries."

He turned, wrapping Ara under his arm as they started the walk back to the main house. "I also received a letter from Fletch. Mrs. Merrywent is settling the latest girl, Clarissa, into the Baker Street house."

Ara nodded. "Good. All is well with him?"

"Yes." Caine quieted with the short answer.

Ara didn't mind. Where at first she had wanted to know every detail of Fletch's dealings with the brothels, as her belly had grown, so had her tolerance for not knowing everything Fletch was doing. Even more so since they had arrived at Villsum House months ago. She trusted Mrs. Merrywent with the new girls that were saved. She trusted Fletch. Most of all, she trusted that Caine was telling her what he needed to.

Funny—and amazing—that the trust had only bred peace in her soul.

Ara's head bowed as she watched Caine's boots stepping even and light in the snow and her hand ducked under the folds of her cloak to rub the hard lump that had become her belly.

She lifted her head, looking to him. "Caine, I have been pondering—our first girl, when we have her, I would like to call her Isabella."

His feet stopped, drawing her to a halt. He rounded her, his hand over her shoulder not leaving her body. Searching her face for a long moment, his left eyebrow cocked before he spoke. "Tell me why."

Ara nodded, drawing a breath as she gathered her thoughts. Her hand went onto his chest. "She was the one that brought us together. You loved her. I loved her for the will she gave me in those few days I knew her. I will never forget how much she meant to me, and I would like to honor her spirit with something beautiful, like our daughter will be, instead of leaving her name to the ugliness in how her life ended."

Heartbeats passed slowly before Caine smiled, his eyes brimming with unshed tears. It took long seconds for him to speak, his voice rough. "I think that would be fitting, Ara. And beautiful."

She nodded, smiling, wrapping her arms around him to grip him hard. "Good."

His face buried in the side of her hair, he cleared his throat. "But this one will be a boy, right?"

He chuckled as Ara shoved his chest away, jumping to the side and bending to scoop up a handful of snow, then throwing it at him with a laugh. "You should be so fortunate."

She scampered from him, scooping up more snow just before he captured her. She mushed the snowball onto his neck, her laughter shaking her.

Caine growled, nipping at her ear.

She settled, letting his hold tighten around her as he caught her eyes in his, serious. "I am, Ara. Boy or girl—no matter what. I am the most fortunate person alive."

She nodded. He was. She was.

~ About the Author ~

K.J. Jackson is the author of *The Hold Your Breath Series,*
The Lords of Fate Series, The Lords of Action Series,
and *The Flame Moon Series.*

She specializes in historical and paranormal romance,
loves to travel (road trips are the best!), and is a sucker for a
good story in any genre. She lives in Minnesota with
her husband, two children, and a dog who
has taken the sport of bed-hogging
to new heights.

Visit her at www.kjjackson.com

~ AUTHOR'S NOTE ~

Thank you for allowing my stories into your life and time—it is an honor!

My next historical in the *Lords of Action* series will debut in late summer 2016.

If you missed the *Hold Your Breath* series or the *Lords of Fate* series, be sure to check out these historical romances (each is a stand-alone story): ***Stone Devil Duke, Unmasking the Marquess, My Captain, My Earl, Worth of a Duke, Earl of Destiny, and Marquess of Fortune***.

Never miss a new release or sale!
Be sure to sign up for my VIP Email List at
www.KJJackson.com
(email addresses are precious, so out of respect, you'll only hear from me when I actually have real news).

Interested in Paranormal Romance?
In the meantime, if you want to switch genres and check out my Flame Moon paranormal romance series, ***Flame Moon #1***, the first book in the series, is currently free (ebook) at all stores. ***Flame Moon*** is a stand-alone story, so no worries on getting sucked into a cliffhanger. But number two in the series, ***Triple Infinity***, ends with a fun cliff, so be forewarned. Number three in the series, ***Flux Flame***, ties up that portion of the series.

Connect with me!
www.KJJackson.com
https://www.facebook.com/kjjacksonauthor
Twitter: @K_J_Jackson

52284173R00180

Made in the USA
San Bernardino, CA
16 August 2017